Banshee's End

Book 4 of Motionless

Daryl Walker

Contents

CHAPTER ONE

Past to Present

*T*he music was deafening, and there were people packed into every part of the club, dancing, laughing, drinking, having a good time.

A smile appeared on Marion's face as she pushed her way through the crowd, heading towards a table with three young women and one young man sitting around it.

The dark-haired woman looked up and saw Marion making her way over to them. "Marion!" she called over the pounding music, getting the attention of her three companions. "You made it! We didn't think you were coming out tonight!"

The smile remained on Marion's face as the young woman got to her feet and pulled her into a hug. Marion hugged her back before moving back a step, forcing the woman to let her go.

"It's really good to see you, Marion," the young man said. He gave her a nice smile, making her smile back.

The woman sat down again, indicating for Marion to join them, pointing at the chair next to her.

"We haven't seen you in ages," the blonde woman said once Marion was sitting. "We really didn't think you'd come out tonight. It's good that you're here."

"I thought it was about time I started to get back out into the world after everything that happened," Marion said. "I wasn't going to come, but I thought about it at work and decided that I should. I can't keep living in fear for the rest of my life, so here I am."

Her friends smiled at her, and the dark-haired woman reached out and touched her hand. "Well, we're glad you're here. It wouldn't have been the same without you!"

Marion smiled again, and her friend smiled back. It really was nice to see her friends again.

As Marion looked around at her friends, her smile slowly faded as she realized something wasn't right. She couldn't remember who any of these people actually were. She couldn't recall any of their names. She knew she'd been friends with these four for years but now she had no idea who any of them were.

"Marion?" the young man said, making her look at him. The look on her face was enough to indicate something was wrong. "Everything OK?"

Marion didn't say anything, finding herself unable to speak. They were all looking at her now and she looked at each one in turn, but the feeling of uncertainty remained.

"Look, we know everything that happened with Kieran really left a mark," the blonde woman said. "But, as you said, it's time to get back out into the world, and now's the time to do it. You're here and you're going to have a good night out."

Marion frowned. Whoever this Kieran was, just the sound of his name was enough to make her feel weak and helpless, which made her angry.

"Yeah, um, yeah, sorry," Marion said, taking a deep breath and shaking her head, trying to get back into things. "You're right, no use holding onto something that isn't worth remembering."

"That's the spirit!" her red-headed friend said. "Kieran was an asshole, anyway. I don't know why you kept him around for so long."

Her other three friends shot her a bit of a look, silently telling her to shut up as Marion looked down at her hands, then across the dance floor.

"Oh, I didn't mean that," her friend said. "You know what I meant...?"

Marion gave a bit of a nod, not saying anything, just watching what was going on inside the club.

The young man looked around at everyone and stood up. "Well, on that note, I'm gonna go buy some drinks. Everyone want their usual or are we changing up what we want tonight to make things more interesting?"

In the background, the song changed, making Marion frown again. Something about this song sounded too familiar.

"The usual thanks," the dark-haired woman said.

"Same," the blonde said.

"Switch mine up and surprise me," the redhead said with a smile.

He looked at Marion. "What about you, Marion?"

Marion kept her gaze on someone on the other side of the dance floor as the music kept playing. This was all wrong. Everything about this situation. Only some of this was what had happened, it was nearly all incorrect.

"Hello? Earth to Marion?" the man said, waving a hand in front of her face. "You still with us?"

Marion didn't move as the music grew louder, if that was even possible.

"Marion? Marion!"

"Marion!"

Marion snapped back into reality, having a brief moment where she couldn't remember where she was. She blinked a couple of times until the all-too-familiar stone walls and the bars at the front of the cell came into focus. Only one candle was lit this deep in the dungeons, and it was over near the door, leaving her mostly in the dark.

Realizing where she was, the anger set in.

"No," she shouted. "No, no, no, no, no!"

The guard on the other side of the bars put the food down as he saw she wasn't about to take it.

Marion screamed, showing her frustration.

The guard left the room, shutting and locking the door after himself as Marion continued to scream. This wasn't unusual but it was becoming more frequent.

He headed up the stone steps and into the upper level of the castle dungeons, aware that someone was watching him from the only other occupied cell.

"You wake her up from her daydreaming again?" the man said, staying up the back in the dark.

The guard stopped briefly in front of the man's cell before walking away. All guards were on strict orders not to interact with the man unless it was to give him food.

The guard left the dungeons, making sure he shut and locked the door once he was out. He needed to have a word with someone about Marion.

He sighed as he walked up the steps and into the ground level of the castle, making sure the final door was shut and locked before he continued on his way.

As he neared the throne room, something small dashed past him, forcing him to stop. He looked to his left just in time to see a small brown tail disappear through one of the open doors. The guard shook his head, then kept walking.

He turned down another corridor, seeing something small and brown disappear into the throne room. The door was open as he reached the room, and he entered without hesitation, knowing he was allowed in, as guards were allowed to go most places in the castle.

"If I'm not interrupting, can I have a word?" the guard said as he stopped in front of the throne.

The woman lounging on the throne had half red and half black hair and, most days, not a care in the world. A small brown cat lay on the floor beside the throne.

"Depends what you want to talk about," Ash said, shifting her position a bit.

"We need to have a word about Marion."

Ash looked at him, more alert now. She sat up properly, startling the little brown cat out of his sleep. "What about her? What's she done?"

"She's getting worse. She's started screaming again. It's getting less and less time in between her fits of anger and she screams for longer each time. Something's seriously wrong, Ash."

Ash nodded and pushed herself up and out of the throne. The little brown cat also stood up and followed her towards the door, followed by the guard.

The guard didn't know where she was going just yet, but she always had a destination in mind. He and the cat followed her all the way to the front of the castle.

Ash dragged open one of the large doors, leaving the other one shut, as she stepped outside. A cold gust of wind rushed through, making the guard shiver.

He stepped outside to find Ash standing on the top step with the cat sitting next to her. The wind was ice cold, blowing Ash's hair every which way as she looked out at the town below her, every bit of it covered in a thick layer of snow and ice. People were still out and about though, not letting the cold weather affect them and their work.

"Wonderland isn't getting any better," Ash noted as the guard stopped next to her on her left, the cat on her right and not liking the snow one bit. It was why he stayed indoors lately. "I've done what I can but even all this snow and ice won't make it any better. This just covers up the damage so no one else can see how bad it is. I thought maybe, somehow, it would help heal Wonderland, but it hasn't seemed to help in any way."

"Would it hurt to tone down the cold just a bit?" the guard suggested, shivering as Ash looked at him, a bit of an amused smile on her face.

"You don't like it?" she asked, making him shrug. She went back to looking out at the town. "I'm surprised you're not used to it. I like it. But then again, I don't really feel the cold much anymore."

"So, what do we do about Marion?" the guard asked as Ash continued to look at the town, watching people move around.

Ash shook her head slowly, thinking.

"Right now, I don't know," she admitted, linking her fingers together as the little cat moved closer to her leg, trying to get a bit of warmth from her. "We don't have any idea of what's wrong with her so we can't really help her or stop it. Not many people down here would be willing to help Marion. *I* don't want to help her, but we don't have much choice."

"Why's that?"

Ash looked at the guard with sadness on her face.

"Because the quicker she deteriorates, the faster Wonderland goes down."

CHAPTER TWO

Life on the Surface

"How long ago did you check on her?" Ash asked as she shut the door, the chill still ever present.

The guard shrugged. "Less than half an hour."

Ash nodded and watched the little cat shake as if trying to get rid of the cold. She picked him up and he meowed at her as she held him close, trying to warm him up a bit.

"I know, Alex, and I'm sorry," she said. The guard didn't understand what was so special about that cat. "I know you hate the cold, but we're inside now, so we don't have to put up with it."

Alex purred, rubbing against her, seeming a lot happier now that he was warmer. He hated the cold and spent most of his time indoors since Ash had made the weather so cold outside.

Ash smiled and looked at the guard as she kept hold of the cat.

"I'll go down to the dungeons and see her," she said, the guard nodding. She looked down at the cat again, a smile on her face. "I'm sure Alex wants to come down there too, don't you?"

The cat meowed at her again, the smile staying on Ash's face as she walked ahead of the guard.

Reaching the door that led to the dungeons, Ash placed Alex on the floor, grabbed her keys, and unlocked the door. She pushed it open, and Alex dashed in. He ran down the steps to the bottom, where he sat and waited for the next door to be opened.

Ash followed, leaving the top door open and walking down the steps. It was quiet, which was nice. She unlocked the next door and pushed it open.

Alex ran in, disappearing into the dark and making Ash sigh. He was so impatient sometimes.

Once again, she followed, seeing Alex standing at the front of the cell Hunter was being kept in. Alex wasn't a cat anymore and he had a frown on his face.

"Alex?" Ash called, but his focus remained on the cell. "You alright?"

"Hunter's not in here," Alex said, the confusion in his tone making Ash frown as she came over. "He was here and now he's not. He was here earlier on when I followed the guard down here."

Ash stopped next to him and looked into the cell, seeing that it was indeed empty. Realizing that he might not be the only one who was gone, Ash ran over to the next door, the one that led down to the cell Marion was being kept in. She'd been put in Alice's old cell as it was more reinforced and less likely that people would see her if they came down to the dungeons.

Ash hurriedly unlocked the door and raced down the steps with Alex close behind. Unlocking one more door, Ash swung it open, hoping that Marion was still there. But all she saw was an empty cell.

Alex came to an abrupt stop behind her as he also saw the issue. He looked at Ash. "What do we do? She can't have gotten far, right?"

Ash shook her head, hooking her keys back onto her belt. "She's long gone by now. We have to find her, Alex, but we're not going to be able to do it by ourselves."

It was a cold and miserable Thursday in Pennsylvania. Chris sighed as he looked out the kitchen window. It looked like he was trapped inside for the day, most likely for the remainder of the week at this rate.

A knock on the door snapped him out of his trance, a frown crossing his face. Who in their right minds would be outside in this kind of weather? And for that matter, why were they knocking on his door?

The knock came again, and Chris headed through the house to the front door. He unlocked it and opened it and when he saw who was standing on his doorstep, he frowned even deeper.

Ash and Alex looked back at him, Alex waving at him in between shivering.

"Hey, Chris," Ash greeted, a smile on her face as Chris looked between the two of them. "Can we come in? Alex's been complaining about the cold since we got here. Well, before we got here, really."

Chris nodded and moved aside to let them into the house. Ash gave him another smile as she walked past him, Alex close behind.

Chris shut the door and stared at them as Ash looked around.

"Thank you, it's so cold out there!" Alex said, still shivering but glad to be inside where it was warm. He looked at Chris. "Why do you have to live in such a cold place?"

Chris shrugged, looking at Ash as Alex looked around a bit more. "What are you doing here and how did you get my address?"

Ash returned the look. "We thought we'd come and see how you're doing. It's got to have been at least a year since we've seen you!" she said cheerfully. She looked around again. "Nice house you've got here."

"I like it," Alex said, smiling at Chris. "I could live here."

"Well, you're not going to," Chris said sternly. Alex pouted at him, and Chris looked at Ash again. "I don't think you came here to see how I'm doing. That doesn't feel like something you'd do, either of you. What are you *really* doing here, Ash? You don't come across as someone who just stops by to see how I'm doing."

Chris crossed his arms as he looked at her, waiting for her answer.

She sighed, giving in.

"Alright, we need some help," she said, making Chris sigh. "Something's happened and we need help."

"What's happened?"

"Marion and Hunter are gone," Ash said. "They were there and now they're gone. Something's very wrong with her but we don't know what. And the longer it goes on, the more Wonderland is deteriorating. We're thinking that she might have some sort of connection to Wonderland, that it wasn't just Abel bringing the curse, if it was ever him. We didn't know what to do so we came up here hoping you guys could help."

"Wait, 'you guys'?" Chris queried. "Who else are we talking about here?"

Ash and Alex exchanged looks, and Ash indicated for Alex to speak. Alex looked at Chris and cleared his throat before speaking.

"We were, um, hoping we could get everyone back down to Wonderland for some help with finding Marion and Hunter before anything bad happens," he said, trying to sound confident but coming across as nervous. "I know where Abel and Matt live, but we had someone tell us where Gates and Zeke are."

"You're kidding, right?" Chris raised his eyebrows. "You're not seriously going to go and harass everyone until they help you?"

Alex and Ash both shrugged awkwardly, and Chris shook his head.

"Chris, look, we didn't know what else to do," Ash said with a sigh. Alex nodded in agreement. "We can't track Marion by ourselves. She's long gone, and we don't have a clue where to start to look for her. We need all the help we can get and everyone we had last time were very valuable assets on this kind of thing. We certainly can't do anything without Gates or Matt."

Chris couldn't believe what he was hearing. It had been nearly ten months and these two just showed up out of nowhere to tell him that Marion had disappeared and Wonderland was dying? Did they think this was acceptable?

The wind picked up outside, clearly making Alex uneasy.

"What are you going to do when we all say no?" Chris asked. "Seriously, Ash. You saw how Gates was at the end there. He won't come back. Matt might, but he's also probably settled back into his life again. You can't go tearing people away from their lives up here for Marion."

"Have you spoken to any of the others since you all left?" Ash asked.

Chris shook his head. "No, I haven't spoken to anyone. I'm pretty sure they all stay with their groups, so Matt would still talk to Gates and Zeke, but not me and Abel and vice versa."

"We have to do something, Chris," Ash insisted. Alex nodded furiously. "We can't let this happen. A lot of innocent people are going to die if Wonderland is destroyed. I know *we* will. There's no way we'll survive."

Chris looked between the two of them, then sighed. He knew he didn't have a lot of options here.

"Alright, fine," he said reluctantly, throwing his hands up. Alex's face lit up and Ash smiled too. "But I'm going to say this now: if no one else will help, you two are on your own. I'm not doing this if everyone else says no."

CHAPTER THREE

California

"See, this is a *lot* better weather here," Alex said as they walked up the stone path that led to the front door of the house. "Feel how much nicer it is? Ash, this is what's missing back home: warmth."

Ash rolled her eyes as Alex looked around the street and Chris checked the address again to make sure that they were at the right house.

"Well, this is apparently it," Chris said, putting his phone in his back pocket. "One of you gets to knock and explain since you dragged me out here."

Ash sighed. "It's so hard to make you boys happy, you know that?"

Alex smiled at her as she knocked on the door. "I'm *always* happy."

Ash glanced at him before turning back as the door opened. "Not always."

A woman stared at the three of them. Chris wasn't sure who this was, and he was now hoping that he hadn't read the address wrong each time he'd checked it.

"Can I help you?" the woman asked, looking between the three of them.

"Hey, sorry, but is Blaine home?" Ash asked, getting straight to it. "We told him a couple of days ago we'd be stopping by, but I don't know if he remembered or not. You must be Skye. I'm Ash."

Ash extended her hand in a friendly manner. The woman hesitated for a few seconds then shook her hand.

"Yeah, I'm Skye," she said. She looked at Alex and Chris. "Who are you?"

"This is Chris and Alex." Ash pointed to each of them as she said their names.

Alex grinned at Skye while Chris just gave her a nod of greeting.

Ash looked back at Skye. "So is Blaine in?"

Skye moved aside, gesturing for the three of them to come inside. Ash gave Chris a slight smirk and went in first, followed closely by Alex.

Once Chris was inside, Skye shut the door and headed quickly past them, going over to the sliding doors that led out to the backyard.

The three of them followed her out. Skye stopped at the edge of a bubbling spa, a step or two away from the pool.

Gates was in the spa on the opposite side to where Skye was standing, clearly having a relaxing time before they'd shown up.

"Some people here to see you," Skye said. "I'll leave you to it."

Skye gave Ash, Alex, and Chris a bit of a smile as she headed past them and went back inside, closing the sliding doors behind herself.

Gates took his sunglasses off and glared at the three people in front of him. "What the *fuck* are you doing here?" he asked, the annoyance clear as he crushed his cigarette in the ashtray next to him. "Get off my property."

"Nice to see you, too," Ash said back with just as much annoyance.

"Go away, I don't want to talk to any of you," Gates said, leaning back a bit and putting his sunglasses back on. "Leave me alone. I don't have time for whatever bullshit you've done."

"No need to be rude," Ash said, placing her hands on her hips as Chris shrugged at Alex. "We just wanted to see how you're going."

Gates scoffed, picking up the cigarette packet next to the ash tray. He pulled a cigarette out and picked up the lighter. "I thoroughly doubt that. So, fuck off because *I* don't care about how *you're* doing *at all*."

"Blaine..."

Gates held his hand up to signal for her to be quiet as he lit the cigarette and put the lighter back down.

"What have I told you about that? You haven't earned that right, Ashley," he said. "Now get off my property before I forcefully remove you three myself. I don't know how you found where I live, nor do I really care, but I want you three gone, now."

"Come on, Gates, just hear them out," Chris insisted. "We're obviously not here just to stop in."

Gates looked at Chris and took a deep drag on his cigarette, clearly not in the mood to be harassed by them today, or any day for that matter.

Gates didn't say anything for a moment or two as he looked back at Ash and Alex. Alex wasn't paying attention and was looking around the backyard, clearly liking what he was seeing.

"You have thirty-seconds to explain to me why you're here before I forcefully remove you, and I don't particularly want to get out of this spa," Gates said. "So, start talking."

Ash rolled her eyes as he took another drag on the cigarette. "We need your help..."

"Aaaand that's thirty seconds," Gates interrupted her. "The answer is no, go away. I'm not helping you with anything."

Ash sighed. "Come on, don't be like that. You don't know what I was even going to say."

"I don't need to know what you were going to say, Ashley," Gates said, making Ash cross her arms and glare at him. "Because I don't care."

Alex looked at Ash before looking at Gates who just ignored him.

"We need you, though," Alex said sadly.

"I don't care," Gates said with a shake of his head. "Alex, look, I don't want to help you guys out. If you hadn't noticed, I'm kind of comfortable back in my own life now. I got my life *back*. I'm not about to get up and help you lot out with some stupid problem just because you're both too fucking irresponsible and unable to do this yourselves. I don't want to risk losing this again. I'm sorry, but I'm not helping."

"Well, then, this was a waste of our time," Ash said bitterly.

"You're telling me," Gates muttered.

Ash shook her head. "You're unbelievable, Gates, you know that?"

He shrugged. "I've been told that by some."

Ash shook her head again. "Apparently, you can't take time out of your *incredibly* busy life to help us, yet all I see you doing is sitting in bubbling water and smoking your life away," she snapped.

"At least I have a life that's more exciting than sitting on a throne twenty-four-seven," he snapped back. "I never intended on going back down to Wonderland or anywhere remotely like it. If I'd wanted to be there, I wouldn't have left. But I *did* leave and now I'm *here*. I was gone for nearly eight years, Ashley. I'm not going to just get up and leave again."

"Well, fine then, we don't need you anyway," Ash said back harshly. "We'll go talk to Matt, then."

"Go for it."

Ash growled and turned to leave, heading over to the closed doors that they'd come through.

Chris sighed as Alex ran after Ash who had gone inside already. "Sorry about all of this."

"Figured it'd happen eventually," Gates said with a shrug. He lowered his sunglasses and looked at Chris. "Don't let her rope you into helping if you don't want to. It's not your responsibility."

The door opened and Vivian smiled at the three people on the other side of the door. Riley stood just off to her side, eager to see who had knocked on the door.

"Hi, I didn't know you were stopping by today."

"Chris!" Riley exclaimed, clearly excited and happy to see him.

He rushed outside and threw his arms around Chris's legs. Chris smiled, leaned down, and hugged him back.

Vivian looked at Ash and Alex. "Matt and Zeke are out the back."

Ash raised her eyebrows. "Zeke's here too?"

"He came around this morning," Vivian said with a nod. "Blaine's not here today, but I'm sure he'll be around later or tomorrow. If he's not at home, chances are he's here."

Ash nodded, not bothering to say that they'd already seen Gates not that long ago. They'd come straight from his place to Matt's, which luckily wasn't too far. Alex had known Matt's address, so all Chris had to do was look up directions on his phone. When they'd got here, Alex told them this was the right house.

Vivian moved aside, letting them all inside. Riley stayed close to Chris and, once everyone was in, Vivian closed the door.

"Make yourselves at home. I'll let Matt know you're here," she said as she moved past them, down the short hallway, and into what Chris assumed was the kitchen.

Ash looked at Chris and Alex stayed quiet, looking around as he always did.

"Let's hope Matt's a bit more helpful," Ash said, Chris nodding in agreement. "Otherwise, I guess we just go and find Abel and see if he can help."

"You're not leaving until someone helps, are you?" Chris asked.

"Someone *has* to help. We can't do this by ourselves, Chris."

CHAPTER FOUR

Matt's House

M att strolled out of the kitchen, into the entranceway where Chris, Ash, and Alex were waiting, then leaned against the wall with his hands in his pockets.

"Hey, guys. Viv said you were here. Gotta say, I'm kind of surprised to see you three. Ash and Alex more so than you, Chris."

Chris glanced at Ash before looking back at Matt. "Well, I was sort of dragged along with no say whatsoever," he said, ignoring how Ash was glaring at him. "They even made me pay for the flights over. But it's good to see you, Matt. How are you doing?"

Matt shrugged. "Oh, you know. Can't complain, nothing to complain about really. What about you three? How's everything?"

Ash and Alex both shrugged and Chris looked at them for a few seconds before looking back to Matt.

"Maybe we should move away from the front door and talk about this elsewhere?" he suggested.

Matt nodded. "Sure. Zeke's outside, so we'll head out the back."

He gave them all a quick smile before pushing off the wall and heading the way Vivian had gone earlier. Chris, Ash, and Alex followed him through the kitchen and out through the open sliding door on the other side.

Matt indicated for them all to take a seat at the table. Zeke looked up, away from his phone, as they sat down and Matt took the chair opposite Zeke.

"Hey," Zeke greeted, putting his phone on the table, realizing he needed to be part of this conversation.

Chris gave him a nod of greeting. Alex smiled and waved at him, while Ash decided not to say or do anything except look at Matt who returned her look.

"We need your help," Ash said, getting straight to the reason they were here. "Gates pretty well kicked us out of his house, so we thought we'd come talk to you about it. In fact, we should have come here first."

Matt looked at her as he thought about what to say, crossing his arms as he leaned back in his chair.

"Well," he began, everyone looking at him now. He glanced at Zeke before looking back at Ash who was waiting to hear what he had to say. "I understand that Blaine doesn't want to help with anything to do with Wonderland. He's happy with how everything's going, right now. I don't think you should pull him away from his life at the moment. But, what exactly do you need help with?"

"Marion's gone," Ash said. Matt raised an eyebrow slightly, but didn't seem surprised. Ash could see him thinking as she spoke. "We don't know where and we don't know how. Hunter's gone as well. He was in one of the cells and they both just disappeared without a trace. They were the only people in the dungeons, they weren't anywhere near each other, and no one was allowed in to see them. The guards were under strict orders not to interact with them except to give them food. We've also noticed a shift in Wonderland. It feels all wrong down there and it hasn't healed in any way since you locked Marion up. In fact, it's gotten worse."

"Hmm," was Matt's response. "Well, I'm sure getting Marion back won't be all that hard. Just got to find out where she's gone. As for Wonderland, we can figure that out as we go. I'm sure we have enough time to figure out what's happening and put it right."

Ash's face lit up with a smile. "So you'll help?"

Matt nodded, shifting his position a bit. "Yeah, don't see why not." He looked at Zeke. "What about you? You in?"

Zeke sighed, resting his head on his hand. "Do I really have a choice, Matt?"

Matt looked at Ash. "There's your answer, we're both in. Just let us know when you want to go."

Ash and Alex smiled at each other. Chris sighed inwardly. It looked like he'd been roped into this once again and he couldn't see any way of getting out of it.

"What about Gates, though?" Alex asked. "If he knows you two are helping, do you think he'll join us?"

"I doubt it," Matt said, watching Alex's expression sadden.

"But we need him, he's part of the team!" Alex exclaimed.

Matt shrugged. "Not my place. If he doesn't want to help, I'm not going over there to force him. If you want him to come along, then you have to convince him. Good luck with changing his mind, though."

Alex didn't know what to say and continued to look at him sadly. Matt gave him another shrug and didn't say anything else.

Chris watched Zeke grab the cigarette packet that was on the table in front of him. He pulled out a cigarette and clicked his fingers, lighting it.

Chris frowned. "Did you just use your ability?"

"Uh, yeah..." Zeke said slowly, not catching on to what Chris was implying. "They work here?"

Chris looked at Ash who, in return, shrugged. She hadn't known about it, either.

Alex nodded and Chris and Ash both looked at him. "I knew they worked. You never asked about it, so I figured you already knew..."

Chris shook his head. "I didn't know. It never really crossed my mind that they'd work outside of the Underground Worlds."

Alex nodded again and Zeke spoke.

"It was, like, one of the first things I tried when I got back home and no one was watching," he said. "But this stays between us. I'm pretty sure we're the only ones who know, well, those of us who came home, anyway."

Chris looked at Matt. "You knew?"

Matt shrugged, linking his fingers together. "Yeah, Zeke told me about it and, of course, I gave it a try. Tell you what, though, it's handy. Viv knows about it, but we don't talk about it outside of the group. Don't particularly wish to get locked away and studied by scientists, you know?"

Chris gave a hesitant nod. "I never really had any reason to try and use mine. There's not really any use for my ability up here, so it never crossed my mind to even try it."

"Does Gates know?" Ash asked.

Matt nodded. "Yeah."

Ash looked at Alex, with a thoughtful look on her face. "How about you go and keep an eye on Gates and talk to him about helping us?" she suggested. An automatic look of panic appeared on Alex's face and Ash sighed. "He's more likely to talk to you about this because you're incredibly timid and less likely to force him into this or punch him in the face when he says no again."

"Why?" Alex complained. "Ash, I don't want to."

"You can get in and out of the house easier than we can," Chris said, Alex turning his attention to him. "You can change into whatever the hell you want. If we keep knocking on the door, we'll eventually be told to get lost and never come back. You're the best option here, Alex."

Alex groaned, majorly slouching in his chair.

"Whhhhhhhhy," he once again complained, dragging the word out to emphasize how much he did not want to do this. "I don't waaaaaaaaanna."

"Just do it, Alex," Ash said harshly, making Alex groan and put his hands over his face. "Chris and I will go and talk to Abel, while you spend a few days here with Gates to try and change his mind."

Alex removed his hands from his face and crossed his arms stubbornly. He was pouting.

"Fine, but I'm not going to try too hard."

Alex was unhappy. He was trying to figure out where in Gates's house he was. All of the lights were out, it was very quiet, and he didn't know the layout of this place. It was nearly midnight, so he was sure he had time to look around, as he was sure Gates and Skye were both asleep.

He'd waited a few hours before deciding to venture inside, as he didn't particularly wish to get caught or seen by either Gates or Skye. Also, it had taken him a few hours to build up the courage to go in.

The little brown mouse had entered the house into what he was sure was a spare room. He scampered through the house, and realized he was now in the kitchen.

The only question was: which way did he go now?

After looking around the rest of the house, Alex finally found the room he'd been looking for: the bedroom. The door was ajar, and Alex easily slipped inside the room, trying to be quiet. Even if he'd been in his usual cat form, he would've been able to get into the room with ease.

Sure enough, this was the right room. Gates and Skye were both asleep in the bed and Alex looked around, trying to figure out the best place to wait.

He didn't plan on leaving the house now that he was inside, so he needed to wait until morning before he could talk to Gates. He would have to wait until Skye wasn't around, but how hard could that be?

Without any more thought, he dashed under the bed, glad there was a lot of space, even with a box or two that had been shoved under. It looked like this was where Alex was spending the night.

CHAPTER FIVE

Convincing Gates

Gates frowned as he felt something move across the bed and settle near his feet. He opened his eyes and sat up quickly, startling the little brown cat who was curled up on the end of the bed.

"Jesus, man!" Gates snapped. "Get the fuck off my bed, Alex!"

Alex meowed at him, continuing to look at him but not moving.

"I said, get off my damn bed!"

Gates got up and grabbed the small cat, who in return meowed at him again. Gates placed him on the floor, put his hands on his hips, and glared at him.

The cat sat down in front of him and meowed once again.

"What do you think you're doing? Get out of my house."

Alex meowed once more, stood up, and rubbed his head against Gates's leg.

"Your adorable techniques aren't about to work on me, Alex," Gates said, as the cat continued to rub against him. Gates sighed again, this time, though, it wasn't as annoyed as it had been. "At least get out of my room. Skye's allergic to cats."

Not needing to be told twice, Alex dashed out of the room, the door moving slightly in the breeze caused by his movement. Gates shook his head and followed, grabbing his phone off the bedside table before leaving the room.

Alex was sitting in the kitchen, on a stool next to the bench, no longer a cat. Gates gave him a sidelong glance and walked past him, picking up a note from the bench and reading it. It was from Skye and said she wouldn't be home for a few hours.

"Sorry about the intrusion," Alex apologized. "I'm under strict orders to keep an eye on you!"

Gates looked at him, still holding onto the note. "Let me guess, Ashley put you up to it?"

Alex gave an awkward shrug as Gates shook his head. He put the note back down on the bench before searching for something in a cupboard.

"What do you want *this time*?" Gates asked, turning back to face him with a box of cereal in his hand.

"Can't we just, you know, hang out instead of talking business?" Alex asked. "Because I haven't seen you in nearly a year! How are you doing?"

"I'm fine, Alex. How are you?" Gates asked with another sigh. He wasn't in the mood for this. He opened another cupboard and pulled out a bowl.

Alex shrugged. "I'm OK, I guess. So, anyway, I see you and Skye are together. How's that going for you?"

Gates stopped what he was doing and looked at him. Alex returned the look with a smile.

"It's fine, we're fine," Gates said, Alex nodding. "It was a bit hard to start with, but we're on track again and we're fine."

Alex frowned. "What do you mean?"

Gates sighed once more. This wasn't Alex's business but now that he'd mentioned it, he felt like he had to tell him.

"When I first got back, it was kind of hard to get back into my life," he began. "Skye was with another guy, which automatically put me in a very awkward position."

"Oh..." Alex said, Gates just looking at him. "So ... what happened?"

"Skye hadn't dated anyone for about five years after I disappeared," Gates continued. "This guy came into her life nearly two years ago and they'd been together ever since. Apparently, he proposed to her, but she turned him down. Her reasoning was that she didn't want the same thing to happen. She didn't want him to disappear like I had. I disappeared a week after I proposed to her, and she was worried that the same thing was going to happen again."

"So, she turned him down, but they were still together?"

Gates nodded. "Anyway, when I finally showed up, he wasn't pleased, to say the least. Which, granted, wasn't unreasonable. I mean, what would you do if your girlfriend's missing ex-fiancé suddenly showed up? It puts everyone in a terribly awkward position."

Alex nodded once more, leaning his chin on his hand as he listened. Gates sighed again and leaned against the bench as he faced Alex.

"Skye didn't know what to do, how to handle it and, truth be told, neither did I," Gates said. "I didn't want to ruin the life she'd built after I was gone, but she insisted I stay here instead of at my parent's place, just for a bit to settle back into life again. Obviously, her boyfriend wasn't overly happy with this and made sure to express his displeasure with me any chance he got."

"Well, I didn't see anyone else here, so..."

Gates nodded. "Yeah. Skye got sick of the way this guy was acting towards me. I don't know how many times she told him off for it. It got to the point that she just said fuck it and told him that if he didn't like it or couldn't accept it, then he should leave. So, he did."

Gates looked away, remembering, as Alex looked at him with a sad expression.

"You feel bad about him leaving her like that, don't you?" he asked, making Gates look back at him. "Like it was your fault?"

"Technically, it *was* my fault," Gates said. "I get it, though. Would you really want to stay in the same house as your girlfriend's ex?"

Alex shrugged. "Wouldn't know."

Gates just looked at him, not impressed at all.

"Anyway," he continued. "Once he left, it sort of went back to being awkward. So, I told Skye that it was probably better if I just went to stay with my parents to give her the chance to fix things with this guy, but she insisted that I stay and one thing led to another and, yeah. That's that and this is where we are."

Gates moved away from the bench, going back to what he'd been doing prior to being roped into the conversation.

"So, I guess it's no use asking if you'll help us, then?" Alex said.

Gates didn't even glance at him. "Alex, do you understand how hard it was to get back into my life?"

Alex wasn't sure where this was going and stayed quiet.

Gates turned to face him again. "Do you know how damn hard it's been to pretend like everything's normal and to not do this around people?"

Gates put both of his hands out, the clear barrier appearing in front of him.

"For nearly eight years, this was my defense whenever I felt threatened," he continued as Alex stayed quiet. Gates put his hands down and the barrier disappeared. "Do you know how hard it is to break those kinds of habits and how long it takes?"

Alex shook his head. "A long time?"

"A fucking long time," Gates said, nodding. "I have to keep reminding myself that I don't need to do that anymore and to just handle things normally, but it's damn hard to break. Skye doesn't know about it, and I don't want her finding out. She's already been through enough."

Alex watched as Gates turned his back on him again, going back to making himself something to eat. Alex was hungry but there was no way he was about to ask Gates if he could have something.

"So, I'll take that as a no then...?" Alex said quietly.

Gates stopped and looked at him again, a bit of a sad look on his face this time.

"Alex, I can't," he said, sounding defeated. "I'm really sorry, but I just can't."

Alex nodded in understanding as Gates avoided his gaze. "It's all good, I get it. Would it help if I said both Matt and Zeke are going to help?"

Gates sighed, running a hand through his hair before meeting Alex's gaze.

"You guys don't need me down there. You can all handle it without me," he said. Alex shook his head, clearly disagreeing. "You've got Matt, he's enough to help you out with whatever your problem is."

"Honestly, Gates, you're the one who did the most for us. I don't know how many times you stopped everyone, or even just one person, from getting killed," Alex said, continuing to try and get him to change his mind. "You may not think so, but we really need you. It won't be the same without you."

Gates sighed once again, looking at Alex as he thought about what to do. He was quiet for a few minutes.

"Alright, look," he said, making Alex's face light up with a big smile. "I seriously mean this: you owe me big time for doing this, is that clear?"

Alex nodded furiously as Gates sighed yet again.

"I just don't know how I'm going to explain this to Skye."

CHAPTER SIX

Winter Wonderland

"These phones are so handy!" Alex exclaimed from the other end of the line, making Chris roll his eyes. "I've been without these my whole life, but they make talking so easy over a distance!"

"Yes, Alex, phones are a good thing," Chris said. "Since you're calling from a new phone, I assume you've managed to convince Gates to help us?"

Chris and Ash were currently at Abel's house. Chris was standing just outside the front door, while Ash was inside, talking to Abel. He'd already agreed to help and now they just needed to arrange for everyone to meet up to get this mission going.

"Yes, he said he'd help," Alex said. "But he also said we owe him big time for it."

"Of course we do."

"How's it going for you? Any luck over there?"

"Yeah, Abel's in. It wasn't hard to get him to agree. He was up for it nearly straight away, really," Chris said. "Ash is still inside talking to him, but we think the best thing to do is all meet down in Wonderland. You go with Matt, Zeke, and Gates, and we'll go with Abel and meet you down there. Sound good?"

"OK, I'll let them know that's what's happening," Alex said. "Any particular place you want to meet up down there or nah?"

"Ash thinks we should meet at the castle as soon as possible. If we're not there when you get there, get Matt to have a look around to see if he can figure out what might have happened, how Marion and Hunter got out. We'll be there as soon as we can."

"Sounds like a plan! See you down there soon!"

Alex hung up and Chris put his phone back in his pocket. He headed back into the house, shutting the front door behind himself. He joined Ash and Abel in the living room, staying in the doorway, not wanting to interrupt their planning. One of Abel's cats sat next to Abel on the arm of the chair he was in.

"What's the verdict?" Ash asked when she noticed him.

"Gates is in, and they're all going to meet us at the castle as soon as possible," Chris said.

Ash nodded, satisfied. "I knew Alex could convince him."

"But, before we go," Chris continued. "I want to head back home and get some stuff because I don't want to go down there unprepared this time."

Ash nodded again. "We can do that."

"Good," Chris said. He looked at Abel. "You want to head down to Wonderland, and we'll meet up in a while?"

"I probably should," Abel said. "I'll make sure Alex doesn't get himself into any trouble before you two show up. I assume you can find your way down there without my help?"

"Just going to go the same way I did the first time," Chris said.

Abel smiled. "Well, then, I guess I'll see the two of you down there."

Abel looked around as the door shut and locked behind him. Snow fell in every direction, blown around by a cold, harsh wind. He pulled his jacket around himself a bit more, unable to see even ten feet in front of himself.

How was he supposed to find his way to Wonderland's main city in this weather? He'd never seen anything like this down here before, weather-wise, and he didn't particularly like it. At this rate, he'd probably die before he even got close to the city or castle, as the cold wind and blustery snow didn't seem close to easing off at all.

He shook his head and grabbed the black key out of his pocket, turning around and unlocking the door he'd just come through. It clicked open and he stepped inside, the door shutting and locking again behind him.

Back in the Room of Doors, Abel shook his head, wondering what had happened to Wonderland since he'd been gone. It hadn't been like this when he'd left, so why the sudden change?

He went over to another door, deciding that getting straight into the castle gardens would be a lot easier than trekking for miles through a blizzard. He wasn't currently equipped for that.

All he wanted was to have a nice walk back through Wonderland and get to the castle to meet up with the others. But it looked like his plans had changed and now he was going to avoid the outside for as long as was physically possible. Well, at least until the weather changed.

He unlocked the door that led to the castle gardens. The same cold, harsh wind blew against him as he went out, the door closing and locking behind him. He could just see the castle up ahead, towering through the snow and ice. Abel was lucky that he knew his way around the gardens.

Braving the cold weather and trying to make sure he wasn't about to slip over due to the snow and ice in his path and in his face, Abel began walking cautiously towards the steps that would lead him up to the castle. He was glad there weren't a large number of steps to walk up. The ice was making it hard for him to do anything right now.

He carefully walked up the steps, making sure with each one that he had a proper foothold before stepping onto the next one. He reached the top and trudged across the deep snow towards the back entrance of the castle.

The door was covered in a thick layer of ice and Abel pushed on it to see if it was locked or frozen shut. Sure enough, the door didn't budge at all, making him sigh.

He made his way around to the front of the castle, the cold seeping into his body even more the longer he stayed outside. It took longer than he would have liked, but he eventually managed to get to the front doors, which were shut as the wind continued to blow snow every which way.

Abel saw a few people out and about during this terrible weather as he went up to the front doors and pushed one of them open. He was glad that it hadn't frozen shut like the back entrance. Once inside, he quickly shut the door again to stop any more of the cold coming inside.

"Alex?" Abel called, hearing his voice echo off the walls.

The castle seemed to be deserted as he began walking down the closest corridor, knowing that the best option right now was to go to the throne room and work from there. It was one of the bigger spaces in the castle and, if he was correct, that was where Alex and the others would be if they were here by now. If not, then he would have to wait.

Walking into the throne room, Abel was glad to see he wasn't the only one here. He felt a bit better when he saw that Alex, Matt, Gates, and Zeke were already here, knowing now that he didn't have to wait around on his own.

Alex was sitting near a fireplace with a roaring fire going, and a smile lit up his face when he saw Abel enter the room and come over to him.

Matt, Gates, and Zeke were standing a little way away, talking about something. Gates didn't look overly impressed, and he didn't seem happy about being back in Wonderland.

Chris and Ash weren't here yet, and they wouldn't be able to do much without them.

"Abel, you made it!" Alex exclaimed, his voice echoing around the large room. Alex frowned, noticing his lack of companions. "Where are Chris and Ash? Chris said they were coming down here with you."

"Slight change of plans," Abel said, as Alex's expression turned to worry. "It's fine, Alex. Chris needed to go home and get a few things. Ash stayed with him in case something happened."

Alex gave a hurried nod but still looked worried. "Alright, well as long as they're still coming to join us." Abel gave a nod of confirmation and Alex looked over to the other three. "Guys, come over here so we can talk!"

Matt said something to Zeke and Gates before coming over and joining them next to the fire, the other two a few steps behind. Abel noticed that Matt was shivering a bit.

Even with the fire, it was cool within the walls of the castle, but nowhere near as cold as outside.

"You called, Captain?" Matt said, arms crossed as he stood next to Alex.

Alex's grinned upon hearing what Matt had called him. "If I'm the Captain, does that mean I make all the decisions?"

Matt shrugged and pulled his jacket tightly around himself. "If you want to. Until Ash gets back and orders us around at least."

The grin stayed on Alex' s face as he jumped to his feet. "Alright, well, I have a few things we need to talk about. But before we talk, I want you to come with me. Something we need to do first. Someone we all need to go and see."

A frown appeared on everyone's faces as Alex smiled at them and headed out of the throne room. The other four quickly followed, no one saying anything as they trailed Alex through the castle, wondering where he was leading them.

They reached a separate quarter and Alex headed to the door at the end. He opened it and gestured for everyone to follow him as he began descending the narrow staircase.

It was then that Abel realized where they were headed. It had been a long time since he'd been down this way, but it was still giving him a rather uneasy feeling.

The staircase was dimly lit, making it hard for them to see where they were going, but when they reached the end, they saw the light coming from the room they were heading to. Stepping through the doorway, Abel noticed it had changed since he'd last been in here.

It was the room that Marion's doctor had used to torture his victims and 'see how they worked'. The curtains had all been removed, making the room look a lot bigger than it had originally seemed. Everything was now neatly organized and there were bits and pieces of different things on the metal tables.

There wasn't any doctor down here today, but there was someone they all knew, and Abel was glad to see him.

"Nixx, look who's here!" Alex exclaimed. "They're back!"

"I can see that," Nixx said. He tore himself away from whatever he'd been working on, turning to face the others, a smile appearing on his face. "It's good to see you, guys. It's been too long. I assume you're here to help with the whole Marion situation?"

"That obvious?" Gates remarked, looking around, seemingly unimpressed like most times.

Nixx gave him a bit of a smile again before looking between all of them. "While you're all down here... You all got phones with you?"

They all gave a nod, Alex included. Nixx gestured for them all to hand over their phones. One by one they obliged, albeit reluctantly.

"Once Chris and Ash get here, I'll hand these back. Better to explain everything while you're all here, so I don't have to repeat myself," he said. "Someone send them down here when they arrive."

Alex agreed, and Nixx turned his attention back to whatever he'd been working on before the interruption.

Alex ushered them all back to the staircase.

"Let's go back upstairs and wait for the other two," he said. "Feel free to have a look around while we wait. We'll discuss some stuff once everyone's here."

CHAPTER SEVEN

Preparations

Ash looked around Chris's house as she waited for him. He was in his bedroom, getting a few things that he said he needed, so she had been left unsupervised while he sorted a few things out.

"How long do you think this'll take?" Chris called.

"Shouldn't be too long," Ash said in response, still looking around his living room. A framed picture on the coffee table caught her attention. "We just need to find Marion and then figure out what to do about Wonderland. Hopefully, not too long."

"Yeah, well, it sounds like it'll take a while," Chris called back. "You guys ever think about completely abandoning Wonderland and the Underground Worlds? It would be a lot safer, and I know Alex seems to prefer it up here now that he's been Upstairs twice."

"Wonderland's our home," Ash said, picking up the framed picture, looking it over with a frown on her face. "We can't just abandon it. Would you want to do that to your home?"

The picture looked rather recent, or at least that was what Ash thought. It was of Chris and a woman. Chris had his arm around the woman, holding her close, both of them smiling and looking happy. Ash hadn't ever seen Chris that happy in the time that she'd known him.

She couldn't help but feel a bit sad as she looked at the picture. Did everyone in their group really make Chris *that* unhappy? Did *she* make him that unhappy?

"I guess it would depend on why I had to abandon my home," Chris said in response to Ash's earlier question, snapping Ash out of her thoughts. She quickly put the framed picture back down on the coffee table, straightening it so it looked like she hadn't touched it. "But it's a bit different up here than down in Wonderland."

"I've noticed," Ash said back with a sigh, moving on to looking at what else he had in the living room as she tried to get the picture out of her head. "You live in a simple world, Chris."

"Sometimes simpler is better."

Ash didn't bother responding, leaving the living room and going into the kitchen with its open dining room. Chris had a nice house, she thought.

Ash picked a white envelope up off the bench and read what was written on it. Seeing that it was addressed to 'Christopher', made Ash smile. Now she understood why he just went by 'Chris'.

She took the piece of paper out of the envelope, leaving the envelope on the bench as she unfolded the paper. She scanned it, not too sure what she was even looking at. None of it made sense to her. It had some numbers on it and what looked like a 'total cost'.

She shrugged to herself, carelessly placing it back on the bench before grabbing the next envelope. This one was addressed the same, with the same name and address. She took the folded piece of paper out like before.

Chris had clearly already looked at all the mail that was sitting on his bench, as it was all already opened. Ash was just having a look at what he'd already seen.

This piece of paper was pretty well the same as the last one, just set out a bit differently with a few different things on it, things that Ash didn't know about and didn't really care about. Chris's world was a strange one.

There was something else on the bench with the mail, not in an envelope. Ash grabbed it and looked through it. It had pictures of different things on it, with a price attached to each picture, telling the reader all about the latest 'specials' and 'deals' that this place had going on.

Ash put it back down and grabbed the third envelope, planning on seeing what was in it.

"What are you doing?"

Ash jumped, startled. Chris was standing in the doorway, an amused smile on his face as Ash quickly put the third envelope down, not sure what to say.

"You going through my mail?" Chris asked, the smile still on his face as he walked in.

Ash crossed her arms defensively and stood a bit straighter. "What else am I meant to do while I wait for you to get whatever you're getting?"

Chris picked up one of the pieces of paper that she'd left out of its envelope and looked at it.

"What even is this stuff anyway?" she asked. "I've never seen anything like this before. You live in a strange place."

Chris looked at her, holding up the piece of paper, the smile still there.

"This is called an 'electricity bill'," he said, the amusement clear as he grabbed the other piece of paper, holding it up as well. "And this is an 'Internet bill'."

The unamused look remained on Ash's face. Like she even knew what 'Internet' was.

"You live in a weird place," was all she could make herself say.

Chris just laughed, putting the bills back on the bench. He took the empty envelopes and threw them into the bin that was by the bench.

Ash grabbed the other piece of mail that Chris hadn't explained. She held it out to him, and he took it.

"This is a 'catalogue'," he said before throwing it into the bin as well. "Shows you what certain stores or businesses have for sale and the prices for them. Complete scam if you ask me. That's why it's called 'junk mail'."

Ash gave a bit of a nod, watching Chris grab the bills off the bench and disappear out of the kitchen as he looked at them.

"You ready to go yet?" Ash called, seeing him head back into his bedroom.

"Yeah, just give me a sec to take care of this before we go anywhere."

Ash rolled her eyes, back to looking around while she waited. She picked up the third envelope, checking to make sure Chris wasn't about to stop her from seeing what was in it. She opened it and pulled out a card, a frown on her face as she read what was written on the inside.

"Happy Birthday, Chris.

"Hope you have a fantastic day and hope we can catch up soon.

"Lots of love, Mom."

Ash couldn't help but smile. It was sweet. His mother clearly cared about him, and he clearly cared about her too. Chris's birthday must have been rather recent. She saw the calendar on the wall and checked the date. The first day of October had something written on it and she read it, seeing that it was a reminder to go out to dinner. Maybe that was his birthday? She didn't even know what date it was today. Ash put the card back into the envelope, leaving it where she'd found it on the bench before moving on.

She moved out of the kitchen, going through the living room and down the hallway. She saw Chris in his bedroom, his back to her as he sat at the desk, looking at something.

Ash went in and Chris glanced over his shoulder at her. She stopped just behind him, looking over his shoulder at what he was doing.

Ash didn't know what he was even looking at. It looked like one of the phones Chris had, only a lot bigger and the screen was horizontal. It had something attached to it with numbers, letters, and a few other symbols that Ash didn't recognize. She saw a few words on it: CapsLk, Tab, Enter, Shift, Backspace, Delete.

None of it made sense to her.

"What are you doing?" she asked, seeing something on the screen. Chris had educated her the best he could on phones, so she figured that it was a 'screen' for this device as well.

"Figured I should probably pay my bills before I leave or else I'll get home and have no electricity and I'll have to rearrange my Internet if I don't pay it," Chris said, tapping at the numbers and letters on the thing attached to the device. Ash watched as what he was typing appeared on the screen.

"Is this like, a bigger phone or something?" Ash dared to ask, feeling a bit silly for not knowing.

The smile appeared on Chris's face again, his focus on what he was doing. "This is a laptop. It's a computer, not quite the same as a phone."

"Riiiight."

Chris looked at her and what was on the screen changed to something else. Ash couldn't help but notice that down in the laptop's right-hand corner it had what looked like the date. By the looks of it, it was the twentieth of October.

"It's like down in Oz, how they got our ID sorted out," Chris explained, Ash nodding a bit as she took in what he was saying, continuing to watch the screen. "That reminds me, I need to find that in case I need it. You still got yours?"

Ash gave a nod. "Do you want me to have a look around and see if I can find it and you can keep paying your 'bills'?" she offered.

"That'd be great if you could."

"Where would you have put it?"

She looked at him as he thought.

"Not sure," Chris said, Ash rolling her eyes. Trust him to forget. "Have a look in the bathroom at the end of the hallway. Might be in one of the drawers. I would have put it somewhere where people wouldn't just find it, because it'd raise a few questions about when I disappeared."

Ash left the room, heading down the remainder of the hallway, seeing the bathroom door open. There was a room on either side of it, both doors open and curtains closed. One of them had a bed and chest of drawers in it. The other room didn't have a lot in it from what she could see. Ash couldn't see much in there as it was dark inside.

Ignoring it, Ash went into the bathroom. Enough light was coming in the window for her to see by. She opened the first drawer that she saw, rummaging through it and finding nothing. It was the same result for the next two drawers and, once they'd been thoroughly searched, Ash looked around the rest of the bathroom, looking into the shower and behind the mirror, coming up empty-handed every time.

"It's not in here!" Ash called down the hallway, still hearing Chris typing away on his laptop.

"Check the spare room on your right as you come out! Maybe I left it in there."

Ash left the bathroom and went into the spare room, pressing the light switch as she went through the doorway. It was weird for her, as they still didn't have electricity in Wonderland. Even though there'd been electricity in Oz, it had felt weird the entire time she'd been there.

Ash began her search, checking in the chest of drawers, the closet, and the bedside tables.

"Not here!"

She heard Chris sigh. "Alright, give me a second, I'm nearly done here."

She left the room, switched the light off, and waited, arms crossed. Chris appeared and moved past her, going into the other room and switching the light on. Ash followed him in, looking around and feeling rather impressed.

There were posters and artwork on the walls, and a desk with another computer on it against the wall on her left. She saw some racks stacked full of things that she didn't recognize, some bigger than others. There was a display cabinet and three bookshelves.

"What is all of this stuff?" Ash asked, going over to one of the racks next to the desk. The things in the racks all had titles, and she read a few of them.

Chris glanced at her as he rummaged through the desk. "You've got CDs, DVDs, books, everything really. CDs are the smaller ones, DVDs the bigger ones."

"What do they do?" she asked, marveling at everything.

"CDs play music, DVDs play film stuff," Chris explained, still looking through his desk.

There was nothing like this in Wonderland. All they had were books and now Ash was starting to wish that it was more up to date, like Chris's world.

Ash stood up straight. She grabbed one of the CDs and held it up to Chris. "These play music?"

Chris gave a nod, and Ash looked at it, flipping it over to see what was on the other side. There was more artwork and words on the back.

"Are these all songs? How do they get so many on such a small thing?"

"Your guess is as good as mine," Chris said. He sighed, shutting the last desk drawer and looking around as he placed his hands on his hips. "Wonder where it is..."

Chris went over to one of the bookshelves.

"So, what's 'film' exactly?" Ash asked, putting the CD back and grabbing a DVD this time, appreciating the artwork on the front.

She turned it over to look at the back, seeing a lot more words than had been on the CD. There were also a few smaller pictures of the people who were on the front.

"It's like ... moving pictures," Chris explained as he looked at the bookshelf, trying to figure out what he'd done with his Oz ID. "Instead of just one still picture, it's a series that all make it move and tells a story. If that makes any sense."

"It's got my interest."

Chris smiled in amusement as Ash continued to read the words on the back of the DVD, then he turned back to the bookshelf.

Suddenly, he remembered where he'd put the ID. He scanned the books, found the one he was after, and took it off the shelf. It was the one he'd left behind on the riverbank when he'd gone down into Wonderland. He opened it to the very back, and there was his Oz ID neatly tucked away out of sight.

A smile appeared on his face as he took the ID out, put the book back, and looked at Ash. Ash looked up, seeing him holding the ID.

"We can go now," he said, putting the ID card in his front pocket. "We good to go?"

Ash looked at him for a few seconds before holding up the DVD. "Think you could show me how film works before we leave?"

CHAPTER EIGHT

Modern Technology

"So, he kills people who kill other people?" Ash asked as Chris put the DVD back into its case, left it on the coffee table, and switched everything off.

Ash glanced at the framed picture again but quickly looked back to Chris, hoping he hadn't seen her.

"Yes, but it's all fictional," he said, taking his phone out of his pocket and checking the time. "Man, we need to get moving. It's nearly six."

"Like, in the evening?"

Chris nodded, put his phone away, and checked his pockets to make sure he had everything: keys, wallet, phone.

"We've been here all day," he said. "They're probably wondering where we are. We need to head out before it gets too dark."

Ash got up from the sofa, stretching a bit. "Guess we should get moving then."

Chris nodded and left the living room, heading back to his bedroom, Ash in tow. He flicked the light switch on and went over to the window. He sighed as he looked outside.

Ash joined him at the window, and saw the snow was coming down hard, with the streetlights the only source of light. She could feel the cold coming off the window.

"Shit," Chris said. "We've left it too late. We can't go out now. It's dark and it's snowing. We're going to have to wait until tomorrow. Hopefully, the others won't worry too much."

"Alex always worries no matter what the situation is," Ash said. "I'm sure it'll be fine. It gives them more time to figure stuff out before we get down there."

Chris sighed again and pulled the curtains closed. "Alright, well, you can take the spare room down the hallway," he said. "The bed's already made, so if you need anything else just let me know. Guess we just go back to the TV and see if there's anything on to watch."

Ash gave him a smile and followed him out of the room, turning the light off as she went out. Chris walked through the living room, then headed into the kitchen. Ash retook her position on the sofa.

"You hungry?" Chris called from the kitchen.

Ash looked over and saw him take the birthday card out of the envelope and look at it. She brought her knees up onto the sofa as she watched him put the card at the end of the bench near the wall.

"I'd be lying if I said I wasn't," Ash said. "You cooking?"

"Was thinking of ordering something, actually," he said as he came back into the living room. He picked up the TV remote and joined her on the sofa. "It's easier."

Ash gave a nod, watching Chris press one of the buttons on the remote and switch the TV on.

"If it's the easier option, then I'm up for it," Ash said.

Chris didn't even glance at her as he pressed another button on the remote, making the TV guide appear on the screen. Focusing on the TV, he grabbed his phone out of his pocket and held it out to Ash who frowned at it.

"I'll direct you in ordering pizza for us," he said, his gaze still on the TV as he found a channel with something on it that he wanted to watch.

Ash took the phone from him and hit the home button as Chris turned the TV volume up. Ash had never heard about 'pizza' before, but it had her interest. She held Chris's phone back out to him, and Chris looked at her.

"Passcode."

"Right, sorry," Chris said, taking it from her and typing in the passcode before handing it back again. "Alright, you ready to learn something new?"

Ash nodded eagerly, a smile appearing on Chris's face. The TV was currently the only light source they had, as Chris hadn't bothered to turn the room's lights on. There was a dull light coming in from the kitchen, but it wasn't nearly enough to light up the entire living room, just a yard or so from the kitchen's entranceway.

Chris looked at his phone as Ash awaited instructions.

"Alright, so you want to tap on that icon there," he said, pointing to one of the little square pictures on the screen as a notification appeared at the top, indicating that someone had messaged him. "Ignore that, I'll check it once this is done. So, press on that icon to start with. This is easy for you, since I already have the app for where I order from. Makes life a lot easier."

Ash gave a laugh, the smile staying on Chris's face. Ash tapped on the icon and the screen changed, saying that it was loading the next stage. Ash had missed being around Chris. She hadn't realized until today how much she enjoyed his company and how much she missed him.

"Alright, now we get to the fun part," Chris said, Ash back to listening. "Deciding what we want. Any ideas on your end of things?"

Ash shook her head as another message came through from the same person as before. Chris touched the screen and swiped away the notification.

"Just scroll through all the options and pick one that takes your fancy," Chris said. "I always order the same thing, so I already know what I want."

Ash nodded and watched him tap on one of the pictures, seeing a message saying it had been added to their order. She hadn't ever seen anything like what she was looking at on Chris's phone, and now she was interested to find out what these 'pizzas' were like.

"Half of this stuff I've never heard of," Ash said as she slowly scrolled through the options. "Any recommendations?"

She looked at him, seeing him thinking.

"Well, it depends what you like," he said, focusing on the phone screen. He pointed to one of the options. "That one's pretty good. It's sort of got a bit of everything on it, but it tastes good. The decision's up to you, though."

Ash gave him a smile, getting one in return. "You know, this might sound crazy, but today's been the most fun I've had in a very long time," she said, glad to see the smile stay on Chris's face.

"I'm glad to hear it," he said. "Shame it has to come to an end tomorrow. But that's what happens. We can't have fun all the time."

He shrugged and Ash looked back at the phone.

"I'll try the one you suggested," she said, tapping on the picture. "Now what?"

Chris took the phone back from her. "I'll do the rest. I'll pay for it when it gets delivered, so until then we can relax and watch whatever's on TV."

Ash sat back and relaxed into the sofa as Chris finished his order. She glanced at him, seeing him responding to whoever had messaged him a few minutes ago, but she didn't say anything.

He finally locked his phone and put it on the arm of the sofa, his attention now on the TV again. "Now we wait. Shouldn't be too long."

They both fell silent, just watching the TV screen.

"So, anyway," Ash said, breaking the silence after a while and getting a glance from Chris. "What have you been up to since we parted ways?"

Chris shrugged, turning his attention to her. "Not a lot. Just been doing bits and pieces of everything. Watching stuff, writing stuff, getting back up to date with things I missed while I was gone. Nothing overly amazing."

Ash gave a nod. "Sounds like you've been having a decent time."

Chris gave a bit of a nod this time. "What about you? I noticed that Alex's hair isn't blue anymore, back to his natural color by the looks of it."

Ash nodded again and looked at the TV again. "Yeah, he wanted a change, so he let it go back to normal. It took me a bit to get used to him being a brown cat instead of a blue one, but it feels normal now. It's not as strange anymore."

"But what about you?" Chris asked again. Ash looked at him. "What have *you* been doing since I last saw you?"

Ash gave a shrug, not looking away from him this time. "Not really anything. I mean, apart from more or less running Wonderland and making sure Marion's still locked away but, as we all see, I've failed on at least one of those tasks."

Chris looked at her sadly, shifting to face her a bit more. "That's not your fault," he said. Ash looked away and shrugged. "I'm serious, Ash. However she got out couldn't have been avoided. I'm just surprised that it didn't happen sooner. You couldn't have prevented it even if you'd tried."

Ash gave another shrug, and Chris spoke again. "Any ideas on how she got out?"

Ash shook her head, looking back at him. "No idea. That's why I was hoping Matt would have a look around since he's good at finding these types of things. But we'll worry about that more when we get there tomorrow. Can we maybe not talk about Wonderland for the rest of the night?"

Chris gave a nod, Ash giving him a bit of a tired smile in return. "Sure. Anything in particular you do want to talk about?"

Ash gave him another smile, and Chris wondered what she was about to say.

"I saw that birthday card from your mom," she said, indicating the kitchen and making Chris glance over his shoulder and into the room. "When was it?"

"A few weeks ago."

"Did you do anything fun for it?"

Chris shrugged. "Depends on what you classify as fun. I spent the majority of the day at home doing nothing and then went out to dinner with a couple of people. It was a good day overall."

Ash gave a nod, shifting her position to face him a bit more. "Well, I'm glad to hear you had a good day. If I'd known, I would have sent you a message."

"You don't have to, not even next year," Chris said, looking down as his phone made a noise. "I don't expect it."

"Well, from now on you should expect it because I'll make sure it happens," Ash said. "So happy late birthday."

"Thanks."

The smile stayed on Ash's face as there was a knock on the front door. Chris got up and headed out. Their order had arrived.

She heard Chris talking to whoever was on the other side of the door. A few minutes later, the door closed again, and Chris came back into the room, carrying two small square boxes.

Ash took the one he held out to her and he sat next to her again on the sofa, putting his own box on the coffee table.

"Feel free to try some of mine if you want. I don't mind," he offered, focus on the TV again. He picked up the remote again and switched channels.

"Thank you. So, what's tonight's plan?" she asked.

"Pizza and TV until we get tired and decide to call it a night," was his response. "Probably shouldn't stay up all hours though, since we have to get moving early in the morning to get down to Wonderland."

Ash nodded in agreement and opened the box, releasing an enticing aroma that made her stomach growl in anticipation.

"Sounds good to me."

CHAPTER NINE

Back Downstairs

"We good to get going?"

Ash nodded and Chris indicated for her to leave first. She headed out the front door and into the cold morning. She waited while Chris checked to make sure he had everything before he followed, shutting and locking the front door before turning and looking at her.

"Alright, let's get moving," he said, walking past her and down the front path. "It's not far. Just not the most fun way of getting down to Wonderland."

"How come?" Ash asked, hurrying to catch up to him.

"Well, the first time I ended up in Wonderland, I went down a rabbit hole, a literal rabbit hole," Chris explained as they walked side by side. "There's nothing wrong with that, apart from the fact that it's dark and dirty and narrow, and you don't know when the ground drops off until it happens."

He gave her a bit of a smile, and Ash looked at him with uncertainty. She hadn't known about the rabbit hole.

"You sure this is safe?"

"Sure."

Ash rolled her eyes, the two of them falling silent. There was still snow on the ground from the night before and they could see their breath wispy and white as they walked.

Eventually, they arrived at the right place. The closeness of the trees and bushes made Ash uncomfortable, but Chris just pushed his way through.

"Do you remember where to go?" Ash asked, roughly pushing a couple of bushes aside as she followed Chris.

Chris didn't bother responding, choosing instead to keep working his way through the vegetation. Ash sighed, stayed quiet, and just followed him. At least she couldn't really lose him, she thought, as his black jeans and black jacket stood out starkly against the white of the snow.

She was glad when they finally made it through into a clearing and onto solid grass, although there was currently more snow than grass. At least there was some space now, as the trees were set further apart here.

They stopped beside a river, mostly frozen except for where a thin stream of water trickled through the middle of the ice.

"It's around here somewhere," Chris said, looking around. "I doubt anyone's stumbled across it in the past ten months, so it might be harder to find, especially in this kind of weather. It was at the base of a tree."

"Guess we just get looking at trees, then?" Ash sighed, hands on hips as light snow started falling around them.

"Guess so."

Everything around here all looked much the same to Chris. He hadn't been back since he'd left Wonderland.

Ash watched him walk over to the closest tree and walk around it, looking at the base. She sighed and headed to a different tree, deciding she should help out and look as well.

Chris moved from tree to tree along the riverbank, going further away from where they'd originally come from. Eventually, something caught his eye at one of the larger trees.

The grass was quite overgrown around the base of the tree, where weeds, grass, and flowers all tangled together. Chris knelt, ignoring the cold dampness seeping into his jeans, and pushed the overgrown mess aside.

His face lit up into a broad smile when he saw a large hole at the base of the tree hiding behind the grass. He looked over his shoulder and saw Ash staring at a tree nearby, looking rather bored with the task.

"Ash, it's over here!" he called, getting her attention. "I've found it."

Ash walked over and crouched next to him.

He removed as much foliage as he could and, once it was clear enough, he looked at Ash.

"You ready for this?"

Abel watched Alex continue to pace back and forth, worry etched on his face.

"They should be here by now," Alex continued to stress for what was at least the hundredth time in the past thirty minutes. "They should have been here last night. It's been too long. Why aren't they back yet? What if something's happened?"

Matt sat back in his chair, arms crossed, watching Alex pace. Zeke and Gates were nowhere to be seen. He knew they were somewhere in the castle, though, as they didn't wish to go outside in this kind of weather.

"Sit down, cat," Matt ordered. Alex finally stopped moving and looked at him. "If something had happened, we'd know by now. If they're not here in another few days, that's when we worry. The weather could have been bad, or something else could have held them up. No need to worry just yet. Sit down, calm down, and stop worrying."

Alex continued to look at him, not saying a word or breaking the stare. Matt sighed and uncrossed his arms, leaning forward on his chair.

"Alright, look," he said, pushing himself out of his chair and readjusting his backwards cap. "If it makes you feel any better, I'll disappear for a bit and see if they're lurking anywhere on their way here."

Alex's face lit up with a smile. "You'd really do that?"

"Only to shut you up," was Matt's response, making a pout replace the smile on Alex's face. "I'll be back soon. If I find them, I'll step us all back here. So, I'll see you both later."

He flashed Alex and Abel a smile before stepping back into the shadow that had been close to where he'd been sitting.

Abel sighed, looking at Alex who was wringing his hands nervously.

"We really need to get moving on finding Marion," Alex said, looking around and fidgeting, not focusing on anything in particular. "She could be anywhere by now and I don't like that she's out there, even if she's not herself and not at her best right now. It's very worrying."

"Once everyone's here we can get moving," Abel said. "Depending on what time Matt gets back will depend on when we can get going. Any ideas on where we should try first?"

Alex shook his head, finally looking at Abel. "Ash was the one who was thinking of what we should be doing. She was hoping Matt would be able to figure something out to get us started, seeing as he's smart and is better at tracking people than we are."

"Well, we can't do anything but wait then, can we?"

Ash dusted herself off as Chris watched her, an amused smile on his face.

"I can't believe this is even a way into Wonderland," she said, the smile staying on Chris' face. "You seriously came down here that way the first time?"

Chris nodded but Ash wasn't very impressed.

"About time you two showed up," they heard, drawing their attention to the other side of the round room. Matt was leaning against the wall in between two of the doors, hands in pockets as he waited in the shadows. "Alex has been a constant worry, and he won't shut up. I'm here to pick you guys up, so that he shuts up about it."

Ash rolled her eyes. Of course, Alex was worrying. There wasn't anything he didn't worry about. He was always like that, so she wasn't overly surprised to hear it.

"Also, didn't think you'd want to go for a wander outside, seeing as the weather isn't the best," Matt continued, earning himself a glare from Ash that he ignored. "So here I am, your own personal chauffeur."

He gave them a slight, sarcastic bow, his trademark smirk on his face. Chris was amazed at how quickly Matt had sunk back into his old, Wonderland ways.

"Have you guys done anything without us?" Ash asked, walking over to where Matt was now standing up straight.

Matt shook his head. "Alex was adamant on waiting for the two of you before we started on anything."

Ash sighed. "Of course, he was."

Before any of them could say anything else, Matt grabbed both of them and, within an instant, they were in the castle. Chris felt his head spinning. It always happened whenever Matt shadow-stepped anyone anywhere. Chris remembered Matt saying it also used to happen to him before he got the hang of it.

"You guys got phones on you?" Matt asked.

Chris had made sure Ash had a phone while they were Upstairs and, as far as he was aware, she still had it with her. He definitely had his.

They both nodded.

"Alright, good, go find Nixx once we tell everyone else you're here," Matt said. "He's been working on some stuff and we've already all been to see him. So, once you go down and give him your phones, you'll find it a lot easier."

"What's he been working on?" Chris asked curiously.

"The good thing about down here is the magic," Matt began. "He's been working on stuff involving both technology *and* magic, so you can guess now that it's pretty cool. Basically, he's managed to do something—I didn't bother asking what because I don't care for science lectures—but it means all our phones are able to communicate down here now and even Upstairs."

The surprise was clear on Chris's face before he even realized that was his expression. "No way, really? That's fantastic. So, we'll be able to contact people at home now while we're down here?"

Matt nodded again. "Also, we can keep in contact down here easier. The wonders of magic, hey?"

"Alright, we'll go find him once everyone knows we're here," Ash said, already moving away from them. "Throne room, I assume?"

Matt nodded. "Actually, if you give me your phones now, I can drop them off while you do this," he suggested. Ash halted and looked back at him. "Saves you both a trip down to Nixx's lair."

Ash rolled her eyes, getting a smile in return before she came back, took her phone out of her pocket, and handed it to Matt. Chris did the same, and Matt smiled at them both before disappearing, making Chris shake his head.

"Alright, let's go let everyone know we're here," Chris sighed.

CHAPTER TEN

Beginning the Hunt

"Ash, you made it!" Alex exclaimed. He was next to her within seconds of her walking into the throne room. He threw his arms around her, making her roll her eyes as Chris entered the room behind her. "I was starting to think you weren't coming!"

"Well, we're here now, so you can stop worrying," Ash said.

Alex clung to her for a couple of minutes, before finally letting her go.

Chris noticed Matt sitting comfortably in one of the chairs, just watching. In the ten months since he'd last seen him, Chris had forgotten just how quickly Matt got things done. He certainly worked fast and had one of the better abilities among them.

Ash looked around the room, a frown on her face, before she looked at Matt. "Where are Gates and Zeke?"

"They're wherever there's a fireplace," he responded lazily. "Because I don't know if you've noticed, Ash, but it's kinda cold in here and outside."

"What did you do to this place while we were gone?" Abel spoke up, making Ash look at him. "The back door is completely frozen shut. I was just lucky that the front doors weren't like that, else I'd have frozen to death out there."

Ash looked annoyed and crossed her arms before speaking. "If you could see what it really looks like out there at the moment, you wouldn't be having a go at me about the weather. Ever since Marion started getting ... like she is now, Wonderland has been falling apart. We always thought you had something to do with it, but even with you gone, it continued getting worse. Something is causing it to change, and a few areas are even deteriorating. This weather is intended to cover up the worst of it to keep everyone feeling safe in their own homes."

"How is Marion connected to Wonderland?" Chris asked, shivering as he realized how cold it actually was in the throne room.

Ash looked at him with no expression on her face. "We don't know."

"Our best guess is something she did when she was in charge," Alex finally spoke up, everyone looking to him. He looked around at everyone. "Shouldn't we be discussing this with everyone here?"

Ash sighed and headed out of the throne room without a word. Alex was quick to follow her, then Chris, Abel, and Matt.

Ash was a few paces ahead and she turned into one of the rooms, everyone following her.

Gates looked over from where he was lounging on one of the sofas. Zeke was on a chair. The only light came from the fire in the fireplace and a few candles on the walls.

"Now that we're all in the same room, we can talk about this properly," Ash said, forcing Gates to move over so she could sit on the sofa next to him. She gestured to everyone else. "Take a seat and we can talk."

Gates didn't look overly pleased when Alex forced him to move along again so he could sit next to Ash on her other side. Once everyone was sitting, Ash looked around at them all.

"To quickly recap what was just said, Marion is somehow killing Wonderland because of whatever's going on with her," Ash began. "It's going to be completely uninhabitable if we let it go on. We don't know how she's connected to the land, but we need to find her and figure it out before it gets any worse. We don't know how long we have."

"Any leads on where she might be?" Gates asked, fishing his cigarettes out of his pocket and looking for his lighter. "Because without leads we have nothing to go on and it'll be a waste of everyone's time coming down here."

Ash shot him a glare, getting one in return. Gates didn't want to be here.

"You didn't have to come and help us," Ash said.

"You forced my hand."

Ash shook her head, not in the mood to argue. She looked at Matt, ignoring Gates who found what he was after. "You're better at finding people than any of us here. We were hoping you could have a look around in the dungeons because you often see things we don't."

Matt returned her look, thinking. He'd already figured he was going to have to be the one to do most of the work. These guys had no idea.

"Alright, I'll see what I can find," he eventually said in response before standing up, taking half a step back, and disappearing into the shadows.

Ash sighed. She hated it when Matt did that. She got up and left the room. Chris and Alex were the first ones to follow, Gates and Zeke moments later with Abel. Abel accepted the now lit cigarette from Gates on their way out.

Ash reached the door that led down into the dungeons, unlocking it and heading down the steps, not waiting for anyone. At the bottom, she unlocked the second door and stepped through, the others in tow, no one saying a word.

Matt was nowhere to be seen within the top level of the dungeons, so Ash continued on her way, heading down to the next level where Marion had been kept.

Sure enough, Matt was in the cell that had recently held Marion. He was crouched in the back corner, running his hand over the cold stone.

He looked over to the rest of them, the candle on the wall the only source of light within the small room.

"Who's been down here?" he asked seriously, still crouched down but having linked his fingers together.

"Recently?" Ash asked, arms crossed.

"Anyone, anytime, since we left."

No one said anything as they watched Ash think about the question. After a minute or two, she responded.

"Alex, myself, and one of my guards," she said. Matt watched her the whole time, his mind ticking over every possibility. "It was the same guard every time. He was down here just before they disappeared."

Matt nodded and went back to looking at the wall. He pointed to something on it, whatever he'd been running his hand over minutes prior.

"Whoever got them out left this behind," he said. It was too dark for the others to really see what he was pointing to. Chris could just make out what looked like a carved marking in the stone. "I've never seen this kind of symbol before but, if I had to guess, I'd say it's some rather powerful magic, dark magic. Probably what I felt when I showed up here."

Gates frowned, moving over to the cell door. He indicated for Ash to hand him the keys so he could unlock it.

She did so reluctantly, watching him unlock the door and carelessly toss the keys back to her. Scowling at him, she caught the keys as he stepped inside the cell and joined Matt at the back wall.

Gates crouched next to Matt, looking at what Matt had pointed out. "This isn't good," he said after a minute of looking at the mark etched into the wall. "Matt's right, this is some really powerful shit. Magic doesn't normally leave etching in walls."

"Any ideas on who or what it was?" Chris spoke up.

Gates leaned in and looked closer at the mark. He shook his head slowly, thinking as he stared at the wall. His expression changed a bit as he came to a realization. He stood up straight and sighed. Matt also stood up.

"What?" Ash asked.

"My best guess?" Gates said. "Carmen. We don't know what happened after we left. We have no idea what's been happening in Oz for the past ten months. We don't know if Carmen's still alive, but my best guess is that she is and she's the one responsible for breaking Marion and Hunter out of here."

"I'll go check the cell he was in," Matt said, Gates giving him a nod.

Matt disappeared and Gates stayed where he was in the cell.

"So, what do we do?" Alex asked, standing close to Ash.

Gates shrugged and Matt reappeared next to him.

"Same deal upstairs in the cell Hunter was in," Matt explained. He looked around at everyone outside the cell. "Looks like we're going to have to take a trip over into Oz, if you're all up for it."

Ash gave a nod. "Whatever we have to do to get Marion back."

"The only problem is, we don't know where they'll be," Zeke said, arms crossed as he stood off to Abel's right. "Because I highly doubt that they'd go somewhere they could be easily found. I doubt they'd be at their castle. We might be searching for a while."

Matt nodded slowly, thinking again, before speaking.

"Zeke's right, we're going to need a serious plan on what to do. We don't know what condition Oz is in, so we can't just go over there without a plan. We also don't know where Carmen would have taken them, so that's certainly another factor. What do we do?"

Everyone stayed quiet for a few minutes, but eventually Chris spoke up.

"Can we send a few of us into Oz to check the conditions and then, depending on what it's like, bring everyone else over?"

Matt looked at him. "That's not a bad idea." He looked at Gates. "You up for a trip?"

Gates nodded. "Sure."

Matt nodded back, looking around at the others again. "Who else wants to come for a trip?" he asked, opening the invitation to everyone. "I'll take one more person, so decide wisely."

Everyone looked at Chris, getting a sigh from him in return.

"Alright, fine, I'll go," he said reluctantly. "I guess it's only fair since I suggested it."

Matt gave a satisfied nod. "Alright, we'll get over there in the morning. It's too late now to really do anything and I'd rather make sure we have a proper game plan before we just go ahead and land in Oz. Everyone who's staying behind here, make sure you're ready to go at short notice. We don't know what it's going to be like over there or how long we'll be, but give us a few days and be ready to leave by the time we get back."

Everyone nodded and Matt nodded back before disappearing from the cell again. Gates left the cell, moving past the rest of them and making his way back upstairs, not wanting to be down in the dungeons any longer than he had to be.

Zeke followed, with Abel not far behind. Ash sighed, looking at Chris as Alex stayed next to her side, not saying anything.

"You sure you want to go back into Oz with them?" Ash asked. "Because you don't have to, you know. It's not compulsory."

"It's fine, it'll be fine," Chris said. "I trust them both. I'm going with the two safest guys we have here, nothing's going to go wrong."

CHAPTER ELEVEN

Bandits are the Least of Your Worries

"**B**e prepared for anything. We don't know what's lurking around Oz anymore," Matt said.

Chris and Gates gave a nod of understanding, not needing to be told twice. Matt put one hand on Chris's shoulder, the other on Gates's. Next thing, the three of them were outside under a tree, Chris's head spinning again in the process.

"Jesus Christ," was the first thing Matt said.

What lay before them was devastating. It was a barren wasteland that stretched out in front of them for as far as the eye could see. From where they were standing, they could see what was left of the Emerald City.

The Emerald City had been big, so the debris covered a lot of the land in front of them. Hardly any of it was left standing, rubble from the houses and other various buildings strewn around the ground.

Even the Yellow Brick Road wasn't fully intact anymore.

"Wonder if anyone managed to survive that," Chris said, none of them able to look away from the wreckage.

"I'd be very surprised if anyone did," Gates said truthfully. "I can't see how anyone could have made it out of that alive. It'd be a miracle for anyone to have gotten out after we left."

Chris gave a nod, neither of them saying anything else.

"We can't hang around, we're here for a reason," Matt said.

Gates tore his gaze away from the devastation and nodded. "So, what's the plan?" he asked, arms crossed.

"We start walking," Matt said. "We'll have to find somewhere to settle for the night because we don't know what still comes out in the dark and I don't think we should take the risk. First town we come across, that's we're staying."

Gates and Chris nodded, agreeing with what Matt had said. Matt began to walk, and the other two followed along quietly.

The sun was nearly gone by the time a town came into view. They headed for it, but Matt suddenly halted near the border of the town, holding his hand up and making the other two stop with him.

"Something's wrong here," he said, keeping his voice down. He narrowed his eyes and tilted his head as if he was listening. If something was wrong, Matt was usually the first one to feel it.

The streetlights were on, lighting up the stone roads and a few places around them, but there was no one out either on the roads or the sidewalks.

Chris and Gates exchanged looks but didn't say anything, knowing it was better not to interrupt Matt. He knew what he was doing.

"You hear that?" Matt suddenly asked, his voice still down.

"Hear what?" Gates asked, equally as quietly.

Matt headed off to his left, pushing a few bushes aside as he made his way around the border of the town. Gates and Chris followed him silently. A little way along, Matt slowed his pace and signaled for the other two to get down as he did the same.

Chris and Gates obliged, following Matt's instructions. That was when they heard the voices.

Matt shifted, pushing some bushes aside so he could see what was going on. Chris and Gates moved closer so they could also see.

"Great, just what we need, fucking bandits," Matt said, more to himself than to his companions.

He fell silent, and the three of them just watched what was happening. It was dark around this part of the town, as it was right on the border and there weren't any streetlights nearby. There was only a small bit of light coming from the other side of the house a few yards away from them, most likely from the street behind it.

A man was standing on the porch of the house, playing with what looked to be a rather sharp knife, his focus on it the whole time.

"You're gonna have to open the door, sometime," the man said, still focused on the knife. "I've got nothing but time, so I'll be right here on your porch when you wanna open up."

He fell silent and Chris took the time to get a good look at him. He was just below average height and dressed all in black, wearing what looked like a cap similar to Matt's. He was wearing it forwards, though, and a jacket with the hood up over the hat and a bandana covering the majority of his face.

"C'mon man, just open the door and we won't have any more problems," the man said, breaking the silence. "You owe me, and you knew I'd be around to collect, so hurry up and answer the door. I know you're home, so don't try and get outta this."

A minute later, the door to the house opened ever so slightly, getting the man's attention. Chris, Matt, and Gates watched as he stopped playing with the knife, still holding it though.

"'Bout time," the man said. "Care to explain why you left me standing out here for so long? I don't know if you've noticed, but it's kinda cold out here tonight. Pay up."

The person who'd opened the door said something quietly. Within less than a second of hearing it, the man on the porch violently stabbed his knife into the wall right next to the door, saying something just as quietly in response.

"Should we do something?" Chris whispered to Matt.

Matt shook his head, but didn't look away from the confrontation. "Best not to mess around with bandits, not the friendliest people around. Easier to leave them to themselves. You don't wanna get mixed up with these kinds of people."

Chris gave a nod, not saying anything more and going back to watching what was going on. The door of the house closed. The man was still on the porch but put something in his pocket, looking around as he did so. Chris didn't know much about bandits but, from this brief interaction, he could tell they weren't good people.

The three of them suddenly heard, close by, what sounded like someone whistling, signaling to another person. The man on the porch stopped what he was doing, clearly having heard it as well.

Matt sighed and Gates and Chris both looked at him, immediately seeing the problem. Someone was crouched next to Matt, just off to his side, holding a knife against his throat. It looked like the man on the porch hadn't come alone.

"Hands where I can see them, all three of you."

Chris, Gates, and Matt all did as they were told, not wanting this to escalate. The man behind Matt signaled for them all to stand up, which they did, as the knife stayed pressed against Matt's throat.

The man holding the knife was dressed similarly to the man on the porch. He had his snapback on forwards and the hood on his jacket over the top of it. He had a mask on, gold in color, with a symbol etched into it that ran the length from the top and down over the left eye.

Matt looked at the other two, clearly far from happy with the predicament they'd landed themselves in.

In the blink of an eye, Matt disappeared, the knife taken out of the man's hand at the same time. Matt reappeared behind the man, knife in hand, holding it against *his* throat this time.

"Hands where I can see them," Matt said with annoyance.

The man sighed and held his hands up as Gates and Chris lowered theirs.

Matt looked at Chris and Gates and was going to say something but was interrupted. The man who'd been on the porch came to a very quick stop, also holding his knife in his hand.

"You stay right where you are," Matt snapped, pushing the knife he held against the man's neck a bit more. "Hand the knife over."

The man hesitated, but realized he was outnumbered. Gates grabbed his knife and tucked it into the back of his belt as Matt spoke again.

"I don't particularly like being jumped," he explained, neither of the bandits saying anything. "But seeing as you're the first people we've seen here, I want to know a few things. First off, where is everyone?"

The bandit who'd been on the porch was the one to speak.

"They don't come outside after dark," he explained, knowing he didn't have much choice but to answer Matt's questions.

"Yet you two *only* come out at night, am I right?"

The bandit nodded but didn't say anything else.

Matt looked between the two of them as he decided what to say next. "You two know anything about what happened at the City?"

The two bandits exchanged looks as a very clear yes.

The bandit from the porch spoke again. "Why do you wanna know?"

"Because it didn't look like that when we left," Gates spoke up, both bandits looking to him. "Did anyone get out?"

The bandit who'd done all the talking frowned as he looked Gates over. He switched his gaze to Matt, looking him over as well, and his expression changed.

"Oh, you're Shade!" he exclaimed. He looked at Gates and Chris. "Which means you two must be part of that group as well, the ones that came over here from Wonderland. Holy shit."

Matt continued to look at him. "I'll take it you know who we are, then."

The bandit nodded. "Definitely. You're all kind of a local legend around these parts now."

"They might be able to help us out," Chris said.

Matt looked reluctant and still didn't release the bandit he was holding.

Both bandits gave a nod of agreement.

"We're more than happy to help you guys out with whatever it is that you need help with," the bandit said. "I'm Ted and this is Danny." Danny continued to stay silent as Ted continued. "Our hideout's not far from here if you need somewhere to stay for the night. We're more than happy to help out."

Matt looked at Chris and Gates for confirmation on what they wanted to do. Gates just gave a shrug, not having anything to say on the matter, and Chris just looked at Matt, not knowing what to say.

Matt sighed. He removed the knife from Danny's throat, pushing him forwards and away from himself.

"Fine," he said, carelessly tossing Danny's knife back to him and watching him catch it without a hassle. "But at the first sign of trouble, you're both dead."

CHAPTER TWELVE

City Below

"Mind the steps, the stone gets a bit slippery in the cold weather."

Chris, Matt, and Gates followed Ted and Danny down the stone steps that led underground.

There were no lights, and Chris was at the end of the line as they made their descent down into the dark unknown. He felt rather uncomfortable and made sure he wasn't about to slip on the steps or step wrong. The last thing he wanted was to miss a step entirely and crash into the four others in front of him.

The steps continued straight down, and it was so dark Chris could only just see the others in front of him. Minutes later they came to a brief stop and Ted knocked on a heavy wooden door.

A few seconds later, a small hatch opened in the door just above eye level, the light from behind the door being blocked seconds later by someone looking out. The hatch closed moments later, and they heard the door being unlocked from the other side.

The sound of the door creaking open made Chris even more uncomfortable as Ted headed in. Danny stood off to the side and indicated for the three of them to forward inside before him.

Matt was the first to move, as he was the closest to the door, stepping inside, but not before shooting Danny a warning look. Gates went in next, followed by Chris, then Danny.

The dim light of the room was a nice change from the darkness of the staircase. Danny shut the door once he was inside, locking it to ensure no one could get in after them. Danny then pushed past them and headed through another open doorway.

"Feel free to make yourselves at home," Ted offered, pulling the bandana off his face and removing his hood. "Just let me go and find the others and let them know what's going on so they don't freak out. Won't be a minute."

Before any of them could say anything, Ted had disappeared through the doorway Danny had gone through moments prior. Chris wondered just how big this underground lair truly was.

"Well," Matt said, breaking the silence. "This wasn't how it was meant to go."

Chris didn't say anything, and Gates also seemed unsure of what to say. Chris took the time to have a look around the room. It wasn't overly large, the ceiling was very low and, if Chris was correct, it was entirely made of dirt, much like parts of the underground home Matt had created back in Wonderland.

There were some Christmas lights strung up around the walls, the colors changing every minute or so. There were also a few dim lights in the corners of the small room, only lighting up small areas around them.

Matt didn't seem impressed with what he was seeing. He kept his arms crossed and moved over to one of the lights, looking it over as they waited for someone to come back and let them know what was going on.

A few minutes passed before Ted came back. The three of them looked over at him as he stopped in the doorway he'd disappeared through earlier on.

"C'mon in, let me show you around." He gave them a smile, indicating for them to follow him as he headed back the way he'd come.

Not wanting to lose him, Matt, Gates, and Chris followed, Matt once again in the lead. Ted was just up ahead as they headed down a long corridor, and they saw him begin to descend what appeared to be another set of steps.

The three of them followed without a word, heading down the spiral stone staircase, with Ted always a few paces ahead. The staircase seemed to go on for a while.

"I swear, this had better be worth our time," Matt said, his voice incredibly low as they followed cautiously. "First sign of trouble and we're out."

Ted stopped at the bottom of the staircase, waiting for the other three to join him. He gave them a friendly smile as they stopped a few paces up from him, standing on the stone steps.

"Welcome, gentlemen, to the City Below," Ted said, pushing open the double wooden doors and gesturing to what lay beyond.

Matt was once again the first one to move. Chris and Gates exchanged looks before hesitantly following. Ted gave them both a cheerful grin as they followed Matt through the doors.

"Oh my God," was only thing Chris could say.

They were standing on a rather high platform, making it possible for them to see the majority of the landscape below.

There were houses, most of which looked abandoned. It wasn't a large area, but it was much like Ted had said: a small city. There was a fountain in the middle of the stone courtyard, with no water running through it. The houses they could see were made entirely of stone. A much larger mansion stood at the very end of the street, with a large waterfall to the right of it.

They were a lot deeper below the surface than Chris had initially thought, as right near the large waterfall, there was a massive gaping hole very high up letting a lot of moonlight into the small city.

A few streetlights lit up the small residential area, lighting the way up to the mansion.

"Impressive, right?" Ted said, looking at the three of them, clearly very proud of their dwelling. He indicated for them to follow him again. "C'mon, let's go say hey to the others."

Without waiting for any kind of response from his three companions, Ted headed off to his left, past Matt and over to the well-maintained wooden steps that led down to the lower level of the city.

Matt went next, followed by Chris who made sure he held onto the fancy steel handrail on his way down, then Gates.

Ted glanced back at the three of them as he reached the cobblestoned street, beginning to make his way into the heart of his little city. Chris wondered a few things as he walked and looked around. How many people actually lived down here? Why did most of the places look to be abandoned? And how many people had Ted had been talking about when he'd said they were going to go and 'say hey to the others'?

They knew about Danny, but the way Ted had spoken made Chris think that maybe there were a few more people here that they needed to be concerned about.

They were quiet as they followed Ted through the almost silent town, the waterfall being one of the only things they could hear. It took a bit longer to walk the distance than Chris had thought it would, but they eventually arrived at the mansion's front door.

Ted grabbed the door handle and shoved the door open with his shoulder. Chris knew he wasn't the only one who winced as the door scraped loudly over the floor as it opened.

Ted gave them a bit of a grin and moved aside, gesturing for them to go inside as he stood off to the side of the doorway. "Welcome to our home, gentlemen." Matt hesitantly stepped inside, giving Ted a warning glare on his way through. "Don't worry, nothin's gonna bite you."

Matt seemed unconvinced but stayed where he was as Gates and Chris stepped into the room after him. The door scraped along the floor again as Ted shut it once the four of them were inside.

"This way."

Ted moved past them in the dim light, heading to a staircase in the middle of the room. Matt glanced back at the other two before following, caution in his every step.

Ted began ascending the stairs, humming something to himself as he walked, seemingly off in his own world.

Gates leaned in to talk to Chris as they followed him upstairs. "Is it just me, or does this whole thing feel ... off to you?" he asked, keeping his voice down and getting a brief glance from Matt who was still in front of them.

Chris nodded as the top of the staircase came into view. "It's not just you."

The house was too quiet, and it was clearly making Gates uneasy. Chris didn't blame him, he was feeling it, too.

They reached the top of the staircase. On the upper floor, all the doors were closed except for one at the end of the narrow hallway. Light and noise came through the partially opened door.

Ted glanced back at the three of them, giving them another grin as he headed down the hallway towards the room.

"Yo, we've got company!" Ted called as he reached the doorway, pushed the door open a bit more, and went into the room.

Matt glanced back at Gates and Chris before hesitantly following Ted into the room. He stopped near the doorway, in case the three of them needed to get out quickly.

"So, you've already met Danny," Ted began, pointing to Danny who wasn't wearing his mask anymore. He was lounging on one of the run-down sofas on the opposite side of the room and he looked incredibly unimpressed.

Ted indicated to the larger man in the room. "This here is Shawn, but we call him S for short." He pointed to the smaller man next to Shawn. "This is Jordan."

Shawn just looked at them, while Jordan gave the three of them a wave in greeting.

Ted looked at his three friends. "This is Matt, Chris, and uh…"

"Gates," Gates said, crossing his arms. "Pleasure."

"Dude, you guys are the ones that took down Marion, right?" Shawn said, pointing to each of them in turn, while Danny watched them judgmentally from the opposite side of the room. "You've no idea how sick that was. So many people owe you guys because of what you did. You guys are like, fuckin' legends around here."

Chris looked at Matt who glanced at him, looking a little thrown off at the greeting and reaction.

"That was like, ten months ago," Matt said, a bit confused at how word had gotten around so quickly. "And we didn't really do shit. We left, the City fell. We didn't do anything."

"Just take the fucking compliment," they heard Danny mutter, most likely having meant it to be to himself. "Jesus."

Matt shot him a glare, but Ted stepped in quickly.

"OK, we get it, there's tension between you guys," he said, trying to lighten the mood. "But like, y'know, can we calm this alpha male shit and save it for later? We've got business to discuss!"

"Bullshit, we don't have business with these guys," Danny said bitterly, taking his feet off the sofa and sitting up, feet now on the floor. He pointed at Ted. "We don't have to do shit for these guys! We've lasted this long without helping strangers, so why the interest in their business all of a sudden?"

Matt looked between the four of them. Danny certainly wasn't the happiest person tonight.

"Look guys, I don't want to be intruding on what you've got going on here," he began, Danny switching his glare to him. "Ted offered to help and, right now, truth be told, we could use it."

"Sure! Anything for you!" Ted said cheerfully. "Just let us know what you want and we're happy to help!"

Danny shook his head, pushing himself up off the sofa as his platinum blonde hair fell out of place.

"What ever happened to us staying outta other people's business? Huh?" he snapped. He indicated to the other three as he pushed his hair off his face, annoyed. "We don't get caught up in other people's problems, especially theirs. You saw what happened to the City. That's on them. You can count me out."

Without another word, he left, roughly pushing past everyone and disappearing out of the room.

Ted sighed, looking at Matt as he readjusted his hat. "He's just upset because you bested him earlier," he explained. "Just let us know what you need, and he'll come around. He just doesn't like being shown up by people."

"I can tell," Matt said monotonously. He sighed. "Alright then, if you're insistent on helping us, guess we should find somewhere to talk."

Ted nodded and indicated for all of them to follow as he headed to the door. "We'll go down to the dining room, more space there. Let's go!"

CHAPTER THIRTEEN

Discussion

"Take a seat wherever, we don't mind."

Matt automatically took the head of the magnificent long wooden table. Gates stayed close, sitting on the first chair on Matt's right. Chris took the seat opposite him on Matt's left.

Ted sat a few seats down from them, and Chris looked around as they waited for the other two to be seated. He figured Danny wouldn't be joining them any time soon.

The few lights that were on in the large dining hall made it obvious that calling it a dining room was an incredible understatement. Pieces of torn artwork and tapestries hung off the walls, chunks of wood were missing from the table, and Chris was sure he could see a sword on the floor near the door.

It made him wonder how this small city had ended up like this, and he hadn't even seen it in the daylight yet.

"So, like, you guys said you left, right?" Shawn said. He sat at the other end of the table, the head of the table opposite Matt, and Jordan was now next to Ted. "Where did you go?"

"Is that really what we're here to talk about?" Matt asked, linking his fingers together and resting his arms on the cold wood as he stared Shawn down from the opposite end of the long table.

"We went home," Gates spoke up, arms crossed as he leaned back in the hard wooden chair.

"Home, as in, back up top?" Jordan asked, looking interested now as he too leaned forwards to look at them all.

"Yeah, and we were all doing fine until someone came and interrupted us," Gates said, shooting Chris a slight glare. He was talking about Ash for sure. "But now, here we are, back down here and stuck until something gets done about this issue."

"You didn't have to come along," Chris commented.

Gates rolled his eyes. "You'd all be fucked without me."

Chris couldn't argue with that. Gates knew they needed him, but that didn't mean he wasn't going to complain about it the entire time.

"I know this isn't what we're here to talk about, but what's it like up top now?" Jordan asked. "I mean, like, how different is it?"

"What year is it up top?" Shawn asked, leaning his chin on his hand as he looked at the others.

"What year did you leave?" Matt asked, also looking interested now.

"2011."

Matt leaned back in his chair, no longer resting his arms on the table. "Boy, you've been gone a while."

Shawn frowned. "How long is a while? Like months, years, decades?"

"Well, it's nearly the end of 2018," Chris said, everyone looking at him now. "So, you've been gone for easily over seven years by now."

Shawn sat back in his chair, looking a bit taken aback upon hearing how long they'd been down here.

"Well, shit," was all he managed to say. He shifted a bit in his seat. "Seven years?" Chris gave a nod, and Shawn shook his head slowly as the reality of it sunk in. "Man, didn't know it'd been that long."

He gave Ted and Jordan a shrug, none of them saying anything more on the subject.

Matt looked around at them all before speaking, taking their silence as his cue to talk. "OK, now before we get into our business, I want to know a couple of things about you four." Matt pointed to Shawn. "What's your ability?"

Shawn frowned, indicating to himself, getting a nod from Matt. "Oh, aah, I'm invulnerable to objects."

"But?" Matt pushed, the frown appearing on Shawn's face again. "Surely there's some downside to that. You can't just be unable to be hit."

"Well, yeah, there is as we've unfortunately discovered," Shawn said. Matt indicated for him to elaborate. "If I get caught off guard, my ability has to reset if I've been concentrating on it. I have to really concentrate and remember it's on to use it."

"So, if you lose concentration, you temporarily lose your ability," Chris stated, making Shawn look to him. "Making you vulnerable."

He got a nod in return.

"Yeah, basically."

Matt nodded as he took the information in. He was glad to know people's weaknesses, as well as their strengths. If they were going to be helping them out, they all needed to know everyone's limitations.

He looked at Ted, indicating for him to speak next.

"I can temporarily borrow other people's abilities," Ted explained. "But when I do, it disables the person I take it from, leaving that person without any ability until it wears off with me."

"Dude, that sucks," Gates said. Ted looked at him and Gates returned his gaze. "Also, that means you stay away from my ability, got it?"

Ted nodded and Gates nodded in return before going back to staring at something across the room.

Matt looked at Jordan, indicating for him to speak.

"Uh, I have duplication, meaning I can multiply myself, if need be," he said. The interest was clear on Matt's face again. "Downside of mine, though, is that sometimes, even though I'm in full control of my duplicants, sometimes they're not the most ... responsive, I guess you'd say."

Matt frowned. "How so?"

Jordan cleared his throat awkwardly and shifted uncomfortably. "Aah, well, we had an incident a couple of months back. Basically, sometimes my duplicants aren't the brightest and don't understand simple instructions. Put simply, there's no longer a town over the other side of the river."

Matt exchanged looks with Gates and Chris, getting a rather concerned look from Gates.

"I can see how that would be a bit of an issue," Matt commented, Jordan nodding and avoiding his gaze by staring down at his hands. Matt looked back at Ted. "OK, what's Danny's ability and do you know the downside?"

"He can summon lightning storms, that kind of stuff," Ted said. "He can manipulate electricity, large and small amounts. But sometimes, if he gets a bit too worked up, he can't control it and it goes quite overboard and takes a bit to get a handle on again."

"That poor town across the river," Jordan said, shaking his head as he stared at the wall, the trauma written all over his face. "Won't ever be the same again."

Ted cleared his throat, linking and unlinking his fingers together. He glanced at Shawn and Jordan. "Yeah, we don't wanna talk about that right now. Best not to scare them off before we've even started helping."

"We don't really scare that easy, sorry," Gates said.

"That's good, very good," Ted said with a nod. He shifted in his chair again. "OK, so what are you guys doing down here again if you all went home? I would've thought that once you're back up top, you'd stay back up top."

"Well, duty calls and we come running," Matt said, crossing his arms as he leaned back into his chair a bit more. Gates rolled his eyes. "How much do you know about what's been going on over the last ten months? Not just here, but in Wonderland as well. Any info, whatever you guys have heard or know."

Ted gave a bit of a shrug, the other two listening in but not saying anything.

"I dunno, not a whole heap," Ted admitted. "But, I mean, we know that the Emerald City fell and there's nothing left there but rubble and ashes."

"Anyone make it out of there?" Chris asked, getting a shrug in return.

"No idea, we didn't hear of anyone making it out, but that doesn't mean no one did," Ted said not-so-helpfully. "To be completely honest, I'd be surprised if anyone survived that massacre. That army tore right through everyone and everything that was in there."

"Do you know if Carmen, the witch, got out?" Matt asked.

Ted shrugged again. "No idea. Haven't seen any witch activity over the past few months, but that doesn't mean she's not out there."

"Knowing her, she'll be laying low for a while," Shawn said, Jordan nodding in agreement. "I don't think she took too kindly to Heather being killed. She's probably planning some sort of revenge scheme against everyone left alive who had something to do with her death."

Jordan looked down the table at Matt, Gates, and Chris.

"Which one of you did it?" he asked. Matt leaned his chin on his hand as he looked at him. "Killed Heather, I mean."

"I did," Matt said, Shawn looking impressed. "Bitch deserved it. It was a blessing to her after everything she did to me when she had me locked up for months. I let her off easy."

"I don't think Carmen knows who actually killed her, though," Gates spoke up, everyone looking to him. "Because she'd have done something by now, not just free Marion, if she's even the one who did it, which, right now, seems likely to me. She'd have done something already if she knew who'd actually done it."

"Carmen takes her time with things, and she'd know it was someone from our group," Matt said, Gates giving a bit of a shrug. "Anyway, she's the least of our worries. We need to figure out where Marion went. That's our top priority."

"So, this is about Marion? She's out? That's why you're all down here again?" Shawn asked.

"Yes," said Matt. "And the sooner we find her, the sooner we can all go back home to our families."

CHAPTER FOURTEEN

Danny's Midnight Talk

"**M**aybe we should discuss this in the morning, it's getting kinda late," Ted said. He pushed his chair back, and the sound it made as it scraped across the floor made Chris wince. "You're more than welcome to stay in here tonight in a couple of the rooms or go out into town and find an empty house. We're not too fussed what you do."

"Danny might be," Gates commented, looking between Ted, Jordan, and Shawn. "He doesn't seem too pleased with our company."

Ted waved his hand, trying to casually dismiss it. "He'll come around," he said, sounding like he was trying to convince himself more than anyone else. "Just gotta ... give him reason to and ... don't make him upset..."

"Too late for that," Matt muttered.

Ted chose to ignore the comment, speaking again. "So, if you wanna find a spare room or more than one to crash in overnight, be our guests. There's plenty of room." He spread his arms out in front of himself. "Our house is your house."

Matt pushed his chair back, getting to his feet. "Well, alright, seeing as we're not going to talk about any more of this overnight, I'm heading back to Wonderland to grab our other companions who also need to be in on tomorrow's discussion." He looked at Ted and the other two bandits. "So, expect more people around when you wake up bright and early tomorrow. Have a good night."

With that, Matt stepped back, past the chair and into the darkness, and was gone.

Gates sighed, pushing his chair back and getting to his feet as well.

"How many other people will he be bringing back?" Jordan asked, looking uncertain.

Chris looked at him and, seeing the concern on his face, he thought about who would be coming back with Matt.

"Um, about four, I think," he said, not sure whether Nixx would be coming or if he was going to stay back in Wonderland. "Either four or five. Is that an issue?"

Jordan glanced at Shawn, then at Ted. He shook his head and crossed his arms as he leaned back in his chair. "Nope, just wondering."

Chris exchanged looks with Gates briefly before looking back at the three bandits. "Well, if there's an issue, let one of us know and we'll sort something out." He looked at Gates. "Alright, well I'm going to go and have a bit of a look around. You up for a walk?"

Gates gave a bit of a shrug. "Guess so, not like there's anything else to do."

"You need a guide?" Ted asked. "Because, I mean, if you do then I'm totally up for showing you the place, the city in general if you wanna have a complete look around. Although it's dark, so, I mean, you may not get the full experience."

He was just too eager, Gates thought. He didn't like the fact that they kept pushing themselves to be on the same team as them. He didn't trust them just yet. "I think we'll be OK. If we get into trouble in your abandoned city, we'll call."

Ted gave a bit of a nod and placed his hands flat on the table, still on his feet. "Ok, cool, cool. Just thought I'd offer, y'know?"

"Oh, just a quick piece of advice," Shawn spoke up. Everyone turned their attention to him. "If you're wandering around out there in the dark, don't go down past the forest."

"Dare we ask?" Gates said with a frown, crossing his arms and wondering what the deal with these guys really was.

None of them spoke for a few seconds, but eventually, Shawn answered Gates's question.

"Things lurk beyond the forest, both in and out of the trees," he explained. Chris suddenly remembered how he didn't like this part of the counties, where everything would kill you when it got dark. "Best to avoid it during the dark hours. Whatever lives in there doesn't show itself in the daylight and luckily doesn't venture onto this side of the trees that often, but you can't be too careful out there at night."

Gates didn't look impressed. He looked at Chris, who in return switched his gaze back to him. "Well, then. Guess we just avoid the forest."

Chris gave a nod of agreement, and Gates headed out of the dining hall, glancing at something on the way out. Ted stopped Chris on his way out.

"He doesn't really seem like he wants to be here," he noted, keeping his voice down. "I just don't want any trouble, y'know? Now that

Danny's kinda on the out with you guys, it might just make things a bit ... hard."

Chris looked at him for a few seconds before answering. "Don't worry about it. Matt won't let anything get out of control."

Ted looked unconvinced, but he let Chris continue on his way, allowing him to leave the room.

Gates looked up from where he was waiting at the massive double front door. "Everything all good in there?" he asked as Chris joined him.

"Yep."

Not pushing the matter, Gates opened one of the doors, ignoring it as it scraped against the floor like it had when they'd arrived. He headed outside into the dark, Chris not far behind him, forcefully pulling the door shut once he was out.

The two of them stood on the top step, looking down at the street below the mansion's front entrance. The streetlights close by were on, but further down the walkway there was very little light. The odd streetlight was on in front of a few houses but, for the most part, the city was in the dark.

"Where do you want to start?" Gates asked, putting his hands in his pockets.

Chris was looking around, trying to decide what to do. He gave a shrug. "I guess we just go for a walk around town and see what's where."

Without waiting for Chris to say anything more, Gates headed down the steps and began to make his way down the overgrown stone street.

Chris hurried along behind him before catching up and walking next to him at the slower pace. As they strolled and looked around, Chris wondered how late it was.

"You ever wonder how somewhere like this ended up in this state?" Gates asked.

"I do wonder," Chris said. "Think it was ever fully inhabited?"

Gates shrugged as he looked down at the ground, watching where he was stepping before looking ahead of himself again. "Most likely. Something clearly happened, though, to drive them all out. Just a matter of what it was that did it."

They fell silent as they continued to walk. Gates came to a halt at the dry fountain in the middle of the street, staring at it in the darkness. There were no lights on in this area.

"Wonder how long it's been like this," he stated. Chris looked around in the dark as Gates thought a bit before speaking again. "Judging by what we've already seen, the overgrown streets, this non-working fountain, and even some of those houses, I'd say it's been like this for a while."

"Maybe it's got something to do with whatever lurks beyond the forest," Chris suggested. "Because if what Shawn was saying is true about whatever lives in there, it could have caused a problem with the residents."

Gates shrugged. "Maybe."

They continued on their way, walking the dark, abandoned streets.

"So, what are we going to do once everyone else gets here?" Chris asked.

Gates glanced at him as they passed one of the lit streetlights. "We talk about what to do."

Chris nodded and stopped talking. Gates was obviously not in a very talkative mood. It had been a long day, though, so he wasn't too surprised that he was being short with him.

Not far ahead, they saw Danny and they stopped walking to watch what he was doing. He was occupied with one of the streetlights, the light flickering on and off. By the looks of it, he wasn't impressed with something. Gates and Chris exchanged looks as they stayed where they were.

"Everything OK?" Gates eventually called.

Danny switched his gaze to them. "Fuckin' perfect."

His response was slightly aggressive, and Chris didn't like it.

Danny gestured to the flickering light. "Does this look like everything's OK?"

Gates and Chris headed over to him as Danny's focus went back to the light and what to do about it.

"Something wrong with it?" Chris asked.

Danny didn't even glance at him as he reached up towards the light. They saw a slight spark jump between Danny's hand and the globe inside the light.

"Nah," Danny said sarcastically, glancing at them both this time. Gates narrowed his eyes and crossed his arms; he really didn't like this guy's attitude. "Yes, something's wrong with it. It shouldn't be flickering, and it's been pissing me off since I was told about it. But, of course, whatever's wrong with it isn't something I can fix, apparently."

"You should be able to though, right?" Chris asked. "Ted was saying you've got a bit of a knack for electricity."

Danny scoffed as the spark appeared again. "Ted doesn't know what he's talking about."

Gates chose not to respond, and he and Chris watched Danny's expression change back to annoyance before he reached up a bit further, getting a proper grip on the flickering light globe. They watched as a slight spark flashed again, then there was a very quick flash of light, and the globe went out completely.

"If it's not gonna cooperate, I don't want it in my town," Danny said as he let go of the now-dead globe. There was a bit of smoke coming off it. "What a waste."

Danny sighed and brushed his hands together before looking at the other two, looking them over as he placed his hands on his hips. "So, what are you guys doing wandering around after dark?"

Gates looked him over in return, arms still crossed as he summed Danny up. "We could ask you the same thing, but you were out here trying to fix something and decided to break it instead." Danny looked unimpressed, but Gates continued. "But seeing as you wish to know, we're out here because we're waiting for Matt to get back with the rest of our group so we can talk a few things over."

Danny looked at him for a few seconds as his words sunk in.

"So, there are more of you," he stated eventually, getting a nod from Gates and Chris. He sighed again, running his hand through his hair. "Wonderful."

"You don't seem overly happy to hear it," Chris noted, Danny switching his gaze solely to him.

"No shit, genius," Danny said. He shifted how he was standing and crossed his arms, mirroring Gates. "Look, everything's been fine around here the past however long it's been. We don't need people coming into our space and fucking things up. Getting us involved in your shit isn't something I really think should be happening, OK? Nothing against you lot personally, but you deal with your own stuff, we deal with ours. We're just simple thieves. We don't go out there and kill people. We rob people, we take things, inanimate objects, not lives. You guys are killers when you have to be, and I don't like that."

Neither Chris nor Gates spoke, so Danny continued with his rant, judgmental annoyance written all over his face.

"So, you'll have to excuse me if I come across as a bit harsh sometimes, because I don't currently agree with what the others are doing. They've all just jumped on board without even knowing the full details of your mission. They do that, that's who they are. You say the one right word and they'll jump. Sometimes it's best to just let thieves lie because it's what we do best."

Gates looked at him for a few seconds before deciding what to say in response.

"You know you don't have to join us and help if you don't want to," he said.

Danny looked him up and down, before making eye contact again. "Well, I don't know if you've figured it out yet but, yeah, I kinda do. Because I don't want my guys getting killed for some stupid mission that you can all do by yourselves. We might know the area, but I know the others will be more than happy to put their lives on the line to help and I don't wanna see someone get killed over whatever this mission is. Not one of my guys, not on my watch."

Gates gave a nod of understanding. Chris could see that Danny had possibly earned himself a bit of respect from his comments. He was loyal to his crew and both Gates and Chris could see that.

"Well, we'll do our best to stay out of as much trouble as possible, so we don't get anyone killed," Gates said.

Danny nodded slightly but didn't say anything. It was obvious his respect for Gates hadn't gone up yet.

Gates looked at Chris. "Anyway, Matt's probably back by now, we should head back inside."

"You remember the way?" Danny asked, his tone not as aggressive or annoyed any more. He indicated back the way they'd come. "I'm headin' back anyway, may as well walk the two of you back so you don't getcha selves into any trouble out here in the dark."

Without waiting for any kind of response, he moved past the two of them, heading back the way Chris and Gates had originally come.

It looked like it wouldn't take as much to get Danny on their side as they'd thought.

CHAPTER FIFTEEN

Explanations

A look of surprise crossed Ted's face the next morning as he came to a sudden halt in the doorway of the dining hall, before moving into the room.

Nearly all the seats at the table were taken and, now that Ted had arrived, they were just waiting on Shawn and Jordan.

"Uh, good morning, I guess," Ted said, awkwardly taking a seat next to Danny and looking sidelong at him. "I didn't think you'd be here with us today."

Danny was sitting with his elbow on the table and his head on his hand, looking bored. "Someone's gotta stop you guys getting yourselves killed."

Danny glanced at Gates who was sitting to the right of Matt, in the same seat he'd been in the previous night, but Gates chose to stay silent.

Matt looked around at everyone. "So, are we waiting for the other two to show up, or do we just assume that they're not coming and we should start?" he asked, directing the question at Ted and Danny.

Ted glanced at Danny who continued to ignore him, so he looked back to Matt and shrugged. Matt shot him an unamused look and went to say something, but Shawn and Jordan walked into the room before he could make any comment.

"Sorry we're late," Shawn apologized as he took his seat opposite Danny. Jordan sat on his left, filling the final place at the table opposite Ted. Shawn looked at Danny. "We're having a bit of trouble down on forty-nine that needs to be dealt with sooner rather than later."

Danny pursed his lips in thought, his head still on his hand as he regarded Shawn. "What kinda trouble we talkin' about?"

Shawn didn't break his gaze as he replied. "They've come back and are kinda refusing to leave. Which means we've gotta deal with them before they push further this way."

Everyone not directly involved in what they were talking about was confused.

"Alright, I'll deal with it," Danny sighed, looking like everything today was quite the chore. "We got time to go through this shit first, or should I get down there now and deal with it?"

Shawn shrugged, crossing his arms and leaning back in his chair a bit. "They're probably not gonna move right now, so we should have time to talk about this before we deal with it." Danny nodded and Shawn looked down the table at Matt, gesturing for him to begin. "The floor is all yours."

Matt wasn't impressed and looked at the four bandits. "Alright, then. I don't know if you met anyone else last night after we got back, but for those of you who didn't, this is Ash, Alex, Abel, and Zeke. Now that introductions are done, let's talk business."

He shifted, crossing his arms and resting them on the hard wooden table as he continued.

"We need help finding Marion," he said, getting straight into it and not wasting any time. "She disappeared from Wonderland, and we think Carmen may have been the one who busted her out. There was a mark on the cell wall that was soaked in some seriously dark magic."

"Would they have gone back to Carmen's castle?" Jordan asked, speaking up and making everyone look to him. "Because that's the most obvious thing to me."

"I doubt they'd be that stupid, that predictable," Gates said with a shake of his head. "Carmen would make sure she wouldn't be easy to track down and, if she does have Marion with her, she'd go elsewhere to keep her hidden from us. She'd know by now that we're after her."

Matt looked around at everyone again. "So, any suggestions on where to start? Because there was something seriously wrong going on with Wonderland before we came over here. We think Marion was doing something, or something was happening to her, that was killing the land and, if that's true, then it could very well happen here, as well."

The four bandits frowned, exchanging looks and shifting uncomfortably in their chairs.

"What do you mean?" Ted asked. "Killing it how?"

"Everything is deteriorating, you should see it," Ash said, shaking her head. She was sitting next to Chris on his right. "We had a problem a while ago when she was the Queen and everything was dying, but since she was locked down in the dungeons, the entire place has been falling apart. Everything's dying again and there are a lot of faults within the county at the moment. It's only getting worse."

"We need to find Marion because we think she's somehow connected to it all," Matt input, all of them back to looking at him now. "Any help would be greatly appreciated because we're running on a bit of a tight schedule."

Ted, Shawn, and Jordan all looked at Danny. Danny sighed, shifting his position so he was mirroring Matt. "OK, say we decide to help you out, where do you propose we start?"

"You boys know the area. We can start around here and work outwards."

Danny shook his head and gave a small unamused laugh. "Look, man, that's a great idea but there's a lot of surrounding area and we only know certain parts of it. If we're on such a tight schedule, we won't have time to go through every single area in Oz. We could easily miss her if she moves around and ends up somewhere we've already checked."

"We can still try," Ash said. Danny looked at her. "Danny, was it?" Danny gave a nod of confirmation. "I get what you're saying, but right now we have to take the chance. We *have* to find her. We can deal with the what-ifs later. We can split into two groups and try to cover more ground. We don't have a lot of options right now."

Danny looked her over briefly as he thought about the best way to respond. Eventually he sighed in defeat.

"OK," he said, running his hand through his hair and bringing a slight smile to Ash's lips. "OK, OK, you win. We'll split into two groups and cover more ground. We'll take the day to prep everything, and we'll head out once it gets dark, sound fair?"

Everyone around the table nodded.

Danny pushed his chair back and got to his feet. "Case closed, I'm going to deal with forty-nine."

"Need back up?" Jordan asked, as Danny pushed his chair back in under the table.

Danny gave him a slight nod before looking at the others. He gestured around at all of them. "Anyone else want to come help deal with this, or you all staying here to talk strategy? Open invitation."

"I'm up for a walk," Gates said, getting to his feet. He looked at Zeke. "You in?"

Zeke didn't seem too enthralled but nodded nonetheless, pushing his chair back and standing up.

Chris followed suit and also got to his feet.

Danny looked at his crew for his current mission. "Alright, meet you all outside in ten."

"So, what's the deal with this whole 'forty-nine' thing? What is 'forty-nine'?" Zeke asked as they stood around outside, waiting on Danny.

Jordan was already outside in the daylight with them, mask on and prepared for whatever they were about to do.

"We have specific areas named or numbered so we know where's where in the town boundaries, our land so to speak," Jordan explained, adjusting his hat then crossing his arms as they waited. "Forty-nine is down near the river, part of our border line."

"Shawn said that 'they' had come back and weren't about to leave," Chris stated. "Who are 'they', exactly?"

"'They're part of the Legion," Danny said as he came out the door, forcefully shutting it after himself before readjusting his mask and looking at them all. "They've been pushing further and further this way, not just into our area either, might I add."

"The Legion?" Chris frowned. This didn't sound good. "Who exactly is the Legion?"

"Vampires," Jordan said.

Chris looked at him now, eyebrows raised in surprise, wondering if he was joking. That wasn't what he'd expected to hear, though he wasn't too sure what he was expecting.

"Vampires?"

Jordan gave a solemn nod.

"Ever since the City fell, they've been pushing further and further into more areas of Oz. I'm surprised they haven't reached Wonderland yet, to be completely honest," Danny said. "They're normally out after dark though, which is what's gotten me concerned. It's not usual for them to come out in the daylight like this, especially this early in the morning."

"They only really appeared in large numbers after the City fell," Jordan input, getting a nod of agreement from Danny. "They've always been around, but they stayed relatively underground up until that point. Ever since then, they've been taking over more and more areas, turning more people for the Legion and then using others as food sources."

"We've been dealing with them for about a month or so," Danny said. "They've never crossed the river, but there's a first time for everything."

"How do we kill them?" Gates asked seriously. They had his interest now.

Danny and Jordan both looked to him.

"Well, that's just it, we don't know," Danny said, looking at the concern on their faces. "From what we've seen, they're your typical vampires: burn in the sunlight, come out at night, bite you and you become one of them, burn down your village because there may be one amongst you, type of vampires. We haven't had any stakes and shit, and we don't wanna get that close to them to test out a damn theory, y'feel?"

"Yeah, I feel," Gates said, rather unamused now. He sighed. "OK, so you don't have any real way to kill them, so how have you been getting rid of them? You said they keep coming back, so what do you do to get them to back off for a while?"

"Intimidation's worked so far, but that'll only last as long as they stay on that side of the river down on forty-nine," Danny said. Gates gave him an unamused look. "What? It's true! But look, either way, if we have to try something, we'll do it. We're not about to let them push themselves and their pointy little teeth onto our land, into our town. It won't happen, but if it does, I won't be around to see it. I'd rather be in LA than down here when the vampires take over for good."

Gates gave a nod this time, choosing to stay quiet. Danny looked at Jordan and indicated to him to begin moving.

Jordan took the lead and headed down the steps in front of the mansion, beginning to make his way onto the street, heading towards the empty fountain.

"Just be careful and let us deal with it for the most part," Danny said, following along behind Jordan, the other three following suit. "But, if it starts to get outta hand, we'd appreciate the help."

CHAPTER SIXTEEN

Down on Forty-Nine

"It's just up ahead. Don't wander off too far, and keep it quiet. Let me do the talking." Danny moved some branches out of the way and stayed at the head of the pack.

They'd taken the route through the forest, and it wasn't anywhere near as terrifying in the daylight as Chris had imagined it would be. Maybe it was worse in the dark. He wasn't about to stick around long enough to find out, though.

Danny stayed a pace in front as they reached the edge of the forest. Chris could hear the sound of the running water of the river not far ahead, but nothing else stirred. It made him quite uncomfortable.

The sunlight was bright as the group emerged from the forest, Danny heading straight for the riverbank.

Chris now saw what they'd been talking about. There were makeshift black tents pitched on the other side of the river, but nothing moved around the area at all.

The ground on one entire part of the riverbank on the other side near the tents was completely dead, the grass all gone, left brown and dead in every aspect of the word. A few of the trees near it were also dead, the leaves having shed, leaving nothing but twisted, skeletal branches in their wake.

"What's with the tents?" Zeke asked, his voice down as they all stopped a few paces back from Danny who was now at the edge of the bank, arms crossed as he observed the other side.

"They've figured out how to make them so the light doesn't penetrate the material, meaning that they won't burn while in there during the day," Jordan informed, his voice down as well. There was worry and concern in his voice, though, and it wasn't very comforting to hear. "Their leader isn't stupid. He knows a thing or two."

They all fell silent. There was no movement and no other sound apart from the rushing river in front of them all.

"Hey!" Danny suddenly shouted, his tone aggressive and making Zeke and Chris both jump from the sudden noise. "Whoever's in charge of this operation, getcha ass out here, right now!"

For a minute or two, nothing happened. Nothing stirred, no sound was heard. Chris glanced at Gates and Zeke, seeing the concern on their faces when there was finally a bit of movement from the front tent.

"Daniel, why so loud?" They all heard the gruff voice coming from within the tent, but Danny didn't even shift. "You don't wish to wake my crew, do you?"

"You need to leave, Graith," Danny said seriously, clearly already knowing who he was addressing, even without seeing the face behind the voice. "I'm getting sick of warning you. You need to leave. I don't wanna have to tell you again."

They all heard the amusement in the laugh from the man inside the tent. Chris wondered if this 'Graith' could see them at all. If the material was as sunlight-proof as Jordan had made it out to be, there wasn't a big chance they could be seen through it. But, then again, these were vampires. Their eyesight was probably better than that of most normal people.

"You can't hold us back forever you know," Graith responded. "We'll pass the river eventually and when we do, you're dead."

Danny scoffed, shifting his weight a bit. "You haven't yet, your threats are hollow. Get away from my river, get away from my property. I'm done warning you. This is your final chance before we take action."

There was another laugh from the tent. "You haven't done anything yet, *your* threats are the hollow ones. You won't cross to this side as long as we're over here. What are you seriously going to do if we refuse to leave?"

Danny didn't say anything in response, clearly not prepared for that question. He glanced over his shoulder at the other four as he thought.

They all heard Graith laugh again. "That's what I thought. Best just leave us to what we're doing, go back to your thieving and pillaging. We don't have time for you lot. I might be nice this time and spare you all."

Danny shook his head but stayed quiet.

Zeke spoke up, getting Danny's attention. "I may be able to help," he said, moving forwards to stand with him on the riverbank. "You said they're basically just like normal vampires, right?" Danny gave a nod and Zeke nodded in return, before turning his focus to the group of tents on the other side of the river. "So, if I were to do this, it should do something?"

Zeke clicked his fingers, and the tent furthest away went up in flames within seconds.

Danny was surprised. He hadn't been informed about who could do what, but now that he knew this was something Zeke could do, it was a lot more reassuring.

Moments later, the screams started from within the confines of the tent. One of the tent's inhabitants fled out into the light, already covered in flames. Within moments of the vampire being outside in the glaring light of the sun, the flames increased, rapidly spreading further over the surface of his body.

The screams got louder but stopped abruptly. All that was left was a pile of ashes. The tent continued to burn, whatever was left inside still screaming as the flames burned right through them.

No more vampires emerged, understanding that the sunlight would kill them quickly and not wanting to take that way out.

The group all heard Graith growl in annoyance. The eerie noise made Chris even more uncomfortable.

Gates and Jordan watched the tent continue to burn, while Zeke's focus turned to the main tent at the front where Graith was hiding away.

"How's that for a hollow threat?" Danny called. "This is your last warning. Next time, all the tents, including yours, go up in flames. Your choice. I'll be back after dark to make sure you're gone."

"Give us an hour after the sun goes down and we'll be out of your way," Graith said bitterly in response, the eeriness still there in his tone. "We can't go anywhere in the daylight. But don't think we won't be back."

"You come back, and you burn."

Graith growled again but didn't say anything more, letting Danny have the win for now.

Danny looked at the others and indicated for them to all head back the way they'd come. The group did as they were told, all heading back into the forest.

There was still no sound as they made their way back, pushing their way through the branches and the undergrowth. None of them spoke on the duration of the short journey, but once they'd made it back to the fountain, Danny spoke.

"I appreciate the help back there," he said, addressing Zeke as they all came to a halt. "Hopefully that'll keep them at bay for a while."

Zeke gave him a slight nod. "Here to help."

Chris saw Ash sitting outside the mansion with Alex who was cheerfully talking to her about something.

"So, what's the plan?" Chris asked Danny. "You check to make sure they're gone tonight and then we all head out for this hunt?"

"Sounds about right," he said with a nod, Gates rolling his eyes at the response. Danny shot him a slight look. "Give my boys a few hours to get a few things together, we'll check the riverbank and then head out. We'll plot a route and figure it out from there. Easier in the dark, as explained earlier."

"What do you want the rest of us to do while you do your planning?" Zeke asked.

Danny gave a shrug. "I dunno, chill? Up to you and your crew. I couldn't care less what you do as long as you don't trash my place and you let us figure out the best route to take in this search. Sound fair?"

"Sounds fair."

CHAPTER SEVENTEEN

Black Flag

"Alright boys, let's see this plan."

Danny placed the piece of paper on the table rather roughly, and Matt regarded it with crossed arms and narrowed eyes.

"Alright, we've spent the day trying to figure out where to go and we think we've narrowed it down to a few places to start with," Danny began, leaning over the table. "Assuming she hasn't left the county, we have six places we think she could have gone."

He shifted how he was standing as he pointed out the names of the places as he spoke.

"First is obviously Carmen's castle. That's quite a hike from here, though. The next place is close to the remains of the Emerald City; the closest town called Crest Hill. Then we have The CornRow. We're hoping she's not hiding out there because it's banshee territory, so we try to stay outta there as much as possible. If she's not at any of those three places, we then have the Morbid Marshes which we also try to stay out of as much as possible. The name should be enough of an explanation, just sayin'. Following them, we have either The Devil's Well, or Belle's Castle."

"The Devil's Well?" Ash queried, Danny looking away from his piece of paper and to her.

He gave a nod. "Some people say it's the way outta Hell, but no one's been able to prove anything. As far as I'm concerned, once you're in Hell, you're gone."

Ash gave a bit of a nod in return, not too sure what to believe.

"What's Belle's Castle?" Matt asked.

"Said to be abandoned most of the year," Danny explained, Ted giving a nod of confirmation. "Ghosts roam the halls, it's well-guarded and not a nice place to be lurking after dark. Supernatural hotspot, brings all the ghosts and ghouls when the sun goes down. Story goes that there was a family who lived there, wealthy pricks. Belle was the daughter of one of the castle owners. She turned up dead one morning, no explanation or nothin'. No one knows what happened, so it's all speculation.

"Mind you, this is all just talk and supposedly happened way back in the day, ever since then it's been supposedly abandoned. Dunno why it's such a hotspot for the supernatural. Whatever happened clearly caused some kind of thing that's attracted them all to it. But every year since that incident, they hold what's called the Funeral Masquerade at Belle's Castle."

"Funeral Masquerade?" Now Matt was interested.

Danny gave a nod. "Yeah, Funeral Masquerade. Cheery, hey?"

"How does this Funeral Masquerade work?" Chris asked, not having a very good feeling about it.

Danny looked at him. "Always takes place on 31 October, their creepy version of a Halloween get-together, I guess. The way it works is that all these people get invited and it's one big cluster of a party. Drink yourselves senseless and if you kill someone, well, that's the point. A death apparently appeases the spirit of Belle, hence why it takes place within Belle's Castle. Doesn't matter who dies and who doesn't. Only rule is that you can't kill yourself and it has to be done before the clock strikes four am. Prime time to watch out is about three am. When someone dies, you'll hear a bell sound. Fucked up shit, let me tell you."

Ash looked at Matt. "We're getting ourselves in way too deep here."

"How bad can it be?" Matt asked back. "We may not even have to go to this damn place, so stop worrying."

"You've gotta be invited to the Funeral Masquerade anyway. It's not just something you can show up to if you feel like it," Ted said. "None of us have ever gone and, hopefully, none of us ever will."

"What happens if no one dies?" Chris asked.

He got a shrug in return. "Dunno, always happens."

Chris gave a bit of a nod, not pushing the matter any further. Hopefully they found Marion before they had to check this supposedly over-haunted castle. If they did have to go into the castle, then hopefully it wasn't during Funeral Masquerade hours.

"OK," Matt said, back on track now as he looked at the paper. "Where are we gonna start? What's closest?"

"Crest Hill," Danny said, Matt nodding with interest as he thought. "If we take Crest Hill to start with, we can then go onto The Devil's Well. They're a bit of a distance apart, but we can make it there and back before sunrise if we move now."

"Alright, let's do that, then. We'll stay as one group for now, in case something happens. I don't want one team getting into some sort of trouble they can't get out of. Let's go."

The moonlight was bright enough to be able to see the road ahead. They'd passed the ruins of the Emerald City a few miles back and had been walking across barren landscape for a while now, following a dirt road that led away from what had once been the City.

They'd tried to skirt around the City as much as possible, not wanting to get too close, as there were signs that some of the Iron Army still remained in the ruins.

Slowly but surely, the small town of Crest Hill started coming into view. What had been a small glow of light on the horizon was now becoming more visible.

"Just keep on guard," Danny said, glancing over his shoulder at the rest of the group. He was in front, Ted not far off to his side. "We haven't been out this way in a while so we dunno what might be out here now. For all we know, Crest Hill could have problems of its own."

"Why's it called Crest Hill?" Alex asked. He stayed near Ash, making sure he wasn't going to get lost in the dark, trusting her to guide him.

"No idea," Danny said truthfully. "Never really thought to ask. I'm sure there's a reason. Some fancy reason like most places around here, anyway."

The group fell silent, no one having anything more to say on any matter. The town got closer still, streetlights finally visible at the main entrance, the dirt road becoming stone a few yards before the first light post. They reached the entrance to the town, a rather nice looking wooden sign saying 'CREST HILL' displayed right at the front.

"Alright, let's have a look around," Danny sighed. "Maybe someone can help us out and tell us what we need to know."

No one said anything in response, just letting Danny lead as they walked into town. The streetlights were on, but no one was out and about at this time of the night. They kept walking, heading into the heart of the town in the hopes of finding someone they could talk to.

Chris could see the town center up ahead as they walked down one of the streets. It wasn't far and it was a lot like the area they'd come from, with the same typical Oz feel to it: the fountain in the middle, though this one was actually full of water, and the housing built around the area making it more of a town circle than a town square.

Just as they were about to walk into the town square, Danny suddenly halted, holding his hand up and forcing the rest of the group to stop dead in their tracks.

"What's wrong?" Ted asked, his voice down as he stayed close by Danny who was focused on something in the town square as he lowered his hand.

"Black Flag," was all Danny said in response, his voice down as well.

Clearly understanding, Ted looked at the others, ushering them back a few paces and indicating for them to move out of the light of the streetlights.

Everyone moved down beside one of the houses. They could only just see the town square through the gap between the house they were standing near and the one next to it. Danny motioned for everyone to crouch down.

"What's going on?" Matt asked.

Danny pointed to something in the town square, everyone looking between the houses to see what he was talking about.

"You see the Black Flag?" he asked, voice down again as everyone tried to see what he'd already seen. "Hanging up on the rafters over the other side of the fountain."

"What about it?" Matt asked, having seen the flag which was gently moving in the slight breeze. He looked at Danny. "Issue with flags?"

Danny looked at him, but Matt was unable to make out his facial expression as he had his mask on like every other time he ventured out of the hideout.

"Black Flag indicates Banshee's End," he said, a frown appearing on everyone's faces, except the bandits' as they all knew what was going on. "If they control this area, there's no way Marion would be here or anywhere near here. We need to move outta here and try somewhere else. She won't be here and the longer we hang around, the more likely it is that we don't get out."

"What in the world is Banshee's End?" Ash asked, feeling rather confused and needing more of an explanation.

Danny looked at her now. "All you need to know is that they're not good. I can guarantee you that if they control Crest Hill, there'll be someone out here right now within town patrolling. We move now, we don't get caught up in their business and that's how I'd like it to stay."

Danny stood up without another word, everyone else doing the same. He indicated for them all to follow him as he began moving back the way they'd just come from.

Ash glanced at Chris and gave him a bit of a shrug, getting one in return.

"You'd better explain it all once we're clear of this town," Matt said seriously, not too many paces behind Danny who was once again in the lead.

Danny gave him a thumbs up in response, keeping quiet as he walked the stone streets, heading back to the entrance of the town.

It wasn't long before they all saw the entrance up ahead, Danny quickening his pace in the hopes of leaving sooner rather than later. Unfortunately, though, for the group of travelers, it was going to end up as later rather than sooner.

A group of people stood just outside the entrance to Crest Hill and Danny slowed his pace, coming to a defeated halt a few yards away, knowing they weren't about to leave. Everyone else stopped with him, and the person at the front of the other group stepped forwards, arms crossed as he regarded everyone.

"Strange to see bandits out here at this time of night," he commented, looking around at them all as he thought. "Didn't think you lot travelled in packs this large, let alone out here at Crest Hill. What business do you have out here?"

"Our business is our own and we've completed what we came out for," Danny said confidently, shifting his weight a bit as he kept his hand on the hilt of the knife he had tucked in the back of his belt. It wasn't his only one either.

"Hands where I can see them, we don't want trouble, and we don't want you starting it." Danny reluctantly did as told, the others all raising their hands as well. The man looked around at them all again as he decided what to do. "We need to know your business, or we have to take you in to be dealt with accordingly. Can't be too careful out here now with the Legion parading around after dark."

"We're not part of their little clique," Shawn spoke up, the man looking to him. "That's the last thing we'd be."

The man looked back at Danny, seeing that he'd pretty well appointed himself as being in charge by speaking first.

"State your business or we take you in."

Danny stayed silent.

"We're looking for someone. We thought she might be here," Matt said, the man looking to him now. "We were wrong, there's no sign of her."

"No one's come through here in a few weeks," the man said. "Who is it you're looking for?"

"Doesn't matter who, just matters that she's not here."

"Her name's Marion and we need to find her as soon as possible," Chris spoke up. "So, if you've seen her, we need to know which direction she went in."

The man frowned. Something about what Chris had just said now had his full attention.

"Marion?" he asked, Chris nodding. "As in, Wonderland's corrupt queen, Marion?" Another nod. The man shifted. "Alright, I need you all to come with me."

He indicated to his men to move in, Danny not in the slightest bit happy as they began to be herded away from Crest Hill.

"Where are we going?" he asked bitterly.

"Banshee's End," the man in front replied. "There's someone there you need to speak to."

CHAPTER EIGHTEEN

Welcome to Banshee's End

The barren wasteland had been dragging on for ages and Chris had had just about enough of seeing absolutely nothing of interest as they walked in the dark, being escorted by the group who had directed them away from Crest Hill.

By the time something came into view, the sun was rising.

He could see what looked like an outpost, the large wooden structure surrounded by a high fence that was made half out of wood and half out of some sort of metal. Whatever it was, the surrounding fence was very well made and looked incredibly reinforced. It all spread out for what looked to be quite some time. Maybe it was more of a small town than an outpost, Chris thought.

The closer they got, the more detail Chris could make out. The entranceway had a gate attached, and a black flag hung from the top of the fence. The gate had the words 'Banshee's End' at the top and the words 'Welcomes You' below, all crudely scrawled into the wood in thick lettering.

"Gentlemen, welcome to Banshee's End," the man said, the first words spoken between any of them in the travelling party since they'd left Crest Hill.

The land around Banshee's End was like a desert. The plain was completely flat and lifeless, the ground beneath it all and the surrounding areas for miles just dirt and sand.

Chris was glad he'd never seen this part of the land before. It certainly wasn't an area he was keen to spend a whole lot of time in. Although, at least having the area completely flat would make it easy to spot an attack if it happened.

"You'll all be given passes to get you in and out of the outpost," the man explained as they continued to walk. As they got closer, Chris could see guards stationed at the front of the gate. "They'll ensure that you have access to all the correct areas within Banshee's End and it'll help with identification, so we know who we have within the walls."

They reached the gate, and the man took an ID card out of his pocket, holding it out to the guard on the right who took it. It looked like the ID cards that they'd used within the Emerald City. The guard looked it over before moving back to the post that held the gate. He pressed the ID card against a small part of the gate which lit up a bright green, the gate beginning to open slowly once the light had disappeared.

The man indicated for them to follow him before he headed inside, the remainder of his men getting their ID cards checked as well before being allowed to enter.

"As I just said, you'll all be assigned cards to get you access," he explained as they all followed him inside. "First, though, there's someone you need to see."

He fell silent as he walked, and Chris took the chance to look around.

The ground inside was still all dirt and desert sand. There was no sign of any paving, no roads or streets, but the area was rather big. There was some housing and what looked like small market areas as they walked further into the outpost.

It was still early, but there were a few people around. Some looked like regular, normal civilians, some looked like guards, and others clearly worked within the outpost. The people they passed gave them strange and curious looks as they passed. By the looks of it, they didn't get a lot of unfamiliar faces within the walls of their sanctuary.

A rather large building came into view. The path they were walking on approached it from the front and was obviously very well used, as there were marks in the dirt where everyone walked. The building was an old stone church, the towers reaching high up into the sky. It was impressive to say the least.

The man leading them glanced over his shoulder to ensure they were all still with him as they got closer to the church. No words were spoken as they walked up the slight incline, reaching the church's front steps. The man got his ID card out, walked up the broken stone steps, and pressed the card face down against a small spot in the large wooden doors.

Apparently, only some people had access to this impressive structure.

The small green light flashed, and the man indicated for them to follow as he grabbed the grand handle of the door on the left, opening the door and going inside. The group followed, the man waiting inside for them as he held the door until he was sure they were all in.

"This way," the man said, heading off into the church after the door closed and locked.

They followed him down a narrow corridor. There were no sounds apart from their footsteps.

Ash nudged Chris in the side, getting his attention as they walked into the main room of the church.

"Who do you think we're going to see?" she asked, keeping her voice down so it didn't echo off the walls and so only Chris could hear what she was saying.

Chris gave a bit of a shrug. "Wouldn't have a clue. Could be anyone but, by the looks of this security, whoever it is, they have to be important."

Ash gave a slight nod of agreement and fell quiet again.

The man led them through the main service area of the church. Chris noticed that it all seemed to be rather well-kept with nothing really out of place. The only source of light that he could see was daylight coming in through the large stained-glass windows set high in the walls.

The man went over to the back of the service area, getting his card out again and pressing it against the door in front of him.

The green light granted him access, and he opened the door and headed inside, holding the door for everyone else who forwarded in after him. Once they were all in, the man closed the door and moved in front of them again, down a dimly lit hallway, heading towards what looked to be a staircase that went down.

As usual, it was a spiral staircase lit by candles placed strategically on the walls. It seemed to be the only style within these counties, Chris thought.

Everyone followed the man down the stairs, the candlelight providing enough light for them to not trip.

At the end of the staircase was yet another door. Once again, the man's ID card and the green light unlocked it. Again, the man held the door open for the rest of the group, and they all forwarded into the room.

The first thing Chris noticed upon entering the room was the light. There was actual light, electric light, lighting up the entire room, making it easy to see what was going on. It was an impressive set up, reminding Chris of some of the crime shows that he used to watch on TV.

Noticeboards lined one entire wall of the large room, notes and pictures alike strung up along the boards. There were multiple desks placed around the room, and there were even a few computers on the desks closest to the noticeboard wall.

"This way," the man said once the door had closed, indicating for them to follow him again as he began walking.

A few people glanced up from their work at the desks, but most didn't pay any attention to them whatsoever.

They followed the man over to the noticeboard wall where a group of five people were gathered around one of the computers. The one sitting at the desk was pointing something out to the rest of his colleagues.

"Gentlemen," the man greeted as they approached, coming to a halt. "Sorry to interrupt, but I have some people you might be interested in talking to."

"No way, hey guys," Jacob greeted them with a large smile on his face as he looked from person to person. "I was wondering how long it was going to be before you lot interfered."

"Jesus, you actually survived it all," Matt said in surprise. "I, honest to God, didn't think anyone would've made it out alive, especially after we saw what happened to the City."

Jacob gave a bit of a shrug, crossing his arms as he addressed everyone. The others at the desk just listened. Chris smiled when he recognized Doug, one of the people who had stayed behind to defend the City and who'd trained with them all quite a bit.

"Some of us got out," Jacob explained, Chris returning his focus to him. "Not many, but there were a few of us. Most didn't make it, though." He glanced over his shoulder at Doug who didn't say a word before he looked back at the group in front of him. "Ben and Ruby didn't make it. They were killed on the front line, unfortunately."

"Sorry to hear that," Chris said. Those two had always been alright with him.

Jacob gave a slight nod before looking at the four bandits.

"Sorry, I haven't actually introduced myself." He held his hand out to Danny first. "The name's Jacob."

Danny reluctantly shook his hand. "Danny. This is Ted, Shawn, and Jordan."

Jacob gave each of them a nod as he shook their hands.

"Well, welcome aboard," Jacob said, crossing his arms. He looked at the man who had brought them here. "You got somewhere to hold them up while they're here?"

The man glanced at the group before addressing Jacob. "We'll get the IDs sorted out first and then we can worry about accommodation."

"You know which ones to give them?"

The man nodded and Jacob looked back to the group.

"Alright, if you go with Cain here, he'll get you all sorted out with ID and whatnot. Once that's all done, make your way back down here, and we'll explain what's going on."

CHAPTER NINETEEN

The Operation

"I can't believe he actually made it out, or that anyone made it out," Ash commented as they followed Cain back up to the main area in the church. "I'm shocked to say the least."

"You're not the only one," Matt said. "Whoever made it out of there is incredibly lucky. Makes me wonder *how* they got out."

"I'm sure everything will get explained," Chris said. He glanced at Matt as they followed Cain. "I'm sure if it isn't, you'll be first in line to knock someone out and find the information on your own."

Cain opened the door at the top of the staircase, heading back into the service area of the church. "Please try to refrain from intentionally injuring anyone while you're here," he sighed. "Much appreciated, thanks."

Matt rolled his eyes as Cain opened the external door and held it open. The sunlight hit everyone as they left the church. It was a lot brighter outside now than when they'd gone in, even though not an overly long period of time had passed.

Once everyone was outside, Cain shut the door and headed down the stone steps, veering off to his left this time. Not a word was spoken between anyone as they walked around the church, passing a few people and heading further into the outpost.

To Chris's disappointment, it was much the same in the way of the scenery: all barren dirt and sand, and some half-constructed houses in the area they were heading into. Unlike the front area that had many complete houses, this section didn't have as many finished products.

There were a few larger scale buildings within the small district that Cain was leading them into, and Chris wondered what they used them for. Were they temporary accommodation for people until they managed to get the proper houses built? Surely there weren't that many people here?

Cain led them past a few people and up to one of the buildings that looked like it had been there for quite a while. Much like the church, it was a bit dilapidated and seemed out of date for this era in the confines of Oz.

It wasn't an overly large building, but it was made of stone, unlike the housing and accommodation that they'd seen so far.

Cain grabbed his ID and scanned himself in, the green light allowing him to open the door. Another top security building, Chris noted.

Once they were all inside, Chris looked around as his eyes adjusted to the change in light. If he had to guess, this looked like it was once a bakery of some sort. Either that or a blacksmith's. He wasn't sure which was more accurate.

"Alright, if you'd all please take a seat," Cain said, sounding rather bored. This was probably something he hadn't wanted to have to deal with, but now he didn't have a choice. "Someone will be with you shortly."

Cain headed further into the building and Ash was the first to do as asked, taking a seat on one of the four available chairs. There weren't enough chairs for them all, so it was going to be first in, best dressed for the seats. Everyone else would be standing.

Danny was the next one to move, quickly grabbing the chair on the opposite end from where Ash was seated. Alex moved and sat next to Ash.

"So, what do you think's going on here exactly?" Zeke asked, taking the last available chair next to Danny who gave him a glance. "They've certainly got quite the operation going on down there in that church."

"Couldn't even begin to hazard a guess," Matt said, crossing his arms. "But whatever they're doing, it sure as hell looks important."

Everyone gave a nod of agreement, but no one said anything more as Cain reappeared with a middle-aged woman.

"Alright, just got to get a couple of details from everyone before we get this under way," Cain said, taking the piece of paper from woman. "I'm going to pass this piece of paper around to all of you and I need you to write a couple of things down for me: first name, last name, where you currently reside, and where you're originally from. Make sense?"

Everyone nodded again, and Cain continued speaking. "Once that's done, we'll move onto the next step. I'll explain what happens next once we get to it."

Chris was wondering how many steps there were going to be before they were issued with the correct identification and could actually find out what was going on.

Cain handed the paper and a pen to Matt who was the closest to him. Matt reluctantly took them and everyone else just watched and waited as he scribbled his name on the paper, followed by the relevant information.

Matt handed the paper and pen over to Gates who was next in line.

After a few minutes, everyone had finished writing. Danny was the final one to write his information down, forcing him to get up from where he'd been sitting to hand the paper and pen back to Cain, which he did rather forcefully.

"Thank you," Cain said, choosing not to comment on Danny's slight aggression. "We'll get this over with as quickly as possible."

"These will give you access to pretty well everywhere around the outpost," Cain explained a few hours later once everyone had been given their ID cards. "We'll head back to the church now, and Jacob can take it from there."

Once again, no one spoke as they made their way back to the church. It was a short walk and a few more people were out and about in the area now.

Cain scanned himself in as before, this time going in without bothering to hold the door for any of them.

They all trooped through the church to the door at the back, scanned in, and followed Cain back down the dimly lit staircase to the underground operations room.

"I'll leave you all to it," Cain said once they were inside the room. He then left, heading back up the staircase and disappearing from sight.

Danny crossed his arms, as he watched as Cain leave. "I don't like him."

He got a slight glance from Matt who decided to stay quiet.

"Hey, guys. Come over." Jacob waved them over to the back of the room, still with the four people he'd been with when they'd come in earlier.

Matt was the first one to move, with the others not far behind. The other workers in the room watched them pass but kept to themselves and quickly went back to what they were meant to be doing.

"So, what's the deal?" Matt asked. "What's going on here?"

"Glad you asked, and we'll get to that in just a second," Jacob said. Matt crossed his arms, just wanting an explanation. "First off, something I need to give each of you."

Matt glanced back at his group as Jacob grabbed a box off the table, opening it and grabbing something out.

"I want each of you to take one of these," he said, handing something to Matt, then to everyone else. "People should leave you alone if they see you've got one of these. They're quite handy, actually."

Jacob had handed each of them a small metallic badge in the shape of a castle with a banshee in the middle of it.

"What are they for?" Gates asked, looking up from the badge and noticing that Jacob had one pinned on his jacket. He looked around and everyone else in the room also seemed to have one.

"It means you work under me now," Jacob said. "Which, in turn, means that people should leave you alone for the most part and not question you or get in your way. A couple of our people did a bit of research over the past few months, and these badges will stop any sort of non-physical ability affecting you as long as you've got it on you."

Gates smiled a bit upon hearing that, giving Ash a glance but not saying anything. Ash in turn just rolled her eyes, not having anything to say back to him, even though she knew what he was implying.

"Alright, so now you going to tell us what's going on here?" Matt asked, just wanting to get answers now.

Jacob looked at him. "Yes, I'm glad you asked. There are a couple of people I'm going to need to introduce you all to, but one of them isn't around at the moment. He's out and we don't know when he'll be back."

"How many more people are we gonna have to be introduced to?" Danny asked with annoyance. He was tired, seeing as they'd travelled all night with no breaks and he just wanted to know what was going on. "Because I think I speak for everyone here when I say that we're all quite tired and would like to know what's going on down here before we go and get some sleep."

Jacob looked at him as he responded. "Once I've explained this, you can all go and get some sleep." Danny still didn't look very impressed. "So, if you'd give me ten minutes of your time and stop interrupting, we can get through this a lot quicker and you can go and do whatever you want afterwards, yes?"

Danny didn't say anything in response, and Jacob looked at him for a few more seconds before he spoke again.

"I'll introduce you to who you need to know tomorrow," he began, everyone listening now. "As previously stated, you might have to wait to meet one of our informants because he's out at the moment and we don't know when he's going to be back. There are two people that you really need to meet and he's one of them but, as for Craig, you can meet him tomorrow. OK, anyway, what we've been doing."

He indicated to the noticeboard wall with the different pieces of paper strung up over it all. Everyone turned to have a better look at it.

"As you can see, we've been working on quite a lot over the past ten months or so," he continued, moving around the table and onto the other side of it so that he was in front of the noticeboard. "We've been keeping track of pretty well everything that's been going on around all of the counties, keeping track of anything that's been happening. We've also been keeping very close tabs on Marion and everything that's been going on with her."

"Does that mean you know where she is?" Matt asked.

Jacob looked at him for a few seconds before he answered. "After she disappeared from Wonderland, we lost track of her. We can't seem to get her exact location now. We think Carmen's managed to mask their whereabouts so none of our defenses or abilities can get past it to find them."

"You're sure it's Carmen who got Marion and Hunter out," Ash stated.

Jacob nodded. "We're pretty sure it was. No one else would be able to do it, and there was a rather big influx of magic coming from the castle in Wonderland when it happened. Not a lot of witches have that kind of power. Carmen's one of the only ones who could have done it."

Ash stayed quiet, having received her answer.

Jacob continued. "We've been trying to track her since she left Wonderland and we think our best shot at getting her is in a few weeks' time at the Funeral Masquerade at Belle's Castle." Chris and Alex exchanged worried looks, neither liking the sound of that. "At this point in time, we're after all three of them: Carmen, Marion, and Hunter. None of them should be allowed to be out in civilization. They're all too dangerous."

"Would you happen to know what's been going on with Wonderland?" Ash spoke up, and Jacob looked at her again. "Marion's clearly connected to it somehow. Any ideas on why it's been deteriorating?"

Doug spoke up, moving and joining Jacob on the other side of the table. "From what we've been led to believe, we think Marion may be the one who created the multiple counties."

Everyone frowned and exchanged looks.

"What do you mean?" Chris asked.

Doug glanced at Jacob, who didn't say a word, giving him the chance to explain.

"Alright, this might sound rather strange and unbelievable, but you need to hear me out," he said. "We've been doing a lot of research on Marion, and we think that something happened to her in her past, way before she came down here. A couple of the people down here with us have been Upstairs, doing a bit of digging, and it turns out that Marion's actually an Upstairs local. She's not from down here."

He glanced at Jacob again before continuing.

"So, with this research, they managed to track down a couple of Marion's old friends," he continued, sounding like it was a bit uncomfortable to talk about. "She's been missing for years. They hadn't seen any sign of her in a very long time. They mentioned that she'd spent a bit of time in and out of the mental health ward over the years due to someone named Kieran who we think had a hand in whatever happened to her."

"They never actually said what it was?" Chris asked.

Doug shook his head. "They wouldn't really talk about it. But they said she'd always be talking about getting out, getting away to a better place, and we think that, somehow, that managed to create all these Underground worlds. We haven't quite figured out how yet, but we think that's why she's so connected to everything down here, especially Wonderland. If she's been having some kind of mental break, it could be what's been damaging the counties."

Doug hadn't been lying when he'd said it was hard to believe, Chris thought.

"Have there been any issues down here in Oz or is it just in Wonderland?" Matt asked seriously.

"We haven't seen anything yet, but it doesn't mean it won't happen," Jacob spoke up, back to being the one in charge. "We don't want to take any risks, so we're trying to find her."

"Hang on," Alex said, trying to get his head around everything they'd just been told. "If these worlds haven't been around forever, does that mean that everyone down here isn't actually from here? I'm confused."

Jacob looked at him and thought for a second, before indicating for him to follow as he moved down to the end of the wall. Everyone else followed, too.

Jacob stopped and pointed to the final noticeboard. There were multiple pieces of paper, all with different people's pictures on them. Alex frowned as he looked through the pictures on the wall.

Jacob indicated one near the top. It was a picture of Alex.

"Birthday 7 December 1987," Jacob said. "Chicago, Illinois, disappeared on 13 August 2012, reported missing by his long-term girlfriend, Sienna."

Alex had nothing to say and just stared at his picture on the wall.

Jacob pointed to the next picture. It was Ash.

"Birthday 2 February 1985," he continued, as everyone looked at the picture of Ash on the wall. "We had a bit of trouble finding information on you, but we know you disappeared on 8 July 2010. You were reported missing by your sister."

Ash and Alex both exchanged disbelieving looks as Jacob crossed his arms and looked around at the group.

"I know some of this might be a bit hard for you to hear, since you probably had no idea that everyone in here, in your group, is actually from Upstairs." He pointed to himself. "I'm from Upstairs too, so it's not just you lot. I already knew that, though. I'm well aware of where I come from. The more digging you do, the more you start to discover." He looked at Ash and Alex. "I know it might be hard to believe, but it's all true. We're still looking into everyone individually."

Ash didn't say anything, not sure what she was meant to say to any of the news that they'd just been told.

Jacob looked around at all of them again.

"You all go and get some rest. It's a lot to take in all at once." He looked at Doug. "Can you show them to their lodgings?"

Doug gave a nod, and Jacob looked back at the group. "Doug will show you where you'll be staying while you're here. We'll talk more tomorrow. We have a lot more to discuss but it will be easier if you're not so tired. Take the time to try and settle in. Come and find me or Doug if there's anything you need to know before tomorrow."

CHAPTER TWENTY

Craig

Chris sat on the edge of the bed next to Ash who was just staring across the room at the wall. She'd been rather quiet since they'd been down in the church.

The small brown cat caught his attention as he wandered past and jumped up onto one of the available chairs and settled down.

"You doing OK?" Chris asked Ash. "I know it's probably a lot to take in, finding out that you're not actually from here."

Ash continued to look at the wall and Chris didn't think she was going to speak.

"I just ... never thought anything of it before now," she said quietly. She looked at Chris and he could see how upset she really was. "I have a family up there somewhere and I didn't even know. I've been missing for at least eight years, Chris. They've probably given up looking for me by now and think I'm dead. How could I not know?"

A few tears ran down Ash's face and Chris put his arm around her shoulders. Ash leaned against him and closed her eyes as he pulled her closer.

"We'll sort it out, that's a promise," Chris said. "We'll sort it out."

Chris glanced over at Alex, and saw that the cat had his eyes closed. It wasn't late, but everyone needed to get some rest. It had been a long few days.

"Maybe you should get some sleep and worry about it later," he suggested.

Ash stayed against him as she nodded, then moved to sit up a bit. Chris indicated to Alex who was already asleep.

"You've got Alex here for you too, you know. He's going through the same thing as you with this. He's just found out that he's not from here either and that someone Upstairs misses him, too."

Ash gave another nod, wiping the tears off her face as Chris removed his arm from her shoulders.

"I'll be just down the hall if you need me for anything," he said, getting up and moving towards the door.

"Thank you, Chris."

Matt continued to look at all the pictures on the noticeboard wall. His arms were crossed, and the interest was clear on his face as he read through the information listed below each person's picture.

"Birthday 28 July 1981."

Matt glanced to his right. Jacob was leaning against the table, also with his arms crossed.

"Went missing and then came home. How did your family take it when you finally showed up?"

Matt shrugged, going back to looking at the wall of mugshots.

"They didn't understand where I'd been and why I couldn't tell them," he said. He looked at Jacob fully, indicating to the picture of Jacob on the wall. "Birthday 22 July 1976. Los Angeles, California. Went missing 4 October 2001. Reported missing by his brother, Michael. Hasn't been seen since."

"Glad you know how to read," he said with a slight smile. The smile disappeared from his face. "I've been gone for at least seventeen years. I think it's a bit too late for me to go home."

"It's never too late," Matt said, Jacob giving a shrug as his gaze went to his picture on the wall. Matt looked him over as he thought. "In all seriousness, though, what are you going to do if something happens and these counties start to collapse because of Marion? You might have no choice but to go back Upstairs."

Jacob looked at him. "I'll consider that when or if it happens."

Matt gave a slight nod, going back to looking at the wall. He gestured to the entire wall.

"So, all this," he began, receiving Jacob's attention and interest. "This is what you've been working on this entire time that you've been here? How long have you actually been here? How did this all come to be?"

He looked back at him, and Jacob regarded the wall before he responded.

"Banshee's End was here before I showed up," he began. "It used to be just a small outpost in the middle of nowhere. It was thought to have been abandoned but there were a few people already here when the group of us found it. After the Emerald City fell, the few of us that were left just had to try and find somewhere to hold up for a while, somewhere out of the way of what was left of the Iron Army. Someone knew of Banshee's End, said it was abandoned, so we headed straight for it, and now here we are."

"There were already people here?"

Jacob nodded. "Not many. Just a couple of people who'd been holding up in the church. They'd been trying to keep out of the way of the Legion. We hadn't heard about them for years until we found Banshee's End. They've been around for a good while, but they'd chased some of these people out of their town just before the invasion of the City. Vampires won't come anywhere near Banshee's End for multiple reasons."

"Which are?"

"We're pretty well out in the open in the middle of a desert, so sunlight is hard to avoid out here." Matt understood now, and Jacob continued. "We've been trying to keep on top of the Legion but they're starting to get a bit out of our control. We've been trying to figure out how we can push them back underground, but we haven't managed to yet. We have someone on the inside at the moment to try and get more of an understanding of what they're after. Hopefully, he'll be back soon to let us know their next move. Honestly, Wonderland has been lucky they haven't crossed borders yet and they're still only here in Oz. As far as we know, they haven't tackled any other counties yet."

"You keep saying 'other counties'," Matt noted. "I thought it was only Wonderland and Oz in the Underground Worlds."

Jacob shook his head. He shifted how he was leaning against the table, and placed his hands flat on the table on either side of himself.

"They're just two of what we believe to be five," he said, the interest clear on Matt's face now. "And that's only on this side of the coastline. For all we know, there are more counties across the sea."

"We have a coastline?"

Jacob nodded. "Strange to think, I know."

Matt looked back to the noticeboard wall. "You've got that right."

"Morning, I hope you're all feeling better today after getting some rest."

Jacob looked around at everyone as they stood around the same table as yesterday, the noticeboard wall opposite them, and Jacob standing in front of it. Doug stood on Jacob's left, arms crossed, and he stayed silent, letting Jacob do the talking.

There weren't many other people in the underground room below the church this morning and Chris wondered where everyone was.

"As I mentioned yesterday, we have a bit to discuss today," Jacob began, linking his fingers together as he looked around at everyone again. "I'll make sure we get you a copy of all the information we have on Marion up to this point. If you have anything else that we need to know about her or any of what we're going to talk about in general, please write it down and give it to myself, Doug, Don, Cain, or Craig."

"Don survived?" Gates said, sounding unimpressed. He'd never particularly liked Don.

Jacob nodded. "He did. You'll find him in the barracks most days with the rest of our protection crew."

"Wonderful."

Jacob chose to ignore the comment and continued.

"One of our main issues and targets right now is the Legion," he said. Danny automatically tensed up upon hearing the name. "But, we'll get to that shortly. First, I need to introduce you all to Craig."

He indicated for them to follow him as he headed to the door that led to the upper levels of the church.

Once outside in the daylight, Jacob led them through the outpost, heading towards the front. He came to a stop at one of the bigger structures, scanned himself in, and opened the door, holding it for the group once he was inside.

It was quite dim within the structure that Chris was now assuming was the barracks. The door shut once everyone was in, and Jacob continued on his way. They started to hear people talking the further in that they went.

Jacob stopped in the doorway of one of the rooms. There were at least fifteen people in there and they all looked up.

"Where's Craig?" Jacob asked, crossing his arms.

For a minute or so, no one in the room spoke. Jacob stayed exactly where he was, waiting for someone to answer him.

"He's out the back with a couple of the guys," someone eventually spoke up. "Cain's out there with them, too."

"Thank you, that's all I needed to know."

Jacob left the doorway, heading back the way they'd come, but taking a hallway on the right instead of going back out the front door. Everyone just followed along behind as they headed further back into the barracks.

They eventually reached the back of the structure. Jacob opened the door at the end of the narrow corridor, the sunlight streaming in as he headed outside. Chris heard voices again as they followed.

There were a few people in the fenced-off training yard, and Chris recognized Don. He didn't know anyone else, apart from Cain who was standing off to the side with Don, arms crossed and no amusement on his face as he watched what was happening.

"Craig!" Jacob called, getting everyone's attention. "Come here."

One of the men who had been with the group of five dismissed himself from whatever they'd been doing and headed over. Craig came to a halt in front of Jacob, looking everyone over but not saying anything.

"This is Craig, he's the head of our defense force," Jacob introduced him, Craig giving them all a bit of a smile. "He helps train a lot of our new recruits in both combat and ability. He's commander of our protection."

Matt looked him over, slight judgement on his face. "What makes you dangerous enough to be commander and trainer?" he dared, always wanting to know what everyone could do ability-wise so he was prepared for anything.

Craig switched his gaze to him and looked him over in return, summing him up.

"Fatal touch," he said. He looked Matt over again. "So, you'd better watch it because if I wanted to, I could also just *wish* you dead."

A slight smirk appeared on Matt's face, but he didn't say anything.

Jacob rolled his eyes. "No one is wishing *anyone* dead. Anyway, this is the group I told you about a couple of months ago, plus a few extras."

Craig looked around at everyone, temporarily letting Matt's unspoken challenge slide as he gave everyone a bit of a smile.

"It's great to meet you. I've heard a bit about a couple of you," he said. He looked at Danny, Jordan, Shawn, and Ted. "If I'm not wrong, you four are the extras, right? You guys drift around a bit, bandits. Correct me if I'm wrong?"

"Not wrong," Ted said with a shake of his head and a bit of a sigh.

Craig gave an interested nod before speaking again. "Well, we're glad to have you all on board. We need everyone we can get." He looked at Jacob. "You talked to them about all the stuff with Marion and the Legion?"

"We've talked briefly on the Marion front, and they'll get all the relevant information before the end of the day," Jacob said. "We were going to talk about the Legion once we'd come down here to get the lot of you introduced. You going to stay down here or come join us?"

Craig looked over his shoulder at the other people in the training yard.

"You guys right down here without me for a bit?" he called.

They all looked over at him and gave nods of confirmation.

Craig looked back to Jacob. "Looks like I'm joining you."

CHAPTER TWENTY-ONE

Relevant Information

J acob looked around the table. Doug was back to standing on his left, while everyone else was sitting on the opposite side of the table. Craig sat at the end of the table, leaning his head on his hand.

"Before we start and I give you information you might already know, what do you already know about the Legion?" Jacob asked, not directing the question at anyone in particular.

"I know they suck," Ted said, a bit of a smile on his face.

Danny couldn't help but smile, and both Jordan and Shawn laughed out loud as Danny high-fived Ted.

"Nice," he said, the amusement clear on their faces.

Jacob rolled his eyes and tried again. "What do you know about them?"

Danny shrugged this time. He was sitting directly opposite where Jacob was standing.

"Not a lot," he admitted. Danny glanced at his usual crew before continuing. "All we really know is that they're vampires and that they showed up not long after the Emerald City fell. We've had a few interactions with them, but it's never gotten aggressive or out of hand or anything, y'know?"

"You speak to any of them directly?" Craig asked, his gaze on Danny who returned his look.

Danny nodded. "Yeah, but we've only ever spoken to the one guy, Graith." Jacob, Craig, and Doug all raised their eyebrows, and Danny looked between the three of them, a bit concerned now. "Is this ... a bad thing?"

Craig looked at Jacob, shifting his position and no longer resting his head on his hand. "If they're sending Graith out, then we've got a serious problem. It means they're getting a lot gamer."

"Graith's the only one we've had to really deal with," Danny said, confused, looking between Craig and Jacob. "Is he someone important or something?"

"Graith Levers has been underground for a very long time," Jacob said. He looked at Craig who was now slouched in his seat with his arms crossed. "If they're bringing out Graith, we're pretty well done."

"What's his role? Why's he so important?" Chris asked. He wanted to know what the big deal was. "He's clearly a serious threat if you guys are so worried."

"Graith Levers is their commanding officer," Craig said. Everyone looked at him. "Same rank as me. He's someone you don't want to mess with. He was one of the first to be turned. If they're sending him out, you know shit's gonna go down. They don't send Graith out for no reason. He's very dangerous."

"He's the only one we've ever interacted with," Danny repeated. "We've never actually seen him, though. Wouldn't be able to pick him out of a crowd, I don't think."

"They ever take any land near you guys?" Doug asked.

Danny shook his head. "We kept pushing them back. I thought they were gonna get through the last time, but Zeke made sure that more than just a warning was sent this time."

Jacob looked at Zeke.

"They needed to know that fire won't agree with them if they fuck us around," Zeke said, shrugging and feeling awkward about suddenly being the center of attention.

Jacob rolled his eyes but didn't comment on it specifically as he spoke again. "Alright, well, now that we've established that we might be in a bit more trouble than we initially thought, let's get a bit of information relayed between this group. That's all you know about the Legion?"

Everyone nodded.

"From what we know, the Legion has been around for quite some time," Jacob began explaining. "They've stayed underground for a good while since vampires and sunlight don't go together every well. The Legion very rarely made their presence known. You'd get your occasional missing civilian because of them but, for the most part, they were very rare sightings and not a lot of incidents. Some towns already had deals with them, so they stayed in the same area for the majority of the time.

"After the Emerald City fell, they started moving in on a few more towns, coming out a bit more and beginning to take over said towns, which is a serious issue. They've been turning entire towns and taking any people who won't accept it to use as their food source. Banshee's End has been one of the main movements against the Legion, trying to push them back underground over the past ten months but we can't be everywhere all at once.

"We've managed to clear a lot of this area, but they're beginning to push back a bit more right across Oz. Since they're turning more people, we're getting increased vampire activity on our radar and they're not going to stop pushing until they've gotten the entire county, which is when they'll most likely start moving onto Wonderland."

"Vampires are pests," Craig noted. "They're the worst to deal with because they're already technically dead, so how can you kill dead people?"

"Fatal touch not so good when the opponent's already dead, hey?" Matt commented, smiling in amusement at the glare Craig sent his way.

"What have you been doing to get rid of them?" Chris asked.

"They're typical vampires," Jacob said. "Stakes work if you can get close enough, but I wouldn't recommend it. Fire is another good one, otherwise it's just a matter of letting them burn in the sunlight."

"So, from what I'm hearing, we don't have many options and they're pushing further and further into Oz," Ash noted, Craig giving her a nod. "So, what do we do?"

"Who's their leader?" Matt suddenly asked, everyone looking to him. "You said Graith was only a commanding officer. Who runs the Legion?"

Jacob gave a shrug. "We don't know, that's one thing we don't know."

"We have someone on the inside, but even he doesn't know yet," Craig said. He looked at Jacob. "When's he due back?"

Jacob shrugged. "No idea, haven't heard anything from him in a while," he admitted. "You know he's going to come and go as he pleases. When he wants to come back and tell us what he knows, he'll show up."

"Can I make a really stupid suggestion?" Matt asked, getting Jacob's and Craig's attention again. "If you manage to find out who runs the Legion, would it most likely be someone that if you kill them, it'll wipe out the rest of the colony?"

Jacob didn't say anything for a minute or so. Clearly that suggestion hadn't even occurred to him until now.

"That's a good question," he managed to say in return. "Always something to consider."

"They're hard to get the upper hand on, though," Craig said seriously. "They'll know we're coming from miles away."

"They clearly don't know you have someone on the inside, though, right?" Ash said, looking between Jacob and Craig. "Because if they did, this guy would already be dead."

Craig smiled a bit. "He's technically already dead."

Ash rolled her eyes, not overly amused by the vague joke. Craig just smiled at her, getting a shake of the head in return.

"What else do we need to know about these vampires?" Danny asked, trying to get the conversation back on track. "Anything else?"

"How do they turn people?" Chris was the next one to jump on board. He wanted to know all he could.

"We're not one-hundred percent sure that all vampires can turn people," Craig said in response to the question. He knew a thing or two about this topic. "From what we've managed to gather from our informant, it can only be certain vampires, high ranking vampires or ones who've been around for a while. Don't quite know how it works, haven't gotten that figured out yet."

"That's why it's concerning if they're sending Graith out," Jacob said, Craig glancing at him and nodding. "He's high up enough that he'd be one of their main recruiters. If he's out and about, it means they're planning on turning more people."

"So, what's the plan for getting rid of them?" Danny asked. "Because I don't know about you lot, but vampirism doesn't appeal to me in any way."

"We're working on it," Jacob said. Danny rolled his eyes. "We've been working around the clock to try and eradicate as many as we can, but we don't have enough people to keep up with the rate that they turn people."

"So, you're saying, for now we just work on killing any we can while we wait for your informant to make his grand appearance," Matt said bluntly. "Which could be tomorrow, or it could be six weeks from now. How about we put our focus onto getting Marion and we worry about the Legion when this guy shows up?"

Jacob gave a nod of agreement. "Sounds like a good plan to me."

"What's the plan for Marion?" Matt asked. "You mentioned the Funeral Masquerade yesterday."

Jacob glanced at Craig who decided to stay quiet this time.

"It's still two weeks or so before the Funeral Masquerade, but from what we've managed to figure out, that's our best chance of getting the three of them," Jacob said. "Marion's always there, hasn't missed one yet. She won't go anywhere at the moment by herself. Carmen's her barricade right now so she'll be there. Hunter will most likely be there as her protection. It's our best shot."

"Last time I checked, you had to be invited to attend the Funeral Masquerade," Ted said.

He got a bit of a smile in return.

"Not when you're part of Banshee's End."

CHAPTER TWENTY-TWO

The Informant

"Man, these guys have way too much power over everything," Ash said as she shut the door of her room.

The small brown cat jumped up onto her bed and Chris stayed near the door.

Ash sat down on the edge of the bed and Alex wandered over, rubbing up against her and receiving a pat in return.

"I don't want to go to this Masquerade either, but if it's our best chance of getting to Marion and fixing everything, we have to do it," Chris said seriously as Ash continued to pat Alex. "I know you don't like it and neither do I, but sometimes you have to do things you don't want to."

Ash sighed, no longer patting Alex. "What's even going to happen when we catch up to Marion? If she's still in mental breakdown mode, then we have to figure out how to fix it in order to fix everything that's wrong, if what they told us yesterday is even true. If we can't do anything to help Marion, then what do we do? Kill her? If we kill her, does that mean everything disappears? If she somehow created these counties, surely her death will undo it all? What happens then?"

Chris gave a shrug. "Honestly, Ash, I don't know. I wish I did, but I really don't."

Ash sighed and stood up. "I want to go have a look at a couple of things. You in?"

"What are we going to look at?"

Ash was already heading past him and back out the door. The cat jumped off the bed and dashed out after her.

Chris sighed. "Alright, then."

He followed her out and down the hallway towards the wooden staircase that led to the lower level of the building they had been lodged in. It was rather quiet as he descended the staircase.

Ash and Alex had already reached the bottom and were heading for the door.

"Could you slow down a bit?" Chris called, getting a glance from Ash who didn't slow her pace at all. "I don't know why you're in such a rush."

Ash didn't bother responding, instead yanking open the door and letting the bright sunlight stream into the front room of the building as she went outside. She left the door open, and Chris made sure it was shut once he was outside.

Ash and the cat were still a few paces in front, forcing Chris to pick up his pace and break into a jog to catch up. They passed a few people who didn't even give them a glance.

"I don't know why you're in such a rush," Chris commented, slowing his pace once he finally caught up. He walked alongside Ash. "Whatever you want to see is surely not going anywhere."

"I want to know what Craig's deal is," Ash said, as the church come into view. "I also want to see who else is a part of that wall in the operations room."

"Why?"

"Why not?" Ash retorted. Chris sighed. She certainly wasn't happy today. "Better to know who we're mixing with rather than go in basically blind! I'd rather know who we're hanging around with in case something happens."

Chris didn't say anything in return, just followed her up the steps of the church. He let her scan herself in and followed once the door had clicked open. Neither of them spoke as the door shut and they headed towards the door at the back.

Alex ran on ahead, then stopped and patiently waited for either Ash or Chris to scan him in so he could get down the stairs to the operations room. Ash let him in, and he disappeared the moment the door opened enough for him to get through.

Ash shook her head and followed. The door shut behind Chris and they headed down. Alex, no longer a cat, was sitting on one of the chairs on the opposite side of the table as they'd done earlier in the day, looking at the pictures on the wall.

There was no one else in the room.

"Wonder where everyone is today," Chris commented as he followed Ash down to the end of the noticeboard wall.

Ash gave a non-caring shrug. They all seemed to have everything under control, so why should she be concerned about where everyone was?

Chris crossed his arms and leant against the table. Alex looked around as Chris and Ash regarded the pictures on the wall.

"There are a few more people here than I thought there would be," Chris said. Ash looked at him and he indicated to the wall. "On the wall, I mean."

"You're on the wall, too, you know," Alex said. He moved his chair over a bit so Chris wasn't right in front of him. He pointed to one of the pictures. "See?"

Chris turned his attention back to the wall and saw where Alex was pointing. He was right. Chris's picture was, indeed, on the wall, with the information below it just like all the other photos. Chris stayed quiet, letting Ash look over the pictures until she found the one she was after.

"Here we are, Craig Taylor," she noted, pointing to one of the pictures.

Chris frowned. Why did his name sound vaguely familiar?

"Birthday 30 April 1987."

The three of them looked over to the door and saw Craig leaning against the doorframe, arms crossed. "Detroit, Michigan. Hard-rock vocalist. Went missing 30 December 2014."

He pushed off the doorframe and wandered over, the other three all staying quiet. He came to a stop next to the table, looking between them all, hands in pockets.

"Anything else you wanna know?" he asked, clearly not overly impressed that they had been prying. "Because I can tell you more if you want."

Ash crossed her arms as she looked him over judgmentally. Craig watched her with a bit of judgement on his own face.

"It's on the wall, so it's public knowledge," Ash said, looking back to his face.

Craig gave her a slight smile and a nod. "Fair enough."

Chris looked at him. Craig was still watching Ash who'd gone back to looking at the pictures on the wall, her interest in Craig clearly done for the day.

"Who'd you used to sing for?" Chris asked. "You said you were a vocalist. Who was it you sang for?"

"Couple of different bands," Craig said, grabbing the vacant seat next to Alex and pulling it around the table to the end. "Alcazar was my main group, though, the one I ended up with."

Chris raised his eyebrows in surprise. "That's why your name sounded so familiar. I remember reading about it when you disappeared. Made the mainstream media as well as around the scene."

Craig raised his own eyebrows in surprise this time. "Really? Mainstream media got a hold of it?"

Chris nodded and Alex was very interested in their conversation, not really caring too much about what Ash was doing. She was still reading through the information under everyone's pictures.

"You ever miss it? Upstairs, I mean?" Chris asked as Craig went back to watching Ash.

Craig gave a bit of a shrug as he leant his chin on his hand. "Guess I'd be lying if I said no," he admitted, his gaze focused on Ash the entire time. "You just ... you just get used to the way things work down here, you know?"

"Boy, tell me about it."

Alex jumped as Matt pulled up a vacant chair, sitting directly between Alex and Craig. Matt looked at Craig and leaned back in the chair, putting his feet up on the table and crossing his arms. "When you're down here for nearly eight years, certain habits become hard to break."

Craig didn't say anything, not really having anything to say in response to Matt's statement.

"I know who most of the people on this wall are," Ash said, the four of them looking to her. She pointed at one of the pictures near the bottom of the wall and looked at Craig. "Not this one, though. Who's Remington Bell?"

"He's our informant," Craig said, shifting how he was sitting. He crossed his arms and rested them on the table. Ash looked back to the picture. "It's been a while since we've seen him, never tells us when he's going to come back. He comes and goes on his own time but, this time, he's been gone a bit longer than normal. Hope he hasn't gotten himself killed."

"High chance he would have?" Matt asked.

Craig shrugged. "You never know with him. He's been doing well with making sure his cover isn't blown but there's always that chance that he'll do or say something to the wrong person and fuck the whole thing up."

"You sound slightly worried about it," Ash noted, finally directing her attention back to Craig.

"If he's found out, our whole operation is blown," Craig said seriously. "We're probably not even going to know for a good while if he gets himself killed. Not like the Legion are just going to leave him on our doorstep."

"How does he get back here?" Chris asked.

"What do you mean?"

"Well, it took us pretty well all night to get here from Crest Hill, we got here as the sun was coming up," Chris explained. "If he's a vampire, he can't go in the sunlight. How does he get back here when it takes so long and there's no cover?"

Craig looked at him for a few more seconds before responding. "In all honesty, I don't know," he admitted. "We always get told when he's back and we have to go talk to him. He never comes directly to either myself or Jacob. He gets here, we get told, we deal with it, he leaves again a few days later. That's just how it works. As far as I'm aware, he walks his way here. He only ever arrives at night, though, as expected. Don't know how he does it, but he does."

CHAPTER TWENTY-THREE

Remington

Craig sighed, pushing his chair back and getting to his feet. "I don't know about you guys, but I think I'm going to call it a night."

He, Alex, Chris, Matt, and Alex had spent the majority of the day in the operations room, talking over various things about the Legion.

Craig hadn't let on much about their plans for the Funeral Masquerade yet, so, for the most part, they were all still in the dark on that subject.

"What time is it?" Matt asked no one in particular.

Craig pulled a phone from his back pocket and looked at it. "Couple of minutes to midnight," he said, before putting his phone back in his pocket and running his hand through his hair. "Let me know if you need anything. You know where to find me. Well, I figure you do. If not, find someone else."

Ash rolled her eyes, not saying anything as the door opened and Cain appeared in the doorway, getting everyone's attention. Craig indicated for him to speak before crossing his arms, waiting to hear what he had to say.

"Remington's outside, he wants to talk to you," Cain said.

Craig looked a bit disappointed that it wasn't something else, then he sighed. "Where is he?" he reluctantly asked. He was tired and really didn't want to deal with this at the moment.

"Just outside the church," Cain said in return, not sounding too impressed himself.

Craig sighed again. "Alright, we'll be right there. Go let Jacob know he's here."

Cain nodded and left.

"I thought you'd want to talk to this guy in private," Matt said. "Why go up there where he's above ground?"

"Remington's a vampire and vampires can't step foot on holy ground," Craig explained. "Which is why we usually have to go to him."

Craig uncrossed his arms and headed to the door. Matt looked at the others, giving them a bit of a shrug before following. Ash sighed, but reluctantly followed too, with Chris and Alex not far behind.

Craig was a few steps in front of everyone else. He opened the door at the top of the staircase and held it for the other four.

"You haven't ever come into contact with a vampire face-to-face before, have you?" Craig asked as he shut the door behind them all.

"Should we be worried? I'm worried," Alex said.

Craig looked at him. "Remington's harmless for the most part."

"The most part," Ash repeated, sounding unimpressed.

He gave her a smile. "Yeah."

He continued on his way to the front of the church.

Ash really didn't like Craig's attitude. It was going to take her a while to warm up to him, by the looks of it. Chris didn't know why she had such a big issue with him. Craig hadn't done anything wrong and, as far as Chris could see, this was just how he was. He hadn't given Chris any reason not to like him or trust him yet.

Craig hauled one of the main doors of the church open and headed outside into the night. The others followed him out, and Chris noticed there were a few lights on around the church, lighting up small parts around the area.

"What's the go?" Craig called to someone who was standing a few yards away from the church, arms crossed. Even in the dark, Chris could see the unimpressed look on the man's face.

"Would it kill you to put up a boundary fence?" was the first question that met Craig as he reached the bottom of the steps. "I'm away for long periods of time, so I don't always remember where the holy ground starts and where it ends."

"Would it kill you to stop complaining every time you show up?" Craig retorted, getting an eye roll in return as he closed the distance between the two of them. "We're not going to accommodate specifically for you. You said so yourself: you're away for long periods of time. You're hardly ever here, so you're not getting a boundary fence."

Craig looked over his shoulder at the other four who were standing a bit away from the two of them.

"This is Remington, our friendly, non-bitey vampire," he introduced. Remington looked around Craig, giving all of them a grin and a wave in greeting. Craig looked back at Remington, indicating to the others behind him. "This is Ash, Alex, Chris, and Matt."

"Hey," Remington greeted them all, the grin still on his face as he gave them another slight wave. "I'd come up there and shake your hands in greeting, but you're all on holy ground and I can't get any closer to the church. Sorry." He gave them all an overdramatic shrug from where he was standing. "Perks of being dead."

"Perks of being the living dead is more like it," Matt commented, making Remington looked at him directly.

"You, sir, have that right," he said in return, indicating to Matt. "The irony of the whole 'living dead' phrase gets me every time."

Matt rolled his eyes, and Remington returned Craig's gaze, waiting for him to speak.

"You get anything useful this time around?" Craig asked.

Remington slightly raised an eyebrow. "I'll have you know, I only come back when I have 'useful' information," he said, sounding slightly offended by Craig's words. "Also, the captain isn't here, so I can't talk about it yet."

This time it was Craig's turn to look unimpressed.

"Really," he stated as Remington gave an authoritative nod. "You do realize that technically I'm your captain? I'm actually the commanding officer, so you report to me."

"And you report to Jacob," Remington shot back with a glare. Chris and Ash exchanged looks. "So, sorry Taylor, but we wait until Jacob gets here because I don't feel like repeating myself, you know?"

Craig's expression turned into a glare in return, and he crossed his arms. "Alright, fine, have it your way. We'll wait for Jacob, then."

A smile replaced the glare on Remington's face now that he'd gotten his way.

"Awesome, thanks," he said. A couple of seconds later a slight frown appeared on his face. "Where is the chief anyway? I thought he would have been in there with you lot, doing whatever it is that you all do down there in your dungeon."

"You don't know what goes on down there?" Chris asked with a frown of his own.

Remington looked Chris over, summing him up, before shifting how he was standing.

"No, I have no idea," he said eventually. He glanced at Craig who'd taken a slight step back to allow Remington a bit more room. "I only get told select things, only what I need to know. Nothing more and nothing less."

"Hey, sorry to keep everyone," Jacob said, coming to a stop on Remington's right and looking directly at him. "We were starting to wonder where you'd gotten yourself to."

Remington gave him a smile and Chris could see that he preferred to deal with Jacob, not Craig.

Remington gestured to himself. "Well, here I am, all flesh, blood, and non-beating heart!" he said, the cheerful look on his face the entire time. "Still dead, might I add."

"Living dead," Matt corrected him.

Remington indicated to Matt again. "You get it."

Matt rolled his eyes like last time, and a grin replaced the smile on Remington's face.

Jacob looked around at all of them. "Let's get somewhere to talk," he suggested. He looked at Matt. "Can you go get the rest of your group, so we don't have to fill them in later? I'd rather have everyone involved in this hearing it all at the same time, so we don't miss anything if we have to relay it back to anyone."

"They won't be happy at being woken up past midnight but, hey, that's not on me," Matt said with a bit of a shrug. "Where are we meeting you?"

"There's a manor up the back of the outpost; you can't miss it. Meet us there and we'll get down to business."

Matt nodded then moved out of the light, disappearing into the darkness. A bit of a shocked look appeared on Remington's face.

"Oh my God, he's the shadow-stepper!" he exclaimed. Craig sighed and shook his head. Remington looked around him at Ash, Alex, and Chris. "I've heard a lot about you and your group. A lot of mixed reactions, if I'm being honest here."

Ash shot him a glare, getting a smile from him in return. Alex stayed close to Ash, still wary of Remington and being only a few paces away from an actual vampire.

Jacob looked at Craig. "Go get Cain, he needs to be in on this as well."

He began to walk, heading past Remington and Craig. Remington followed Jacob, making sure he avoided the church's boundary.

Craig sighed and spoke to Chris. "You lot go with him, and I'll meet you all there." He started to head off to do as he'd been told, but stopped and looked back at Ash, Alex, and Chris. "I know I said he's harmless, but just ... keep alert. You never know when something might happen."

Without another word, he headed off, Chris and Ash exchanging looks as he disappeared down the dirt road.

"That's reassuring," was all Ash said.

CHAPTER TWENTY-FOUR

Group Meeting

"This has got to be it," Ash said as they stopped in front of a large house. "It's the only one it can be."

Ash, Alex, and Chris had walked along the dirt road in the same direction Jacob and Remington had gone. The other two had disappeared rather quickly, so they'd had to find their own way to the manor at the back of the outpost.

The building was impressive, definitely worth being called a manor. It made sense to Chris why Jacob had decided they should hold their meeting, or whatever they were calling it, here.

It was easily one of the biggest buildings Chris had seen within the outpost, besides the church which was probably the largest building in the entire area.

By the look of it, this manor was not a recent addition but had been here the entire time. Like the majority of the houses and buildings within the fenced outpost, the manor was made of stone, but there were pieces of wood that looked like patch jobs, fixing the structure up to make it complete again.

Ash pointed to the scan-pad next to the front door, getting her ID card out of her pocket. "Limited access, apparently."

It didn't surprise Chris that this building was one they needed to scan themselves into. Most of the places they needed to access were like that, mostly to stop civilians and any uninvited guests from getting in the way.

Ash scanned herself in and the door clicked open. She held the door for Chris and Alex, then entered after them.

Ash made sure the door was closed before she joined the other two in looking around the grand, dimly lit front room. It was a lot like the mansion where they'd stayed with Danny and his crew, though this one was a lot neater and nowhere near as neglected as that one had been.

"Where do we go?" Alex asked, gripping Ash's forearm, his voice barely above a whisper. The silence of the manor made him uncomfortable.

Ash shrugged, not sure where they were meant to go from here.

Chris looked around, a bit of a frown on his face as he tilted his head and listened for a few seconds. When he heard faint voices, he headed to his left, past Ash and Alex who exchanged looks before following, not wanting to be left there by themselves.

The voices got louder as they walked deeper into the building. After a few minutes, they came to a brightly lit room, the door ajar and the voices obviously coming from in there. Chris cautiously pushed the door open and saw a dining room with Remington and Jacob seated at the long table.

Remington was sitting at the head of the table furthest away from the door where Chris was standing. Jacob was at the opposite end, closest to Chris.

"You made it! Thought we'd lost you!" Remington exclaimed with a smile. He gestured to all the vacant seats. "Come on in, pull up a chair."

Chris pushed the door open a bit more and entered the room. Alex kept very close to Ash as they followed.

"Doesn't matter where you sit," Jacob said.

Remington picked up a half-empty glass, leaned back, and put his feet up on table. He mindlessly studied the red liquid in the glass.

Chris gave a nod, deciding where to sit. Alex took the seat closest to Jacob, preferring to be as far away from the vampire as possible. Chris moved around the table and sat opposite Alex.

"Dare I even try and guess what's in that glass?" Ash asked, her tone unimpressed.

Remington looked away from the glass towards Ash, smiling. "Put it this way, sweetheart, it's certainly not wine."

"Then ... what is it?" Alex hesitantly asked.

Remington switched his gaze to him now, the smile no longer on his face. Alex didn't like it.

"I'm a vampire, what do *you* think it is?"

The worry returned to Alex's face but all it did was make Remington smile in amusement before taking a sip from the glass.

Ash took a seat next to Alex who couldn't take his eyes off the vampire at the end of the table.

"He won't hurt you," Ash said with a sigh. She was over Alex's dramatics for now.

"You don't know that," Alex said seriously, making Remington roll his eyes.

"He certainly won't," Jacob said, his tone equally as serious. Remington and the other three looked at Jacob. Jacob was watching Remington with no smile on his face. "Because he knows what will happen if he dares to try anything."

"I sure do, Captain," Remington said. He raised his glass slightly, the grin back on his face. "Which is why I have to drink from glasses while I'm here, not from real, living people. Believe it or not, there's a *huge* difference in taste."

Ash just shook her head, while Alex sat wide-eyed and worried. Remington clearly found Alex amusing and flashed his teeth, making Alex shift uncomfortably in his seat.

"Alright, why are we all here at nearly one o'clock in the morning?" Danny was standing in the doorway. He indicated to Remington. "The fuck's this guy?"

"Dead," Remington said before taking another sip from his glass.

"Living dead," Matt said as he pushed past Danny to enter the room.

Remington gave him a nod. "Yeah, that."

Danny stood there for a few more seconds as Matt's words sunk in.

Matt took the closest seat to Remington who gave him a smile of greeting. Some of the others moved past Danny to get into the room, deciding where to sit.

"You're a vampire?" Danny asked in disbelief, crossing his arms. He didn't like vampires.

Remington frowned and looked down at himself before looking back up at Danny. "Am I?"

Danny wasn't in the least bit happy and glared at Jacob. "You've got to be kidding."

Jacob looked at him as everyone else took a seat. Abel sat next to Chris, Jordan was next to Ash on her left, Ted on his left with Shawn opposite him. Gates and Zeke moved to the other end of the table and Gates sat opposite Matt while Zeke sat on Matt's right.

"Not kidding, sit down," Jacob said, gesturing to the few remaining vacant chairs, all close to Remington's end of the table. "We have a lot to talk over, so find somewhere and sit down."

Danny shook his head in disbelief, reluctantly moving and taking the available seat on Ted's left, not liking that he was only three seats away from Remington.

"You all look tired," Remington noted. Danny shot him a glare and Remington focused his attention on him. "What? You do!"

"Well, I dunno what you were told, but we were all in bed, asleep," Danny snapped, making Remington roll his eyes. "I dunno about you, but I don't particularly like being woken up at nearly one in the morning to be told that we're needed for a team meeting!"

"Wouldn't know, been a long time since I've been woken up," Remington said. "Now that I come to think of it, when *was* the last time I actually slept?"

"Perks of being the living dead?" Matt queried.

"Don't know if I'd call it a 'perk' as such. It gets boring after a while when you don't sleep," Remington admitted. "I have a *lot* of spare time nowadays."

"So, who *are* you exactly?" Danny asked seriously.

"Remington Bell," Remington introduced himself, once again with a smile. "Banshee's End's dead—sorry, living dead—informant."

Danny crossed his arms and leant back in his chair with a shake of his head, looking ahead of himself now. "Wonderful."

Remington looked at Matt, giving him a bit of a shrug before finishing off what was left in his glass.

"We'll wait for Craig and Cain," Jacob said, breaking what was most likely going to become an awkward silence. "Once they're here, we'll hear what Remington has to say."

"I'll happily talk if I can go get another glass because I'm starving," Remington said, ignoring the disgusted look on Danny's face. He saw the same look on most of the other faces around the table. "What? Guys, it's a long walk, alright? Man, judge a man for being hungry?"

"I'd rather him go get something than have him sit here and see us all as meals," Alex spoke up, everyone looking to him.

Remington pointed to him. "You're smart, I like you."

"Shame he doesn't like you," Ash muttered to herself.

"Just so you know, I did hear that," Remington said, pointing to his ear. "Vampire hearing, you see?"

Ash rolled her eyes, not saying anything more as Remington took his feet off the table, pushed his chair back, and grabbed his now empty glass. He exited the room through the door closest to him, opposite to the door they'd all come in.

"I don't like him," Danny said straight off, his voice down. "Fucking vampires, man. You serious?"

"Vampire hearing!" they all heard Remington call from the other room. "At least pass notes or something so I don't have to hear you bitch about me."

Danny sighed and shook his head but didn't say anything else.

Alex watched the door Remington had left through, still uneasy.

"How long does it usually take for the other two to get here?" Matt asked Jacob. "Should they be here by now?"

"They shouldn't be too far away," Jacob said. "Depending on where Cain was when Craig went to get him will depend on how long it takes them to get back here. If they're not here in a few more minutes, we'll go see what's keeping them."

CHAPTER TWENTY-FIVE

What's Keeping Craig?

"It's been at least twenty minutes, should they be taking this long?"

Jacob shook his head, checking the time on his phone. It was nearing two in the morning.

"Alright, we need someone to go find out what's happening," he said. "They should have been here by now. He looked around at everyone. "Who wants to go for a walk?"

Matt pushed his chair back, always up for finding out what was keeping people from what they were meant to be doing. Danny was the next one to push his chair back and get to his feet, preferring to be in any other place besides the one he was currently in. Preferably one that didn't have a vampire in the room.

Matt looked around the table. "Anyone else?" He indicated to Danny. "Or just us?"

Remington didn't bother volunteering himself and when no one else volunteered either, Matt looked at Danny, indicating for him to head out. Danny didn't hesitate in the slightest and Matt headed out after him.

Jacob caught Matt's eye before Matt disappeared through the door. "Try to make it quick."

Danny was already at the front door by the time Matt caught up.

"He doesn't seem that bad, you know," Matt said as he followed Danny out the door and into the dark of the night. There were only a few lights on in the surrounding area, like most areas of the outpost.

"He's a vampire, Matt. They're all the same, no matter what anyone else says," Danny responded as they walked, heading in the direction of the barracks. "You can't trust them, no matter what you might think. Vampires need to be wiped out, not let into your house."

"Well, if you turn out to be right, you can kill him yourself."

Danny scoffed but didn't say anything more on the subject as they walked on in silence. There was no one else outside at this time of the night.

The barracks eventually came into view and Matt hoped it wasn't anything too drastic keeping both Craig and Cain from their meeting. He didn't wish to deal with something major right now, especially since he hadn't gotten much sleep the previous night.

He approached the door of the barracks, scanned himself in, and pushed the door open, not bothering to hold it for Danny. It was rather dark inside, and quiet, but Matt assumed most of them were either out on patrol or asleep before their shift started. Hopefully, they wouldn't have to search the entire outpost for Craig and Cain.

One of the lights close to the door suddenly lit up, and Matt looked over his shoulder to see Danny light another one.

Danny looked at him as the spark disappeared from his hand. "What? I'm not walking around in the dark."

"Let's just try and find someone who's awake," Matt said. "Maybe someone can tell us if Craig's here or not."

He headed off to his right, Danny trailing along behind him. They walked in silence, until they saw some lights on in a room up ahead. Matt went to it and pushed the door open a bit.

Don was sitting on the bed, looking at a book, and he looked up at the intrusion. A surprised look crossed his face when he saw Matt.

"Craig's not here," he said before Matt could say anything. "He and Cain got called down to the gate for some kind of disturbance."

Matt frowned, looking back at Danny briefly before looking back at Don who decided to wait for him to ask his question this time.

"What are you doing awake at this time of night?" Matt asked.

Don gave a bit of a shrug. "My shift starts at two, so I should probably get down to the gate and relieve one of the guards."

He shut the book, stood up, and headed to the door where Matt and Danny were standing. He turned the light off and left the room, Danny sighing and following him, seeing as they were all going to the same place.

Matt followed along behind, knowing he could easily shadow-step down to the gate, but then he'd have to wait for the other two to get there. He didn't really wish to make Danny any angrier than he currently was. Luckily, the gate wasn't too far.

"I could be asleep right now," Danny commented as they headed out of the barracks. "All this for a damned vampire and his most likely irrelevant information."

"You guys finally met Remington?" Don asked as they walked.

"Unfortunately," Danny sighed.

"He's not so bad, you know," Don said. "Just gotta get used to the fact that he's a vampire, that's all."

"I thoroughly doubt I'll ever get used to it," Danny stated. Why did everyone like that guy? It didn't make sense to him.

Don glanced at Matt who gave him a slight shrug, not wanting to input anything into the conversation, as it would only make Danny unhappier. After a minute or two, the gate came into view.

The left gate was open, with a few recruits hanging around it and Craig and Cain standing in the middle of it, Craig just in front of Cain.

"I'm sorry, we *can't* let you in," they heard Craig say as they approached. "We can't just let people in, especially at this time of night. No ID, no entry. I'm sorry."

"Please, you have to let us in," they heard from the other side of the gate. Matt frowned. He knew that voice, he just couldn't pick it. "You don't understand! They'll track us down if you don't let us in!"

"What's going on?" Matt asked as they finally reached the open gate. A few of the recruits stepped aside to let the three of them through, although Don hung back a bit.

Craig looked at Matt as he stopped off to his side. Danny stopped next to Cain.

"Sorry, we were heading up to the manor but got called down here," Craig apologized. "I thought we'd be finished here by now, but I've got to do my job."

"Please, you have to let us in or else they'll come for us and kill us, maybe even make us one of them!" The tone of the man on the other side of the gate was desperate.

Craig turned his attention back to him. "Sir, seriously, I need you to take a step back," he said authoritatively as he held his hand up in a stop gesture. "I won't warn you again."

Matt wondered how often he had to deal with these kinds of situations. Surely this was more Cain's job than Craig's. As far as Matt knew, Craig was above Cain in the hierarchy of Banshee's End and yet, here he was, dealing with someone who just wanted to be safe inside the walls.

Matt moved slightly, forcing Cain to move a bit, so he could see the person on the other side of the gate.

A surprised look crossed his face. "Well, shit," he said, Craig looking to him. "Would you look at that."

The two people looking back at him were the last people he'd expected to see. It was an older man and his young son. Matt recognized them straight off. They were the family with the banshee daughter who'd held their group up the first night they'd been in Oz ten months or so ago. If he remembered correctly, the man's name was Colin. He didn't remember the boy's name, but it looked like it was only the two of them as there was no sign of Colin's wife.

"You know them?" Craig asked, his gaze still on Matt.

Matt nodded. "I do. More or less, anyway. They helped our group, they're good people."

"Please let us in, we're begging you," Colin pleaded, Craig's attention back on him.

Craig sighed and ran his hand through his hair, trying to make up his mind on the best thing to do. "Why did you seek us out? Why do you need sanctuary? We need to know what we're dealing with. We can't just let you in."

"Vampires! Vampires took over our property," Colin rushed, desperate and panicked. "A whole group of them. They killed my wife, and we only just managed to get out. Please, they're going to track me and my son down."

Craig looked over to Cain who returned his gaze. "They're moving further inland. We've got to get back on top of this situation. Get the observation team together, we leave in an hour."

Cain nodded and turned, heading off towards the barracks.

Craig looked back at Colin and his son who were waiting to hear the decision. "OK, we'll let you in, but you're going to have to go through a lot of processing so we can make sure you can stay. Is that clear?"

Colin gave a rushed nod. "Whatever you need us to do."

Craig nodded in satisfaction, moving aside. After everyone was in, Craig gestured for someone to shut and lock the gates.

He pointed to a couple of the recruits. "Get them to the processing building. Someone will be with them as soon as possible."

The two recruits nodded and did as they were told, saying something to Colin and his son as they led them away.

Craig looked at Matt and Danny. "We're gonna have to make this meeting quick because I have a team to get out into the field."

CHAPTER TWENTY-SIX

Informant's Information

Everyone looked over as Matt came back into the room, with Danny close behind, and Craig a few seconds later.

"About time you showed up," Remington said as Matt and Danny retook their seats. He had his feet on the table again and he held his glass up. "I'm already on my fourth glass."

Craig rolled his eyes, taking the available seat on Danny's left, one seat over from Gates.

"Cain coming?" Jacob asked.

"No," Craig said, looking down the table at him. "He's getting the observation team together, so we have to make this quick. I have to get out there with them in about an hour. The Legion's moving further inland. We're going out to see how far they've gotten and what we need to do in terms of taking them out in that area. We should only be a couple of days."

"OK, but remember you have to be back by the weekend," Jacob said, Craig nodding. "Sunday night at the latest. We leave for Belle's Castle on Monday since the Funeral Masquerade is on Wednesday next week."

"I know. Don't worry, I won't miss it. If we're not back by Sunday, I'll meet you at the castle on the Wednesday night."

Jacob nodded, fine with Craig's proposal. "As long as you're there, we won't have any problems."

He turned his attention to Remington. "Alright, we're now running on limited time, so we need to know what you know. What have you found out since you last spoke to us?"

Remington took his feet off the table and straightened up in his chair. "Alright, so there's been a bit of chatter amongst some of the guys the past few weeks. It's honestly starting to look like this problem isn't about to just go away."

Danny wasn't impressed with Remington's choice of words, calling them 'the guys', but he kept quiet and just listened.

"We figured it wasn't about to just go away," Craig said. "We've been doing what we can to reduce the threat as much as possible, but we don't have enough people to defend here *and* go out to all the places the Legion has taken over."

"So, what have 'the guys' been talking about?" Danny asked, wanting to go back to bed and not sit in the same room as a vampire for any longer than he had to.

Remington switched his gaze to him. "There's been a lot of talk recently about what the next phase is."

Concern appeared on Jacob's and Craig's faces.

"What do you mean, 'the next phase'?" Jacob dared to ask, not liking where this was going.

Remington stared down the table at him. "Well, you see, this is the issue," he said, stalling for a second as he tried to figure out the best way to word the situation. "From what I understand, from hearing what everyone's been saying, the next phase is moving through the counties. Wonderland seems to be next on the list. After that, it's onto the other ones. From what I gather, they're not about to stop until they have full control of the entire Underground Worlds."

"Jesus," Craig sighed, leaning forwards and putting his arms on the table as he switched his gaze to Jacob. "See, this is what I was talking about. We seriously need more people or else this threat is going to take over and we're all fucked. If they're planning on taking Wonderland and the neighboring counties, we *have to* get a move on and take down their captains. Anyone who can turn people."

Jacob leaned back in his chair, thinking while everyone watched him. He was the one in charge, so he had to make the decisions.

"If we get on top of taking out their higher ranks, we can get on top of the whole threat," Craig continued. "Which means we need more people on the ground, more people who can help take them out. Look, we seriously need more outposts with people, because if we can get solid bases throughout each county, we stand more of a chance."

Jacob looked at him directly. "Alright, what do you propose we do?"

"Like I just said, we need to start setting up more outposts," Craig explained. At least Jacob was listening to what he was saying. "Sure, we've taken a few towns already and we do regular patrols of them, but that's not good enough anymore. We *need* to set up outposts and have people there *all* the time. No more weekly patrols, we need full time residents there so we have a more solid base."

"OK, how do we do that?"

"After the Funeral Masquerade, I'll take a couple of guys out and we'll have a look at where we can set up outposts," Craig said, having thought this through many times. "We'll try get other people involved and get some more protection and defenses up and running. We *have to* get on top of this situation before it gets more out of hand."

"Are you only talking about setting up outposts within Oz?" Jacob asked.

Craig shook his head. "We need to push into the other counties, too, find their borders and get into their areas and get them on board, including Wonderland."

"You're not setting *anything* up in Wonderland," Ash spoke up defensively, everyone looking to her now. "That's not your call on whether we need outposts there or not."

"So, you're willing to let vampires push through to your county?" Craig asked seriously.

"We've got enough in the way of defenses to keep them back for a while."

"Bullshit, don't you give me that. We're all very aware of what's going on in Wonderland, Ash. We know for a fact that you *don't* have the resources or defenses to keep the living dead out."

"Well, clearly neither do you!" Ash exclaimed.

"They're going to take Wonderland if you don't let us put some outposts in place," Craig said sternly, not happy with Ash's accusation. "This is a serious issue. If what Remington just said about them pushing through all the counties is true, Wonderland is going to need as much protection as you can get. *We're* the ones who know what we're doing. We have people trained up for this kind of thing. Your county has *nothing* and *no one* trained for this. Wonderland *will* fall if you don't let us pass this."

"Ash, let them do this," Chris tried, Ash looking across to him.

"No! Why should I?" she snapped. "Chris, Wonderland isn't *their* land. *I* run it now. They're *not* pushing into our county and setting up useless defenses."

"It's probably too cold for them at the moment, anyway," Alex said with a bit of a shrug, trying to defuse the tension as best he could. "Snow isn't fun when it's all the time."

"Just so you know," Remington spoke up, everyone looking to him now. "We don't actually feel the cold. We're technically dead so, yeah, cold is not gonna stop them. Just so you know..."

Alex looked down at the table, not saying anything more.

Craig looked back to Ash. "You've got to let us do this if you don't want them to take over your land," he said, trying to get his point across. "Think of the people you already have there, that live there, everyone who resides there. If they knew what kind of threat was coming, you think they'd blatantly say no to any help they could get, all because *you* don't like the people who are offering to help? What is your problem?"

"My problem is that it isn't your concern if they come into Wonderland. We'll deal with it *if* it happens."

"Alright, whatever, have it your way," Craig said, shaking his head and throwing up his hands in frustration. "We'll set ourselves up on the border, how does that sound? Or is that still too close to you?"

"As long as you're still on the Oz side of the border, I'm not going to care."

Craig shook his head again, falling silent now.

Abel was the next one to speak up. "Can I input something here? Might make a bit of difference," he said, everyone looking to him. Craig indicated for him to speak, so he did. "If they get into Wonderland, there's a very high chance that they'll find the way

Upstairs. I don't know about you guys, but I don't think we can afford to let that happen."

That hadn't even occurred to anyone else in the room. Abel was the one who had always gone back Upstairs more than any of them, which is why he would be the one to have thought of it.

Craig looked at Ash. "He's got a point. Does that change your mind?"

Ash leaned back in her chair, arms crossed. "Not yet. I don't live up there, so I have nothing to care about if they do. Not yet, anyway."

Craig shook his head, dropping the subject for now.

"Once we get back here from the Masquerade, we'll discuss it more in depth about what to do and where to set up," Jacob said. Craig nodded, glad at least *he* was on board. Jacob looked back down the table at Remington who had been minding his own business while they'd been discussing options. "Is there anything else we need to know for now? Found out who's running things yet?"

Remington shook his head. "Not yet, sorry. Believe me, I've tried. Whoever it is keeps very underground, that's all I know."

"The moment you find out, contact us," Jacob said, getting an understanding nod from Remington. "You don't have to come back here if it's too early, just find a way to contact us and let us know so we can get on top of it. Nothing else you need to tell us?"

Remington thought for a few seconds before shaking his head. "Not that I can think of. That was pretty well the only thing, about them pushing through to the other counties. Oh, and Graith's gonna be at the Masquerade as well, just a head's up on that one. There'll be a couple of us there, so keep alert."

"Any idea how many of you will be there?" Danny asked, hating the idea even more now. He'd never wanted to go to the Funeral Masquerade in the first place and yet, here he was, knowing he had to and now there were going to be multiple vampires there as well. His luck just kept getting better and better.

"Not sure, ten max," Remington said. "I'll be there, but I'll have to stay away from you guys as best as I can. Last thing I want is for them to find out I actually work for you. That wouldn't go down well *at all*."

"Just keep clear of us," Jacob said. "Shouldn't be too hard since I'm sure the majority of the vampires you hang with know not to mess with anyone from Banshee's End. Keep clear for as long as possible. If you have to tell us anything, either wait until the night's over or, if it's urgent, I'm sure you can figure out a way to get the information to us."

"Will do."

Craig moved his chair back, getting to his feet. He looked around the table.

"Alright guys, I'll see you all most likely on Wednesday," he said, pushing his chair back under the table. He looked at Jacob. "I'm taking the observation team. You know how to contact me if anything happens, if you need any of us back here. Otherwise, I'll see you at Belle's Castle."

"Don't get too close," Jacob warned, Craig giving a nod to indicate that he'd heard him. "Come back straight away if anything happens and contact us if you need anything."

"Will do," Craig sighed as he left the room.

Jacob looked around at everyone left in the room.

"Alright, you can all go back to bed," he said. Danny was the first one on his feet. "Sorry about dragging everyone out at this time of the morning but we'll talk more later, when the sun's up. We'll discuss the plan for the Masquerade later in the day."

"No one is to talk to me until at least midday," Danny warned, indicating to everyone in the room. "If anyone tries to wake me up again, you'll regret it. Goodnight."

He left the room. Ted, Jordan, and Shawn stood up moments later and followed him out without a word.

Remington watched them leave, shaking his head. "I don't like them very much."

"You don't really get used to it," Ash sighed, resting her head on her hand as he switched his gaze to her.

Jacob was the next one to move. "You know where to find me. Have a good night."

He left the room, leaving Matt, Gates, Zeke, Abel, Chris, Ash, and Alex in the room with Remington who was now mirroring Ash's position of head on hand, boredom on his face.

"Guess we should all probably go get some sleep," Matt commented, all of them looking to him.

"You do that," Remington said, sounding bored, just like his expression. "I'll be around somewhere, not sleeping, if you, for some odd reason, need me. Though, I doubt you will because you all seem to have everything handled pretty well without me."

"Wish you could sleep?" Ash queried.

Remington shrugged. "You get used to it."

CHAPTER TWENTY-SEVEN

Remington's Background

"So how long have you been ... like this?" Ash asked Remington who kept his gaze on her.

"A vampire?" Ash nodded and Remington shrugged. "Not that long. At least six years."

"How old are you?" Alex asked, interested now as Remington switched his gaze over to him.

"Twenty-six," Remington said, still sounding bored.

"Twenty-six? When you were turned?" Alex asked, a bit confused.

Remington shook his head. "Twenty-six this year."

Alex nodded, understanding what he meant now.

"How did you become a vampire?" Ash asked, wanting to know a bit more about Remington. Now seemed as good a time as any to ask, as she didn't know how long he would be sticking around for. If he wasn't going to the Funeral Masquerade with them, he surely had to leave soon.

Remington once again looked at her as everyone else in the room just listened in. "How does anyone become a vampire? I got bitten."

"Did it hurt?" Alex asked, looking intrigued again.

"Hell, yeah, it did," Remington said seriously. "Like, it *really* hurt. Not the initial bite, that wasn't so bad but, after that, no thanks. I wouldn't wanna go through that again and honestly wouldn't wish it upon anyone. Once you get bitten, it kills you. It's basically like poison and it's uncomfortable and downright unpleasant. It hurts and there's nothing you can do, it lasts for *hours*. Honestly, if I were any of you, I'd try to avoid being turned into a vampire."

"I assume you weren't someone who was really up for being turned?" Matt input.

Remington shifted how he was sitting, no longer resting his head on his hand, and looked at Matt. "Sometimes you don't have any other choice and it's your best option when it presents itself."

Matt raised an eyebrow in interest, but Remington didn't elaborate and looked away from him, avoiding his gaze.

"Have you got any abilities or anything?" Ash asked.

Remington shook his head. "No. Once you die, you lose any abilities you had, anything like that disappears. I never had one to start with, not that I discovered anyway. If I did have one, though, it'd be gone by now. I'm dead so I wouldn't be able to use it."

That was something about abilities none of them had known.

"So, if someone dies, they lose their ability?" Ash repeated, getting a nod of confirmation.

"You'll hear a lot of this bullshit about abilities being 'born in the bloodstream' or whatever the hell people say," Remington said. "Part of that *is* true and, excuse me for having to say this, but it's actually noticeable and makes people taste a bit different. But that aside, yes, there is a part of it that's in the bloodstream but it's only active like that when you're alive. The core of everyone's abilities is actually in the soul. That's what makes everyone's abilities different and unique to them. So, when you die, that's why your ability stops, and why vampires don't have abilities. They're connected to the soul, so once you're dead, you technically don't have one anymore and that dispels your abilities."

"Just on the hypothetical," Matt spoke up. "If you were to be cured of your vampirism, would you get your ability back? If you knew what it was, anyway?"

"In all honesty, Matt, I don't know," Remington admitted with a bit of a shrug. "My best guess is no because I've been dead for six years. The souls of the dead only hang around for a certain amount of time before they dissipate and are gone forever. Even if I *were* to be cured of my vampirism, it'd be very unlikely that I'd get my ability back in any form."

He gave a shrug, not seeming too fazed about the matter, back to resting his head on his hand. "I've come to terms with it. It's one of those things that takes a while to get used to, but the longer you deal with it, the easier it becomes. Like I said, I've been dead for six years now, and you get used to the way things go."

"Don't you miss normality?" Chris asked.

Remington gave a bit of a shrug again. "This *is* normal to me, now. Sure, there are a few things I miss, like actually being able to go outside during the daylight hours, but I've gotten used to the dark and only coming out during the night. I do miss real food, though. I would kill for that again."

Ash could see that statement made Alex uncomfortable.

"You can't eat real food, at all?" Chris asked.

"Can't physically stomach it," Remington said with a shake of his head. "Can't taste it and can't eat it. There are a lot of downsides to being a vampire. Don't get me wrong, it has its perks, but it also—excuse me for this—sucks a lot."

"What kind of perks are we talking about here?" Matt asked curiously, wanting to know more about how vampires worked.

"Wicked hearing, which can also be a downside, unfortunately. It's good when I need to know what's happening, but it also sucks when there's a lot of commotion and lots of people around. It sometimes all gets mixed up into one noise and it's so annoying. But it helps if you guys are down in the church and I have to sit outside because I can still hear what you're all saying. Another one is that my reflexes are pretty good. That's helped me out in a lot of situations. Eyesight's pretty damn good, too. Believe it or not, strength is another. It's basically all the typical vampire stuff."

"So, what are the downsides?"

"The hearing obviously happens to be one, as I mentioned just before," Remington continued. "But there's also the sunlight thing, you know, where I'll burst into flames if I'm in the sun for about thirty seconds. Um ... being able to control the hunger is a major issue for a lot of newer vampires, something you learn to control over time. Fire is not my friend, nor are stakes. Not being able to eat real food, not feeling the heat or cold, not being able to step foot on holy ground, or sleeping. That kinda stuff."

"What happens if you do step onto holy ground? You burst into flames?" Ash asked, her tone a bit sarcastic.

"Eventually, yes," Remington said seriously. "It burns to start with and then, eventually, yes, I'd burst into flames and be reduced to nothing but ashes. Then I truly would be dead."

"Can I ask something?" Chris said. Remington looked at him and indicated for him to speak. "I know you're undercover within the vampires and everything, so I assume that's why you don't have one of the Banshee's End badges. That the reason?"

"Big part of it," Remington said. "But also, not really much need for it. Non-physical abilities don't work on the dead, so I don't have a lot of reasons to need one unless I want to show that I work for these guys. Eventually it'll happen, but for now I can't risk it. If anyone finds out I work for Jacob, I'm gone. I'd rather stay living dead than be just dead, you know?"

Chris nodded in understanding, not saying anything more.

Remington sighed, pushing his chair back and getting to his feet. "Anyway, it was nice meeting you all and having a chat, but I think I'm gonna go find something else to do before the sun comes up. Jacob'll let me know what I need to know before I leave in a couple of days. If I don't see you all before I leave, I'll see you all at the Masquerade next week. Have a good night, everyone."

He left the room, leaving the door ajar on his way out.

"I think we should all call it a night," Matt said, looking around at who was left in the room. "It's after three and we're expected to be somewhere in the morning to find out what we're doing next week. It's been a long day, and I'm done."

"Agreed," Gates said, the first thing he'd said all night as he pushed his chair back and got to his feet. "I'm going back to bed."

Matt got to his feet as well, Zeke following suit without a word. The three of them left the room, leaving Ash, Alex, Chris, and Abel.

Abel looked at Ash. "I really think you should take them up on their offer of setting up some outposts in Wonderland. I know you don't want to, and you don't really care if they make it through and to the doors that lead Upstairs, but some of us *do* care." He indicated to Chris, his gaze still on Ash. "Chris and I both have family up there and the last thing we want is for vampires to make their way through to our home and possibly take that from us. You also have family up there, and Alex does too."

"We don't even know them!" Ash exclaimed, making Abel sigh. Why was she always so difficult? "I get it, Abel, but as of right now, the answer's no."

"What about everyone else down here who has family up there?" Abel asked seriously. "I'm sure Jacob has family up there. Matt does, Gates does, Zeke does. I'm sure Danny and those guys do. Shit, even Craig probably has people up there. You're really willing to let your ego ignore a serious threat that could potentially wreck this world and another? Really, Ash? That's just selfish."

Ash didn't say anything for a few minutes, thinking over what Abel had said.

"Let me sleep on it and I may change my mind."

CHAPTER TWENTY-EIGHT

Plans

"Alright, everyone, listen up!" Jacob called, silencing everyone who had been talking. "This is important, so I need everyone's full attention."

There were a few more people than usual in the operations room. Chris hadn't realized there were this many people this deeply involved in the situation.

Once he was sure no one was going to interrupt him, Jacob spoke again, addressing everyone in the room. "We've had an update on the Legion. They've been pushing further inland, so Craig's gone out with the observation team to do what they can over the next few days to try to get that area back under our control.

"We've been informed that after the Legion gets as much of Oz as they can, they're going to start pushing into the other counties, starting with Wonderland.

"Once Craig gets back from this operation, we're going to be discussing what our best move is. At this point in time, it looks like we'll be setting up multiple outposts, more throughout Oz and then we push into the other counties and try to get them on board with letting us set up in their lands. We can't have the Legion taking any other counties, we have to get on top of it now and, if that means recruiting more people, then that's what we're going to do."

He paused, looking around at everyone in the room. As expected, Remington was nowhere to be seen as he couldn't get anywhere near the operations room, and it was also broad daylight outside. There were a lot of people at this briefing who didn't actually know Remington, having only seen his picture on the wall and never having come into contact with him. He was someone who was on a need-to-know basis.

Jacob continued. "With that said, our next move is the Funeral Masquerade." He looked around at everyone again, seeing a few unsure faces. "Not everyone in here will be going, but you all need to know the plan in case something goes wrong. We're going after Marion, which is why we're heading to Belle's Castle come Monday. Craig will be meeting us there if he's not back by Sunday. Remington will be there, but he won't be with us, so to anyone who's there, do not approach him in any way. We don't want his cover blown, clear?"

Everyone nodded, and Jacob spoke again.

"If he approaches you, there'll be good reason for it. Leave him to himself and everything should be fine. Now, we'll go through the plan and then, if there are any questions, I'll be more than happy to answer them. Everyone knows by now whether they're going or not. So, here's how it's going to go down. We're leaving on Monday since it'll take us a couple of days to get to the castle. We're all Banshee's End, so we won't have any problem getting in. Make sure you've got your ID and badges on you at all times because you never know what might happen.

"We're not undercover this time around, we want people to know we're there for a reason. You'll be assigned a partner so you're not by yourself within the castle. We don't want anyone getting into trouble, which is why we want pairs, in case something happens. We've had word that Graith and a few more vampires will also be within the castle, so keep a very close lookout. We don't want anything happening to anyone. If anything does happen, you come to myself, Craig, Cain, or Doug. Understood?"

Everyone nodded again, Jacob giving a slight nod back.

"The whole reason we're there is to get Marion," he continued, still having a lot to say. "We're there for her and the other two. Be warned, Carmen is very dangerous and so is Hunter. If you come into contact with any of the three people we're after, keep your distance until we're ready to move. Craig and myself will take care of Marion, Carmen, and Hunter. Our main target is Marion, though, and once we know she's there, we'll make our move."

"What are you going to do with her once you've got her?" Matt asked. Gates and Zeke nodded, sitting next to him, as always. "We don't know what kind of state she's in at the moment. If she's still mentally unstable, we could be in for some serious trouble."

"We have a plan, don't worry," Jacob said.

Matt was not happy to hear that there was a plan he knew nothing about.

"It's a need-to-know thing," Jacob continued. "And not everyone in here needs to know. I'll inform you guys a bit later when we're clear to talk. I can't have everyone knowing, but you will definitely be told, don't worry."

"Alright, then." Matt felt better hearing that.

"Is everyone clear on their role for next week?" Jacob asked, back to looking around at everyone in the room. Everyone nodded. "Well, alright, then. If there's anything else anyone needs to be told, you'll be spoken to. Any questions before we adjourn?"

When no one spoke up, Jacob gave a slight nod, indicating for everyone to get back to what they'd been doing. A few people left the room, and Jacob looked at the usual group in front of him.

"Let's get out of here and talk about what's happening when we get Marion."

He headed over to the door, the group of them following him, the little brown cat out in front and dashing out the door the moment it was opened. Ash shook her head as they followed Jacob and Alex up the stairs.

"Why's this on a need-to-know basis?" Matt asked as they reached the front of the church.

Jacob opened the door, and the cat dashed out in front of him into the sunlight.

"Because if everyone knows, word could slip out and the whole thing could be ruined. You can't trust everyone with everything," was his answer.

The sunlight hit them, Chris shielding his eyes from the harsh light. He understood why Remington didn't like the sunlight, even though he had more reason not to like it than just the glare.

"What are you doing out at this time of day?" Jacob suddenly said, seeing Remington standing in the shade by one of the houses. "You sure it's a good idea?"

"No, and I regret it," Remington called from where he was leaning against the wall of one of the houses, sunglasses on and jacket hood up.

"Then why're you lurking in the shade?" Danny asked, arms crossed and with the usual unimpressed look on his face.

"Heard the words 'need-to-know basis' and figured that involved me so I came out for a wander." Remington shrugged. "This sunlight is damn bright, might I add."

He readjusted his hood, making sure it was sitting right. Jacob sighed. Trust Remington to come out during the day when he wasn't meant to be around.

"Thought you couldn't walk in the sunlight," Danny commented.

"I can't, which is why I'm over here," Remington called back. "If it touches my skin I'll burn, so covering up is my best option right now and even that's limited to only a couple of extra minutes."

Jacob shook his head. "Your risk. We're heading to the manor, so we'll meet you there, I guess."

Remington gave him a grin before Jacob and the rest of the group headed off, the little cat once again out in front as he dashed ahead. Nobody spoke as they walked along the dirt road to the back of the outpost like the night before.

Jacob scanned himself in once they got there, holding the door for everyone, and going in after they were all inside, making sure the door was shut. They all followed Jacob through the manor, going to a different room this time, not the dining room where they'd been last time.

They came to a living room further back in the manor.

"Everyone find somewhere to sit. We'll just wait a few minutes for Remington since it'll take him a bit to get here," Jacob said, going over to one of the chairs and taking a seat.

"Already here, Chief." Remington carelessly pushed past everyone as he entered the room. "Sorry for keeping you all waiting, I'm sure you've been here for a while."

Danny rolled his eyes and sat on one of the sofas, his usual crew joining him as everyone else found somewhere to sit.

"So, what are we talking about?" Remington asked, trying to get comfortable as he lounged on one of the chairs. "If it's a need-to-know basis, then it's gotta be important, right?"

"You knew it was need-to-know, so clearly you heard something about what it was," Ash shot at him.

"I have selective hearing, sometimes," Remington remarked drily.

Jacob spoke before anyone could say anything else. There was just too much tension in the room, and he was sure it was because of the whole vampire-in-the-room situation.

"We're talking about what's going to happen to Marion once we get her," he began explaining. Remington nodded, understanding now. "I'm going to tell them now so we're all on the same level of knowledge." He looked around at everyone. "He already knows this, so he's wasted his time coming out during the day."

Remington gave a lazy shrug. "Gets me outta that room, so I'm not fussed."

Jacob chose to ignore his statement, speaking again to explain what was going on. "We've been trying to figure out what the best thing to do with Marion is. We've decided it's not wise to kill her in case something happens that makes things down here worse and possibly irreversible. We can't keep her locked away again as long as Carmen's around, so we're going for the next best thing."

"Which is?" Matt asked, arms crossed as he stayed leaning back in his chair.

Jacob looked at him. "We're going to send her into a different dimension." Interest crossed a few people's faces at that. "That way we don't have to worry about killing her and causing more damage."

"Are you sure that won't cause things to worsen?" Ash asked.

Jacob nodded. "We're pretty sure it'll help stabilize everything. It won't make things worse."

Ash wasn't sure whether she could believe that or not, but she didn't push the matter. If something happened, then they'd deal with it when it occurred.

"How are you going to send her into another dimension?" Chris asked.

"Right near the coastline is the Dimension Portal," Jacob explained. "It's got access to every dimension."

A frown appeared on Matt's face now and he wasn't the only one.

"You sure it actually exists and isn't just some … myth made up to scare people or make people believe things are real when they're not?" Ash asked skeptically.

"Oh, it's real," Remington spoke up, all of them looking at him.

"We scoped it all out once we heard about it. We wouldn't be going just on hearsay for something like this," Jacob said seriously. "We know it's there and it's currently active. This is our best shot at getting rid of Marion humanely. This is the way we go."

CHAPTER TWENTY-NINE

The Funeral Masquerade

"You ready for this?" Chris asked as he watched Ash get a few things together, making sure she had her Banshee's End badge on.

"Not really, but what choice do we have?" she responded. She stopped what she was doing and looked at Chris who was leaning, arms crossed, against the wall of her room near the door. "As long as we all stay out of trouble, we should be fine. This is going to go fine."

Chris gave a slight nod but didn't say anything in return, not really sure what to say. If it was one thing he knew, it was that nothing ever went exactly how it was planned when they were down here in the Underground Worlds. Something always went wrong. He just didn't know what that something was going to be this time.

"We'll all be fine," Ash repeated, Chris giving another vague nod. "If anything happens, we've got a lot of backup, and we can't afford to panic."

A light tap on the door got their attention, the door opening a few seconds later.

"We're heading out," Matt informed them, getting a nod from Ash and Chris.

The little cat had been lying on his usual chair, but he now jumped down and trudged out through the open door as Matt watched him.

"We'll be right there," Chris said.

Matt nodded and left.

Chris looked at Ash and pushed himself off the wall. "Let's get going."

Ash made sure she had what she needed before she followed him out into the hallway.

They were heading out with the entire Banshee's End group of people, so there was going to be quite a lot of them.

Remington had left a few days prior, knowing that he needed to get back to wherever he'd been before he headed out to Belle's Castle with whichever other vampires were going to the event.

"Everyone remember who they're paired with in case something happens?" Jacob asked, standing at the head of the group as Ash and Chris arrived. Everyone nodded, Ash glancing at Chris but not saying anything. "Alright then, let's get moving. We're heading straight to the castle. We'll stop a few times along the way, so keep alert. Let's go."

It was Wednesday night, and they all stood outside the massive front doors of Belle's Castle. The guards on duty had stepped off to the side of the doors once they'd seen that these were all members of Banshee's End.

"Everyone keep a serious look out and if anything happens, contact one of your captains," Jacob said. "Remember, we're here for Marion. If we don't get Carmen and Hunter, don't worry too much. We leave once we have Marion. Let's go."

The guards opened the doors for them without a word, Jacob heading in first with a few of the others not far behind him. They weren't all going inside at once, as they didn't want that many people disrupting the flow of what was already happening inside.

Matt looked at the few of them in their usual group as a couple more of the Banshee's End crew went inside.

"Alright, everyone try to stay alive, OK?" he said, all of them nodding. He looked at Gates whom he'd been paired up with. "Let's go check this place out."

He and Gates headed in, as the guards kept holding the doors open, knowing to close them once everyone was inside.

Alex loitered close to Ash, unhappy at having been paired up with Abel and Zeke. There'd been an uneven number within their group, and Jacob figured they'd want to stick together.

Ash looked at Chris who was looking at something on his phone as Danny and Ted headed in, Jordan and Shawn not far behind. Knowing them, they'd all stick together in their group of four instead of their inconspicuous groups of two.

"You OK?" Ash asked, getting Chris's attention away from his phone. "You've been constantly checking that phone all day. Is something happening at home?"

Chris looked at her for a few seconds as Abel grabbed Alex and headed inside. Alex reluctantly left Ash and Zeke followed them in, not too impressed with being paired up with them and not Matt and Gates.

"Yeah, just waiting to hear back from someone," Chris said as a group of people passed them, also heading inside. He put his phone back in his pocket. "Let's get inside, we're wasting time being out here."

Without waiting for a response, he headed inside with Ash hurrying to catch up.

There were a lot of people in the castle's grand entrance room, the impressive staircase leading to the next level above them.

"Where do we want to set up for the night?" Chris asked as a few people passed by, some from Banshee's End, some not.

"We should find somewhere that the others aren't covering yet," Ash suggested, Chris nodding in agreement. She indicated to one of the rooms on the right. "Let's check there and see if there's anywhere worth being stationed?"

"Sounds good."

The two of them headed through the groups of talking people. Chris was getting an uneasy feeling from a few of the people, and he was starting to wonder if vampires were the only threat within this castle at the current time.

"This place gives me the creeps," Ash admitted as they went through the entranceway and into the room. It was a living room of some sort, and there were a lot of people already in there.

"Glad I'm not the only one," Chris sighed as they moved further into the room. He saw Matt and Gates not far from them across the room. "Keep going, Matt and Gates have this room."

Ash nodded, carefully moving past more people, Matt catching her eye and giving her a nod of greeting, letting her know he'd seen them.

Ash nodded back as they went into the next room, but there were a few Banshee's End recruits already there as well.

"They've probably got a lot of this place already covered," Ash said as they continued to move through the castle, trying to find a room where there weren't any other recruits. "We might have trouble getting anywhere and have to just settle for the same room as someone else."

"We'll keep looking," said Chris. "It gives us a bit more of the layout, anyway."

Ash nodded in agreement, moving past more people who were standing around, talking and laughing in groups.

They were nearing the back of the castle and Chris could see they were heading to the ballroom. It reminded him of the masked ball in Wonderland where he'd first met Ash.

"Let's just set up in here somewhere," Chris said as they entered the ballroom, masses of people already in there, talking loudly over the band who continued to play some classical song that Chris didn't particularly like the sound of.

Ash nodded, moving over to the other side of the room near one of the entranceways, figuring they could get a better look and stop anyone from leaving that way if they had to.

"I guess now we just wait and see what happens," Chris commented as he leaned back against the wall.

Ash did the same, leaning against the wall next to him as she looked around. "Guess so. Might be here for a while, it's only just ten o'clock. Heard the party doesn't get started until just after midnight."

Chris sighed. "Wonderful."

Ash looked at him as he crossed his arms, just observing what was going on.

"It surely can't be that bad," she tried, getting Chris's attention back onto her and away from what was happening on the ballroom floor.

"Well, seeing as someone always dies at these things, I think it can't be that good," he said truthfully. "There are a lot of people here, sure, but you never know what could happen. A few of these guys are our guys and the last thing I want to see happen, is one of them get killed."

Ash couldn't argue with that. She didn't say anything in response, so Chris went back to looking around the crowded room. It was really hard to see anyone in particular within the crowd and he was wondering if there was somewhere better they could station themselves so they could get the full view of what was going on in the ballroom.

"We need to find a better spot, I can't see anything here," he said. He looked up and saw the balcony on the floor above. He pointed it out to Ash. "Let's go check it out. We need a better view."

Without waiting for any sort of response, he headed out through the entranceway they were standing next to. Ash followed, not wanting to lose him.

Just outside was a narrow staircase that hopefully led up to the next level. Chris and Ash headed up, and, sure enough, the stairs led to the balcony.

Chris went over to the small balcony, avoiding the few people who were already up there. It was a good vantage point, as he could see the entire ballroom floor below.

Across the room, on the opposite balcony, he saw Abel, Alex, and Zeke, the three of them clearly having had the same idea.

"Any sign of anyone yet?" Ash asked as she joined Chris who was now leaning against the balcony's railing, looking down at the room below.

Chris shook his head. "Nothing. Haven't seen any sign of Craig yet, either. Wonder if he's even here yet."

"I'm sure he's here somewhere, he said he would be."

"Doesn't mean he's arrived yet."

Ash gave a nod of agreement, looking down at the ground floor, the masses of people still astounding to her. Even when Marion had held her gatherings, there hadn't ever been anywhere near this many people. It made Ash wonder where they all resided, if they were all Oz residents or if there were people from all the neighboring counties.

Chris pointed down to someone on the floor, Ash's gaze following where he was indicating to.

"Remington's here," he noted. Remington was observing people from the other side of the room on the ballroom floor. "Which means if he's here, there are bound to be more vampires down there."

"Probably best we stay up here, then," Ash said.

Chris gave a nod of agreement. "I think that's a good idea."

CHAPTER THIRTY

Graith

"Craig."

"Hunter."

Craig kept his gaze forwards, not looking away from the people he was currently observing as Hunter leaned against the wall next to him. Craig tried not to let Hunter's presence faze him, and he kept his arms crossed. He saw Jacob over the other side of the room, keeping his eyes on what was happening throughout the ballroom.

He could see Ash and Chris on the balcony on the floor above and he knew Abel, Alex, and Zeke were on the balcony opposite them.

"Not surprised to see you here," Hunter said, following Craig's gaze and seeing him watching Jacob now. Hunter indicated across the room. "Didn't think he'd get out of the Emerald City but, I mean, I guess I was wrong."

"I assume there's a reason you came over to me," Craig said, finally breaking his gaze and looking directly at Hunter. "Also, I hope you know that I'm going to make sure you don't leave this castle unescorted."

Hunter smiled in amusement, summing Craig up as Craig watched him with no amusement on his face.

"I truly thought you weren't down here anymore," Hunter said, ignoring Craig's comment. "I thought you would've packed it up and gone back home by now."

"I assume you're not here alone," Craig said, choosing to ignore Hunter's remark. "Because that'd be damn stupid of you to come to something like this unaided."

"It would be, wouldn't it? Guess you'll have to stick around and find out for yourself." With one last smile, Hunter pushed off the wall and left the room.

Craig shook his head, looking across the room again, seeing Jacob watching him. Not needing to be told, Craig headed out of the room, planning on finding out where Hunter was going.

Up on the balcony, Chris and Ash had seen what had happened, and they both watched Craig follow Hunter out of the room.

"That's not good," Ash sighed. "If he's here, then we're in the right place. Marion won't stray too far from her champion."

"Oh, she's here, she's lurking somewhere."

Remington leaned against the balcony railing on Ash's right as he observed the lower level of the castle.

"Didn't think you were meant to be talking to any of us," Ash commented, looking him over as he ignored her gaze and continued to look down at the ground level, thought on his face.

"I'm not talking to you, I'm looking for my next unsuspecting victim," was his response, scanning the ground for someone. "I've been here for a few hours and I'm getting hungry. Better to get on top of it before it gets too bad because that's when bad things happen and people die."

"Really? You're seriously preying on people while you're here?" Ash was appalled.

Remington tore his gaze away from the floor and looked at her. She could see the look in his eyes and immediately wanted to retract her previous statement.

"Yes, because I don't have much choice," he said, keeping his voice down. He leaned in slightly, making Ash uncomfortable. "You'd also better keep it down a bit because there are some people down there who won't take too kindly to hearing you speak, especially about this kind of thing."

He moved back, giving her the space back. He could be scary when he needed to be. He went back to looking down at the masses of people on the floor, trying to decide who might be an easy target.

"We're vampires, we prey on people all the time," he continued, moving and placing both of his hands on the railing, gripping it tightly as he scanned the crowd again. "Oh no."

Without warning, he quickly ducked down and was now sitting with his back against the stone of the balcony railing. Ash frowned, exchanging looks with Chris who gave a shrug. The two of them looked down at him, seeing the worry on his face.

"You OK? What's going on?" Ash asked, making sure to keep her voice down this time.

Remington urgently signaled for them both to be quiet, not wanting whatever, or whoever, he'd seen on the lower level to hear them. Chris and Ash exchanged looks again as Remington stayed where he was, leaning his head back against the stone railing, closing his eyes and muttering something to himself.

"Go away, go away," he said a few times, his voice almost inaudible.

He opened his eyes and looked at Chris and Ash, then scrambled to his feet and roughly grabbed the two of them. Without any explanation, he dragged them off to the side of the balcony, moving the dark red curtain out of the way and pushing them back behind it before moving the curtain back into place.

Ash peeked around the edge of the curtain and saw that Remington had gone back to his position at the balcony, hands flat against it as he stared down at the floor below. Chris looked around the other side of the curtain to see what was going on.

A man came to a stop on Remington's right, getting his attention. Neither Chris nor Ash recognized the man, but there was something about him that gave both of them a rather uncomfortable feeling.

"Banshee's End certainly have their defenses here tonight," the man said. As soon as Chris heard the voice, he knew who this was. "I'm surprised they haven't tried anything with our group yet."

There was no way Chris was about to forget that eerie back-tone. There was no doubt in his mind that this was Graith Levers, the Legion's Commanding Officer.

"They seem to be more focused on something else," Remington said, turning his gaze back down to the ballroom, the band having changed to something slightly more upbeat and not as depressing. "Still have the rest of the night, it's only just nearing midnight."

"Keep a close watch, never know what they're planning and what they're really here for," Graith said, getting a nod from Remington who continued to avoid his gaze. "What are you doing up here?"

Remington looked back at his commanding officer, a bit of an unsure look on his face now.

"Ah, was looking at who's available down there because it's been a while since I've had anything," he said, his unsure tone matching his look. "I mean ... if that's OK with you?"

Chris was glad he'd managed to cover that one up. The last thing he wanted was for Remington to get caught out in a lie.

Graith looked him over again, thinking. Then he nodded and Remington nodded back, clearly having been given the good-to-go signal. Graith turned to leave, speaking as he did so, Remington watching him the entire time.

"Just don't turn or kill anyone and we won't have any problems," he said as he walked away. "Also watch out for their commanding officer. Craig Taylor isn't someone you want to run into on a good day."

With that he left, not having anything more to say to Remington. Remington sighed and turned back to face the front of the balcony, hands flat on it once again as he looked out across the room.

Chris and Ash waited a few minutes before moving out from behind the curtain, Remington didn't even glance at them as they kept a bit of distance from him this time, so it didn't look too obvious this time around.

"You can turn people, and you didn't think that was something we needed to be told?" Ash asked. Her voice was down as she looked out over the balcony. Remington kept watching the crowd, while Chris looked over his shoulder to make sure no one was lurking in the shadows. "Does anyone else know?"

"No," Remington said. He glanced over at them, lowering his voice again. "And I'd appreciate it if you two kept that to yourselves. This isn't something I wanted anyone to know."

"Were you *ever* going to tell them?" Chris asked seriously, as someone on the lower level caught Remington's attention.

"Eventually," he said. He pushed off the balcony. "If you two will excuse me, I've just decided on dinner."

He turned and left the balcony, disappearing quickly down the narrow staircase. Ash shook her head and went back to leaning on the balcony next to Chris.

"I can't believe this," she said with another shake of her head, watching Jacob on the opposite side of the room where Craig had been before he'd left. "You'd think that would be something they'd need to know since they said only certain vampires can turn people."

"Remington might be a higher rank than we all thought," Chris said, putting it out there and getting a glance from Ash. "They said only ones who've been around for a while and high-ranking vampires can turn people. He's only been a vampire for six years. I wouldn't think that would be long enough to be able to convert people."

"Great," Ash sighed, leaning her head on her hand as she watched Remington talk to a young woman not too far from where Jacob was stationed. She saw Jacob watching him as well. "I don't think it's something he's going to tell anyone."

Chris couldn't do anything but agree.

"Daniel, so this is what you look like without your mask on. Not hiding your identity tonight."

The bitter look appeared on Danny's face as he turned to face Graith, knowing it was him. There was no way anyone else sounded like that and he'd heard Graith's voice many times since they'd been trying to invade his land.

"And this is what *you* look like without your sunlight-proof tent, not hiding from the light tonight," he retorted, looking Graith directly in the eye. He noticed Ted, Jordan, and Shawn were just a few paces away, ready to back him up if they were needed.

Graith looked different to what Danny had initially thought. He was slightly taller than Danny, and his hair was dark brown and pushed back off his face. The thing that Danny didn't like about him—besides the obvious thing about him being a vampire and being rather pushy—was that his eyes were a dark red. It made him uncomfortable, but he wasn't about to let Graith know that.

Graith looked Danny over, summing him up quite a lot before he looked back at the bitter look on his face. He indicated to the Banshee's End badge Danny was wearing.

"Didn't think you'd ever sink that low," Graith noted, linking his fingers together in front of himself. "Banshee's End? I thought you didn't like them. You never called upon them to help you out when we tried to get onto your land, and you lot are bandits. Bandits don't mix with law enforcement."

"We're not technically law enforcement," Craig said, coming to a stop on Graith's right. Graith was quite a lot taller than Craig, but he wasn't letting that intimidate him. "I'm surprised you're willingly showing your face in public, Levers, especially since this is where people come to die."

"That why you're here, Commander? Ready to die?" Graith shot back. Craig crossed his arms and a slight smile appeared on Graith's face. "Or are you here to kill *me*?"

"You're the least of my worries tonight," Craig said. "You can go about doing whatever it is you normally do. You're not our focus tonight. We have business here and it's got nothing to do with you or your army."

The amusement stayed on Graith's face.

"Well, that's a relief. I won't have to worry about pulling any of my men from their night out at the all-you-can-eat buffet," he said. Danny looked even more unimpressed now. Graith looked Craig over. "Also, it's funny you should mention that you're not here for me, because if I remember correctly, I saw a lovely blonde woman heading up to one of the areas above the ballroom where some of your people are stationed. The girl with the red hair and her friend, I think. Tell you what, that blade looked *pretty* sharp."

Craig's expression changed, the amusement still there on the vampire's face.

Craig looked at Danny. "Move out, they're up on the left balcony in the ballroom."

Without waiting for any word of confirmation, Craig was out of the room. Danny gestured for the other three bandits to follow Craig.

"Better get a move on," Graith said to Danny before passing by and disappearing into one of the other rooms.

Danny shook his head, watching him for a few seconds before he joined the others, heading out of the room and straight for the ballroom.

CHAPTER THIRTY-ONE

The Bell Tolls

Chris shifted how he was standing. He was getting tired and there hadn't been any sign of anyone yet, only Hunter and Graith. There hadn't been a lot happening throughout the night and he was rather bored.

"I don't understand how we've gone this entire time and only seen Hunter," he said, trying to strike up another conversation with Ash who was also looking tired. She glanced at him, then back at the ballroom floor. "Seriously, how has Marion gone this long without showing herself? Surely *someone* has seen her by now."

"Well, we got word a few hours ago about her being around somewhere," Ash said, shifting how she was standing as well.

She saw Craig come back into the ballroom and look up at her and Chris. Ash frowned and Chris followed her gaze, seeing Craig indicating for them to get down to the ground floor.

"Looks like we're needed for something," she said.

They left the balcony and headed back to the stairs that would take them to the lower level.

"Wonder what that's about, what's going on," Chris commented as they reached the staircase.

They waited for a couple of people to come up before they could head down, as the staircase was so narrow that it could only take one-way traffic.

Ash shrugged as they began descending the stairs. Chris was in front with her a step behind.

"Don't know, but it's clearly important," she said as they reached the bottom.

"What time is it?" Chris asked as Ash stepped off the last step and onto the floor. "How long do you think we're going to have to be here? What time's this thing finish anyway?"

Ash got her phone out of her pocket, checking the time, before putting it back in. "It's just after three. I assume this whole thing probably finishes up before sunrise. Wouldn't be much later than that since it goes all night or so."

Chris nodded again, sighing. Realization crossed his face as he looked back to Ash. "Have you heard any bells yet? Because if it's just after three, then there's less than an hour left before someone has to die for this whole night to come to a conclusion, right?"

"Was it four o'clock Danny said it has to be done by?" Ash asked as Chris nodded. "And three was the prime time to watch out, right?"

Chris nodded again. "Yeah."

"So, I guess you'd both better watch out, then." Marion gave the two of them a smile from where she was leaning against the wall just behind the staircase they'd just come down. "Long time, no see, Chris. Not surprised Ash dragged you all the way back down here since she couldn't handle it herself."

Marion moved around the staircase, Chris automatically backing up, making sure Ash was behind him as he moved her back a bit as well.

"Ash, signal Craig," Chris said, never taking his eyes off Marion who was now pretending to study the very sharp blade she had with her. "Get him over here, *now*."

Marion looked away from the blade and at the two of them with a bit of a smile. "Last time I checked, he was over the other side of the room."

Chris was still in between her and Ash, and he shuffled backwards a bit more.

"It'll take him a bit to get through the crowd in there and over to here." Marion continued to smile. "By then, though, I'm afraid it might be a bit too late for him to do anything."

"Ash, signal Craig," Chris repeated as Marion moved forward another step, once again pretending to study the blade she was holding. "I don't care how, just signal him over *now!*"

Ash finally moved from behind him and over to the entranceway that led into the ballroom.

Marion stepped up until she was standing just in front of Chris who stood his ground, not wanting to make any movements.

"Just so you know, seeing as I can see you're trying to figure out what kind of state I'm in, I'm doing fine," Marion said, her voice low so Chris had to really listen to hear her. "Carmen's magic works quite well with fixing things. Everything should be just fine with the world, now."

"Glad to hear you're not having a mental breakdown, anymore," Chris said.

There was no way he was about to take his eyes off her. She could try something at any point, and he wasn't about to risk it.

Marion looked him over, thinking a bit before glancing over to where Ash had disappeared into the ballroom.

"I don't think she's coming back," she noted, back to looking at Chris who didn't dare look around to see where Ash had gone. "Shame. She'll just have to see the end result, I guess."

"Was this your plan the whole time?" Chris asked. "You plan on killing us all off one-by-one until you have no threats left?"

Marion shrugged lazily. "Maybe. I mean, you've *all* always been thorns in my side and every time I spare one of you, it ends up bad for me. I can't risk that anymore, Chris. I have to just take the chance and end it the moment I have the opportunity."

Without any sort of indication, Marion moved too quickly for Chris to try and defend himself.

"You just happened to be the unlucky first one," Marion said. She pulled him forwards a bit and Chris felt the sharp pain as she pushed the blade deeper. "Sorry, Chris. One down, seven to go."

She moved backwards, yanking the blade out and letting Chris fall to his knees. Within moments, she'd disappeared from the room, leaving Chris on the floor trying to stop the bleeding.

Back in the ballroom, Ash was desperately trying to get Craig's attention from the other side of the room. She couldn't see him from where she was on the floor, as there were too many people in the way. She started pushing her way through, knowing she was running out of time but unaware of what had happened minutes before.

"Where are they?" Craig said. He, Danny, Ted, Jordan, and Shawn were on the other side of room to where Chris and Ash had been on the balcony. "They should've been down here by now. You guys see either of them?"

His four companions shook their heads as they looked around, trying to find any sign of Ash and Chris. Craig shook his head, looking around again. Someone caught his attention. It was Remington and he was in the middle of the room.

"Something's happened," Craig said, the other four looking to where he was looking. "Remington's sensed something. He's not the only one, either."

Remington and four others, from what Craig could see, had all sensed something. The other four were clearly vampires as well, as they were the only ones that were fazed.

Without waiting for anyone to move or say anything, Craig began pushing his way through the crowd in the same direction he'd seen the vampires head a second before. He wanted to get there before they did.

Ash, by this point, had given up on trying to get Craig's attention, as she still couldn't see him. She moved back the way she'd come, back to where she'd left Chris.

"Oh my God, Chris!" she exclaimed when she saw him on the floor as she came back into the small room.

She rushed over, crouching down in front of him. Chris looked up at her briefly as she tried to see what was going on, seeing the blood seeping through his fingers, his shirt already soaked with his blood.

"She disappeared out into one of the other rooms," Chris managed to say as Ash saw someone appear in the entranceway. It was Remington and a few others she didn't recognize. "You can't let her get out."

"Right now, she's the least of my worries," Ash said seriously, seeing the pain on Chris's face. This wasn't good. "I'm not about to go anywhere and leave you here, OK? Marion can wait. This is serious."

Chris glanced at her again, staying where he was. Ash saw Craig push past Remington and the other people. He was over to them in less than a second, crouching down next to Ash as the four bandits moved away from the entranceway, staying near the staircase.

"What happened?" Craig asked urgently, looking between Chris and Ash.

"Marion's gotten out through one of the other rooms, I don't know which one," Chris whispered through the pain, starting to feel the weakness from the amount of blood he was losing. He looked at Craig. "You can't let her out."

Craig seemed reluctant, but he looked over at the bandits. "Search this entire place," he ordered. "Go through every room until you find her. No one leaves until she's found."

Danny gave a nod and indicated for the other three to begin in the other rooms. They all headed out and Craig glared at Remington and the vampires with him.

"You all need to back the fuck up," he warned. Remington was at the head of the pack and Craig looked straight at him. "All of you."

Remington stared Craig down for a second or two before looking back at the vampires and signaling for them to back up. They all did as they were told, dispersing back into the ballroom, Remington gone with them.

Craig looked back at Chris. "We can't move you. If we move you, it'll make it worse and you'll bleed out faster."

"What can we do?" Ash asked urgently. She indicated to Chris. "We have to do something or he's gonna die!"

"I know!" Craig snapped back, silencing Ash. "I know that, OK? I'm doing what I can but right now, it looks like that's gonna happen. I'm sorry, Ash, there's only so much I can do, OK?"

Ash stayed quiet, and Craig looked back at Chris, seeing that he wasn't faring too well now. "What do *you* want us to do? The longer we stay here, the more likely it is that you don't make it out of this castle. We can move you to another room away from everyone and everything and try to fix this but, as I said, I don't like your chances if we move you, and I'm truly sorry about that. I need to know what *you* want us to do."

Chris looked at him for a few seconds as he tried to quickly decide what to do. He felt dizzy which made it hard to think. "I can't stay here," he ended up saying.

Craig gave a nod and looked at Ash. "Help me get him up." He looked at Chris again. "This is most likely gonna hurt, so just bear with it for a minute or so and we'll get you out of this room, OK?"

Chris nodded, a slight smile on his face. "Right now, everything hurts, so I don't think you could do any worse."

Craig smiled back slightly before he and Ash carefully took hold of Chris, helping him to his feet. Chris managed not to cry out in pain as the two of them carefully moved him towards the closest room.

"Get out," Craig commanded the couple of people who were in the room, and they quickly left when they saw the blood trail Chris was leaving as he moved.

They sat him on one of the sofas, Ash sitting on his left and putting her arm around his shoulders, knowing there was nothing either she or Craig could do at the current time.

Craig stood with his hands on his hips, looking at Chris while trying to figure out what to do.

Craig and Ash looked over as someone appeared in the open doorway. Chris stayed where he was, not game to move.

"Right now's really not the best time," Craig said with annoyance as Remington stayed in the doorway, looking at Chris.

"I know, and I'm really sorry about crashing the party," he said in return. He looked to Craig. "But I might be able to help if you let me."

"How in the world would you be able to help?" Craig asked, the annoyance clear in his tone.

"Remington can turn people," Ash spoke up. Craig stared at her as her words sunk in. Ash looked at Remington. "He's able to turn people into vampires."

Craig returned his gaze to Remington. "You're joking," he said, the disbelief clear in his tone. "Why the fuck didn't you think about telling me this before now?"

"Because I didn't want anyone to know!" Remington snapped back. "I've only been a vampire for six years, so you can kinda see how it'd be a really awkward situation for me to have to try and explain myself and why I can turn people, since only high ranking vampires can turn! You see what kinda issues this was going to cause? You see this, Craig?"

Craig stayed silent, staring Remington down.

Remington indicated to Chris, speaking again. "If you let me help, he doesn't have to become tonight's sacrifice. You just have to give me permission to do it, because I won't do it if you say no."

Craig looked at him for a few seconds before he forced himself to speak. "It's not up to me. It's up to Chris, because he's the one who would have to live with it. It doesn't matter what I say."

Remington looked over at Chris and Ash. He started to say something, but forced himself to stop, the look on his face changing.

"What?" Ash asked urgently, still in the same position as before. "What is it?"

Remington looked at her briefly, then back at Chris.

"It's not going to matter, anyway. There's nothing I can do," he said sadly, then sighed. "His heart's stopped. He's gone."

Ash's expression changed to panic. She looked at Chris and saw that Remington was right. Chris wasn't moving and she was pretty sure he wasn't breathing. She could see no signs of life.

"No, no, no," Ash sobbed. She held him tight, the tears running down her face as she looked at Craig. "You have to do something!"

Craig looked at her sadly, repositioning himself and putting his hands behind his head, looking down at the ground, not saying anything.

Ash looked over at Remington who looked at her sadly as well, knowing there was nothing that could be done now.

Moments later, the three of them heard a loud bell toll, causing a cheer to rise up from the ballroom.

Craig moved, sat down on one of the chairs, and put his head in his hands.

CHAPTER THIRTY-TWO

Saying Goodbye

"What do we do now?"

Jacob shook his head, trying to think of an answer. They'd all returned to Banshee's End the moment the Funeral Masquerade had ended and now they were trying to figure out the best thing to do.

"We're going to take a few days," he eventually said, breaking the silence that had fallen upon the group. "Anything we were planning on doing can wait. I don't care how urgent it is, we're taking a few days."

No one said a word.

"We bury Chris, and we take a few days," Jacob said, repeating himself. He sighed, looking around at everyone. "Look, I'm really sorry about this. I know you all probably blame me for this since I'm the one who put us into that situation, but I want you to know that I'm incredibly sorry this has happened. I take full responsibility for this."

"It's not your fault," Abel said. "We were all doing what we thought we had to and so it's on everyone, not solely on you."

Jacob gave a nod, though it didn't make him feel much better. He reiterated his plan yet again.

"We'll bury Chris and then take a few days before we get back into the swing of things. I don't care what anyone has to say, we're taking a few days because this is a significant loss. I don't want to see anyone down here all week and even for a few days after that. Chris was part of this team and we're going to do the right thing by him. We're going to make sure he didn't die for nothing."

A knock on the door made Craig look over his shoulder. Ash was standing in the doorway of his room.

"You coming?" she asked.

He nodded and put down the book he'd been looking at before the interruption. He headed over to where she was standing and stopped in front of her.

"Ash, look..."

Ash held her hand up to silence him. "If you're planning on apologizing to me, please don't. Because I know you did everything you could and that if you could have done something else then you would have done it. So please, no apologies because I don't want to hear it."

She lowered her hand, and Craig looked at her for a couple of seconds as he decided what to say.

"Well, then, I guess I have nothing left to say," he ended up saying, getting a sad smile from Ash in return. He sighed. "I really am sorry about this, though, Ash. I know you and Chris were friends."

"That's all we were, friends." Craig couldn't help but smile slightly at her words. Ash looked him over briefly. "Now come on, the last thing I want is to be late for a funeral."

She turned and left, and Craig followed, shutting the door behind himself, as he didn't like leaving it open for prying eyes. Ash didn't even bother waiting for him as she headed out of the barracks and back outside into the daylight. It was getting late, and the sun would be down soon enough.

Ash stayed a few paces ahead of Craig as they went to meet up with everyone else near the back of the outpost, having decided that the best place to start was the graveyard. It was just a shame at who was going to be the first one buried within the boundary fence of that graveyard.

Everyone else was already waiting as the last two arrived. They joined them, standing around the recently filled in grave, having decided as a group that this was what they wanted to do.

Jacob looked around at everyone, making sure they were all there before he started.

"So, this isn't exactly what any of us wanted to do," he began, not too sure how to go about this kind of thing. It was the first time he'd had to run something like this and so he was going to just go with it and hope for the best. He sighed. "No one's ever ready to say goodbye to someone and I know when you're close to someone, it's a lot harder."

"Chris never wanted to be down here in the first place," Ash spoke up, everyone looking over to where she was standing between Alex and Craig. She shook her head, feeling a few tears trickle down her face. "And I'm the one who convinced him to come back down here to help us because we couldn't do it by ourselves. He wouldn't be dead if I hadn't asked him to help."

"Ash, come on, it's not your fault," Alex tried to say, but Ash shook her head and everyone else stayed quiet.

"I should have just dealt with it myself instead of relying on someone else, like Chris, who I knew would say yes to helping because his heart was always in the right place," she said. "I left him in the same room as Marion when we both knew not to leave anyone by themselves. It's my fault."

Alex looked at her sadly but didn't try to say anything else, knowing it was no use.

Ash didn't even bother trying to get rid of the tears off her face. "This whole thing is my fault and I'm sorry."

No one said anything for a minute or two.

"Anyone want to say anything?" Jacob asked, being the only one game enough to try and speak. He looked around at everyone. "If so, now's your chance. If not, we can all go our separate ways for a few days."

No one spoke up, having nothing to say, and Jacob nodded.

"Alright, then," he said awkwardly. "You're all dismissed for the next week or so. You know where to find me if you need anything. Try to take this time to grieve. I'm really sorry about all of this, and I truly hope we can work through this. If anyone needs to talk, please come find me."

He headed off without saying anything more.

The sun was nearly gone for the day and a few of the others left, too, but Ash stayed where she was. Alex was not about to move until she was ready to go, and Craig also stayed beside her.

"Ash, you can't blame yourself for this," Alex said quietly, seeing someone a few paces away in the shade of one of the buildings.

It was Remington, trying to keep himself out of what was left of the sunlight. He had clearly wanted to be a part of this but couldn't yet come any closer.

Ash shook her head, staring down at Chris's grave as she let her tears flow freely.

"He can't be gone, Alex," she said quietly. "This was not meant to happen."

Alex moved and put his arms around her tightly, feeling her return the gesture and bury her face in his chest.

Once the sun had completely disappeared and night had taken over, Remington cautiously walked over to them, hands in pockets, gaze on the ground.

"Here for a reason?" Craig asked, not happy to see him right now. "I don't remember anyone inviting you to this."

Remington kept his gaze on the ground, kicking the dirt beneath his feet.

"I know, but I thought I should come by and pay my respects," he said quietly, not wanting to deal with confrontation right now. "I want to apologize for not being able to help. I feel partially responsible."

Craig wasn't in the least bit happy with him, but he could see that Remington genuinely felt bad about not being able to do anything when it had happened.

Craig sighed. "Just try to keep away for a few days, OK?" he suggested, getting a reluctant nod from Remington. "Let them grieve. They don't need any more problems to deal with for a few days."

Remington nodded, then turned and headed back the way he'd come.

Craig looked at Ash and Alex, everyone else having left now. Alex returned his look, but Ash still had her face buried in his chest.

"You know where to find me if you need anything," Craig said, trying to keep his tone soft so he wouldn't upset Ash any more than she already was. "Just knock on the door and I'll answer. Try and have a good night."

With that said, he headed off, leaving the two of them where they were, confident they'd seek out either himself or Jacob if they needed anything.

CHAPTER THIRTY-THREE

Welcome to Hell

The last thing Chris expected to do was open his eyes. The confusion set in very quickly as he sat up and looked around cautiously, no idea where he was. It was very hot and very unfamiliar. The vast empty landscape spread out every which way with no end in sight.

"It finally awakes."

Chris looked to his left, a frown appearing on his face as he saw who'd spoken. "Heather?"

Heather was sitting on a large rock a couple of feet or so away from him and she looked him over disapprovingly.

"Glad you remember who I am," she said with disdain in her voice. She gave him an amused smile. "How's it feel to be dead?"

The frown appeared on Chris's face again. "I'm sorry?"

Heather rolled her eyes, jumping down off the large rock and wandering over to where he was still sitting on the hot, cracked ground. She offered her hand to him, and Chris reluctantly accepted it. She helped him up off the ground, then stood back.

"You don't know what's going on, do you?" Heather asked, crossing her arms as she watched him brush himself down.

"Am I *meant* to know what's going on?" Chris asked. He looked around again as Heather just watched him, then he looked back at her. "You said I'm dead?"

Heather gave a bit of a nod, that unimpressed look back on her face.

"Only reason you'd be here," she said, her tone serious. She shifted, holding her arms out to each side. "Welcome to Hell, Chris!"

Chris's expression dropped. "Hell?"

Heather rolled her eyes. "You hard on hearing? Did dying ruin your ability to listen? Yes, Hell. H-E-L-L. You know, as in, where you go when you die if you don't go the opposite way?"

Heather pointed towards the sky, Chris following her indication.

He looked back at her as it started to sink in, and he remembered what had happened. "Oh no."

"There we go, memory's back!" Heather exclaimed unenthusiastically. She shifted her position as Chris thought. "So? How'd you go out? Got a body to get back to?"

Chris looked at her. "You know how to get out of here?"

Heather looked him over, arms crossed once again. "I might. But it'll cost you. I can't get out of here without someone on the outside helping me, so if I get you out of here and back to the land of the living, you have to help me once you get back up there. Deal?"

She held her hand out, but Chris hesitated. Was making a deal with Heather the wise thing to do? She couldn't be trusted when she was alive, so how could she be trusted when she was dead? But then again, if she couldn't get out of Hell without someone's help from outside, what could she seriously do if he didn't follow through with the deal?

"Alright, fine," Chris said, shaking her hand in agreement. "You have a deal. Get me out of here and back to life and I'll help you. What do you need me to do?"

"Better not try to screw me over, again," Heather said, narrowing her eyes at him.

"Same goes for you."

Heather smirked, liking his attitude. She always had.

"Guess we'd better start walking then," she said, already beginning to move. "Keep up if you don't want to get lost."

Chris quickly followed along, picking up his pace until he was walking next to her. He was hoping she knew where she was going as, if she didn't, there would be a real big problem.

"You're going to have to explain to me how I'm meant to help you once I'm out if you want me to *actually* help," Chris said, glancing at Heather as they walked across the barren landscape, nothing in sight at all.

"It'll come in due time," she said. "I'll have to write it down for you, your memory might be a bit fuzzy when you get back. Always happens when you climb out of Hell and I don't wish to wait forever to be brought back to the land of the living, you know."

"You going to explain how *I* get out of here?"

"Eventually."

Matt watched Craig who was currently focused on a book he was reading. Craig was sitting with his feet on the table, leaning back in his chair as he read.

"What do you know about the Devil's Well?" Matt suddenly asked, making Craig jump and almost tip backwards in his chair.

He'd known Matt was there in the shadows, but it had been quiet between the two of them for a while. Craig looked at him, a frown on his face upon hearing Matt's question.

"The Devil's Well?" he queried, Matt nodding. "Why do you want to know about the Devil's Well?"

Matt gave a careless shrug. "Just wanna know. Why so suspicious?"

Craig gave him an unamused look. He put the bookmark in the book, closed it, and set it on the table before placing his feet firmly back on the ground.

"It's said to be the way out of Hell, but it's just a myth that's never been proven," Craig said.

"How does it work?" was Matt's next question, the confusion still evident on Craig's face.

"Dunno," he said, which wasn't what Matt wanted to hear. "The story goes that the soul gets out through the Well and automatically re-merges with the body, assuming there is one. Once again, it's never been proven. You also can't get back to your body if you don't have one. Why are you asking this?"

Matt shrugged again. "Call it curiosity."

Craig shook his head, checking the time before sighing.

"Alright, keep your secrets, I'm going to bed," he said, getting up and grabbing his book off the table. "Research it or ask someone else because I really don't know a lot about it."

Matt gave him a nod, watching as he left the room.

Craig shut the door of the church as he left, heading out into the darkness and back to his place in the barracks. He passed a few people on the way, getting a hesitant greeting from a few of the recruits. They'd all been told to keep some distance from anyone who had gone to the Funeral Masquerade and so they were rather hesitant to even greet their commanding officer right now.

Craig didn't mind too much. There were some days that he didn't really wish to deal with a lot of people. He liked having time to himself every so often.

He scanned himself into the barracks and headed through the building to the back where his room was located. He was glad that his room was near the rear of the building, as there weren't a lot of others' rooms this far back.

He frowned as he approached his room. The door was ajar, but he always left it closed. The light was also on, signaling that someone was in there. He cautiously pushed the door open and looked in to see Ash reading through one of his notebooks.

Craig sighed and pushed the door open fully, getting Ash's attention away from what she was reading.

"What are you doing?" he asked as Ash turned her focus back to the notebook.

"You wrote all this?" she asked, turning the page as Craig came into the room and shut the door properly. Ash looked up as he passed her and put the book he had with him on the desk. "I didn't know you wrote poetry."

Craig grabbed the notebook from her and shut it as he looked directly at her.

"They're lyrics and I've only recently gotten back into writing them," he said, going back over to the desk. "Invading other peoples' privacy won't earn you any bonus points."

"Hmm, it's lucky I'm not after bonus points from you, then," Ash said in return as Craig put the notebook back in the correct desk drawer.

He turned around to face her, leaning against the desk and crossing his arms as he addressed her.

"Then what *are* you here for?" he asked. "I know I opened up the offer to talk or whatever, but you don't look like you're in the mood to talk."

Ash looked him over, pretending to think. She raised her eyebrows at him, but Craig didn't say anything more.

"Is that right?" she said, getting a slight nod. "Then, what do *you* think I'm here for?"

Craig gave a bit of a shrug. "Don't know."

Ash rolled her eyes, moving from where she was over the other side of the room, going over to where he was leaning against the desk and stopping right in front of him.

"You said to come find you if I needed anything," she said quietly, looking him up and down as he did the same to her. "So ... here I am."

She looked back up at Craig's face, seeing him watching her.

"OK, so what do you want, then?" he asked, already having a pretty good idea of why she was there. He indicated to the Banshee's End badge he had on his jacket. "I also hope you know this'll stop you from trying anything."

Ash smiled in amusement. "Only while you're wearing it."

Craig rolled his eyes but couldn't keep the smile off his face. "In all honesty, Ash, if that's the reason you sought me out, I completely understand. And honestly, all you have to do is ask."

Ash crossed her arms as she stayed rather close to him. She raised her eyebrows again, the interest clear in her eyes.

"Is that so?" she asked, getting a bit of a nod from Craig. "Well, someone's a bit more willing than a few other people I happen to know."

"No one in your group too keen on you?"

Ash hit him rather hard on the arm but all it did was make him laugh.

"One mistake, OK? That's all," she said, the smile still on Craig's face. She sighed. "Look, I know this probably isn't really the best time to even be considering this kind of thing since it's only been two days since we lost Chris, but I just..."

"Need the comfort?" Craig asked, a bit of sadness in his voice now, all amusement gone.

Ash gave a bit of a shrug. "If that's what you want to call it, I guess."

Craig sighed this time. "You should go back to your room," he suggested, Ash avoiding his gaze. "I honestly think you just need some time to think this whole thing through. I don't want you doing something you think you'll regret later."

Ash looked at him for a few seconds before sighing, Craig just watching her and offering no words.

"Maybe you're right," she said, starting to rethink her earlier intentions. She moved back slightly.

"Either way, you know where I am most of the time," Craig said. "So, if you need anything else, you come find me. Go back to your room, get some rest."

CHAPTER THIRTY-FOUR

The Devil's Well

"How far do we have to go and how exactly am I meant to get out?" Chris asked again.

Heather rolled her eyes and glanced at him as they walked. "Do you ever stop asking questions?"

"Not until I get told what I need to know, and you still haven't said anything about how I'm meant to leave this place," Chris shot back at her, already sick of her and her attitude. "Look, you can't keep me in the dark forever, you're going to have to tell me sooner or later."

It felt like they'd been walking forever and there still wasn't anything in sight. It was all the same dry, barren, cracked wasteland that it had been the entire time. They hadn't even come across anyone else and Chris was starting to wonder what the deal with Hell really was.

"I thought we'd at least have come across someone else by now," Chris commented, Heather glancing at him again. "If this is really Hell, I would've thought there'd be a lot more people."

"Hell's bigger than you think," Heather said with a sigh. "Yes, there are a lot of people and other ... things down here but out here in the barren landscape of it, you're less likely to run into anything or anyone that can hurt you."

Chris raised his eyebrows. "This is only a minor part of Hell?"

Heather nodded. "That's right."

Chris sighed. This was going to take a lot longer than he'd initially thought.

"I know how it works."

Gates switched his gaze to Matt, a questioning look on his face. "I'm sorry?"

Matt looked across the table at him, the look on his face saying all. "The Devil's Well, I know how it works."

The confusion was clear now on Gates's face. "Well done?"

Matt quickly got to his feet. "I'm a genius, Blaine. You don't get it."

"Are you now?"

"Despite popular belief, yes, I am," Matt said, Gates looking him over with a non-believing expression. "It's simple and I don't know how no one else has figured it out yet."

Gates sighed. "I'm still confused at what this has to do with anything."

"Right now, it doesn't matter, I'll explain later. We need to go get Craig."

Matt was already heading for the door by the time Gates responded.

"Matt, it's eight o'clock in the morning!" he called after him, getting to his feet. By the time he got to the door, Matt was already halfway down the hallway. "You really think he's gonna be up and about at this time of morning?"

"If he's not already, he's about to be!" Matt called back.

Gates sighed and just followed his friend.

Matt went out the front door, not having to shield his eyes from the sudden light change this morning. It was coming over dark, and it looked like it was going to rain. Gates quickly caught up as Matt headed for the barracks, knowing that was where he would most likely find Craig. If he wasn't there, he'd search the entire outpost until he found him.

Matt scanned himself into the barracks, not holding the door for anyone but himself this morning. Gates quickly grabbed the door to stop himself being locked out and having to scan himself in. He stayed a pace behind Matt as they headed through the barracks, passing a couple of people who glanced at them and got out of their way but didn't say a word.

Matt came to a stop at one of the rooms and knocked on the door. A few seconds later, the door opened to reveal Don, who raised his eyebrows when he saw who it was.

"Craig's room is up the back, last door on your right as you go down the hallway," he said, already knowing what they wanted to know. Gates still didn't like the kid. "He's not by himself so I wouldn't knock on his door for a while if I were you."

Matt glanced back at Gates before returning his gaze to Don. "Is that so?"

Don gave an awkward nod, not looking too comfortable with discussing this specific subject. Matt looked back at Gates again who returned his look. "We'd best go and pay Craig a visit then."

He gave Don a smile before he continued on his way through the barracks, Gates not far behind.

"Are you sure this is still a good idea?" Gates asked as they passed a few more people headed the opposite way.

Matt glanced over his shoulder, giving him a smile. "Definitely."

Gates rolled his eyes and stayed silent, not wanting to talk about it anymore. If this was what Matt wanted to do, then there wasn't much chance of changing his mind. Sometimes Matt couldn't care less about other people's privacy.

They turned down the last corridor in the barracks, Matt heading down to the last door on the right. If what Don had told them was true, this would be Craig's room. The two of them came to a stop outside the door, which was closed.

"Why do you need Craig for this exactly?" Gates asked, his voice down as Matt looked at him. "Can't you just do whatever it is you wanna do, without him? Why's he so important to this?"

"Besides him being their commanding officer?" Matt asked back, voice down as well because of how quiet it was within the barracks at this time of the morning. "I don't know if you've noticed, Blaine, but he's very overpowered with his ability. If I'm right and this is how things work, it might be a good idea to have him with us."

Gates didn't bother trying to argue. If Matt had an idea and he knew what he was doing, he'd go with it and wouldn't question it anymore.

Not saying anything else, Matt knocked loudly on the door, making sure the sound echoed off the hallway walls before he opened the door moments later.

"Jesus, what are you doing, Matt?" Craig said with annoyance. He was now sitting up in bed, trying to wake himself up. He gestured to the door. "The door was closed for a reason!"

"Which was ... what?" Matt asked, shutting the door. He crossed his arms and stood watching Craig, who seemed a lot more alert now.

He gestured around the room. "Doesn't look like there was any reason to me." He looked back at Craig, who was watching him with no amusement. "So, why the closed door?"

Craig just looked at him for a few seconds before he responded. "Unlike some people, I like my privacy, hence why my room is right at the back of the barracks. Clearly, you don't know anything about that."

Matt smiled in amusement before he wandered over to the desk, Craig watching him the entire time.

"You see, I'm thinking slightly different," Matt said, sitting down on the chair and linking his fingers together. He indicated between himself and Gates who had decided to keep quiet. "We were told something else. We were told you weren't here by yourself."

"And yet you *still* decided on entering my room the way you did?" Craig asked with disbelief, getting a shrug. Craig shifted how he was sitting. "What would you have done if I wasn't the only one here? Seriously, what would you have done if that was the case?"

Matt shrugged. "Probably would've laughed."

Craig glared at him, but Matt chose to ignore it and looked around the room instead.

"What do you want, Matt? Why are you here this early?" Craig sighed.

Matt switched his gaze back to him.

"I say we talk over breakfast," he said, getting another sigh from Craig. Matt smiled in amusement, indicating to something on the floor near the end of the bed. "Also, you might wanna return that to Ash."

"Oh, fuck off."

"So, what's this about?" Craig asked tiredly as he leaned his head on his hand, looking at Matt and Gates who were on the opposite side of the table.

"Remember how I mentioned the Devil's Well to you yesterday?" Matt began, deciding to get straight to the point.

Craig gave a nod. "What about it?"

"I think I know how it all works," Matt continued.

"How? Matt, the whole thing's just a myth, nothing more. You can't prove it works."

"But there's a chance it could."

Craig sighed, shifting his position as a few recruits entered the room, taking a few of the available tables. Gates could see them trying to listen in to their conversation.

"Why do you suddenly care so much about a myth?" Craig asked, rather far from the mood this morning. It was too early for this kind of learning.

"I don't know if you've noticed, but one of our team members is dead," Matt said, his tone a bit harsh and making a few of the recruits who had been listening in look away for a minute or so. Matt readjusted how he was sitting. "I also don't know if you know about the way things work when you die, what decides whether you go up or down."

"Any type of supernatural ends up down," Craig said, still too tired to deal with this. "Others go up."

"Exactly, which means that anyone who has an active ability goes down."

That got Craig's attention. He frowned, shifting and no longer resting his head on his hand. He crossed his arms, placing them both on the table in front of him.

"Which means that Chris is down," he said, picking up on what Matt was implying. "Which is why you've been interested in the Devil's Well because it's supposedly the way out of Hell."

"Now you're getting it," Matt said, pointing at him, glad that Craig was starting to wake up and think properly. "You see where I'm going with this?"

"He also hasn't been dead that long which means his soul is still most likely active," Craig continued, looking down at the table in thought as the recruits still listened in. "Which means he's got a chance at getting out and back to the land of the living."

"There we go! Now you're up to speed."

Craig looked back at Matt who was watching him closely.

"OK, so how does it work? You said you know how it works, so go ahead and tell me."

"From what I can figure out, there has to be some sort of sacrifice," Matt said, the frown back on Craig's face as a few more recruits entered the room. "I don't know what type of sacrifice just yet, but it has to be a sacrifice, a permanent one. There's apparently a guardian near the exit of Hell that leads through the Devil's Well. It changes with each decade that goes by or when one gets killed to allow a soul to exit through the well."

"So, Chris's going to have to kill this … Guardian of the Exit, which will initiate the sacrifice?"

Matt shrugged. "Possibly. As previously mentioned, I haven't figured the sacrifice bit out yet."

"Surely this guardian is the permanent sacrifice, right?" Gates spoke up, Matt and Craig both looking at him. "It's not going to have to be someone else's life, is it?"

"Let's hope not."

CHAPTER THIRTY-FIVE

Burn the Scarecrow

Heather came to a stop outside the city gates. Chris did not like the feeling he was getting from it. There was a long line waiting to enter and he was wondering if this was where they were meant to be going.

"Here's the deal," Heather said, Chris switching his gaze back to her now as someone passed them and joined the end of the line. "Once we get in there, we have to head for the middle of the city. Once we get to the middle of the city is when we can get on with this and we can get you out of here. Sound good?"

"You've still neglected to explain to me *how* I get out," Chris reminded her. "We've walked for days to get here, and you still haven't told me what I'm meant to be doing."

A group of four joined the line, making it that bit longer. Heather indicated for them to join the line, Chris obliging and following her to the end, the two of them cementing their place in the city's waiting queue.

"The city's main building is in the dead center, hard to miss," she began explaining. They miraculously moved up a place in the line as a few more people joined behind them. "It holds a lot of the inner workings of Hell. There's a ladder that goes right up top and also even further down. All you have to do is climb on up and get to the top which will lead you out and you'll wake up in your body again. Simple."

Chris gave her a non-believing look. "Something makes me think it's not going to be that easy."

Heather gave him a questioning look as they moved up another place. "Why would you think that?"

"Nothing's ever that easy," Chris said. "If getting out of Hell was that easy, there'd be a lot more people having done it or at least giving it a go. You see where I'm going with this, Heather?"

Heather rolled her eyes, arms crossed as they continued to move up in line.

"OK, it might not be that simple," she said, giving in. Chris knew it wasn't going to be as easy as she'd made it out to be. "There might be a few other ... things to go with it. But the whole ladder thing is true. You have to climb to the top and get out to be able to return to life. I wasn't lying about that."

"So, what else does this involve and what happens if I fail?"

Heather looked at him for a few seconds before returning her gaze to the front, the line moving at a better pace now.

"If you fail, you'll most likely end up in the lower levels of Hell, which are far worse than here. You could also end up permanently dead and no longer exist at all, but it's a small chance that could happen."

"Something in there going to have a shot at killing me by chance?"

Heather shifted a bit, looking uncomfortable. "Maybe."

Chris sighed. This wasn't what he wanted to do. Surely there was a better way to go about this rather than having to confront something that would try to kill him, even though he was already dead. If that was even what he had to do. Heather wasn't being very specific.

"OK, so we get inside the city gates, we go to the city center, and we confront whatever horror awaits in front of this freaking ladder that will lead me back to life," Chris said. Heather was listening, but looking ahead, as the city entrance got closer. "If I fail, I end up either permanently dead and non-existent, or I end up in the even lower levels of Hell, which is worse than here. How could anything possibly go wrong here?"

Heather shrugged. "You'd be an idiot if you messed this up, just saying."

The two of them fell silent as they continued to move up in the line and get closer to the gates. After another few minutes, they were allowed to pass into the thriving city, Chris still uncomfortable with the vibe the entire place was giving off.

Heather led the way without a word, and Chris made sure he wasn't about to lose her in the crowds that were throughout the entire area. A large building came into view, the structure pointing high up into the sky, Chris unable to see the top of it.

"That's it," Heather said, pointing it out to Chris who'd already seen it as they walked. "It'll take us a bit longer to get there, but once we're inside, we can get this show on the road."

She picked up her pace, Chris having to increase his as well to keep up with her and not lose her. As much as he didn't like her, the last thing he wanted was to be left by himself in Hell with no idea of what awaited him or what the rules were.

They kept up their pace, and Chris saw a line of people waiting to enter the structure. Heather slowed down and joined the end of the line, Chris with her.

"Let me guess, people all trying to get out of here," he stated.

Heather crossed her arms again, staring ahead of herself, while the line moved a bit.

"Most likely. Always a lot of people having a shot at leaving and getting back home. I would have, but I have no body to return to, as you well know, so until *you're* back up there, I have to suffer down here." She looked him over. "I have enough faith in you, Chris, not to fail this. You're smart enough. A lot of these guys ... most likely not."

The person in front of them glanced back at the two of them, clearly hearing Heather's words. He shot her a glare, getting one in return before turning his attention back to the line in front of him.

"Might be here a while," was all he said.

There were only two people left in front of Heather and Chris. They'd been in the line for what felt like an eternity. Chris was wondering how long he'd actually been dead for. Did time go slower or quicker down here? How long had he been away from home? What would happen if he never made it back?

"You need to stop worrying so much," Heather said, watching the next person in line go in. The doors shut behind him once he was inside. "I'm sure you've got this. You've survived other things."

Chris gave her an unamused look as Heather just looked at him.

"Marion stabbed me," he said unenthusiastically. "She killed me within minutes. I may have survived a lot of different things, but the fact that she was able to take me down like that, doesn't leave a lot of faith in myself, you know?"

Heather rolled her eyes, focus back on the front of the line, only one person away from being let into the structure.

"You'll be fine. Toughen up."

The doors opened to allow the next person in. That had been a lot quicker than the last time. The amount of time between when the doors opened varied, and it made Chris wonder if they opened once the fate of the last person had been decided.

It looked like some people lasted longer than others.

"Any ideas on what I have to do when I'm in there?" Chris asked seriously as the person in front of them entered, the doors swinging shut moments later.

Heather looked at him, seeing the concern on his face. She sighed. She knew she'd have to tell him sooner or later.

"You're going to have to take on the guardian," she said, confusion on Chris's face now.

"Guardian?"

"Of the ladder to the outside world," Heather continued. Chris was very unsure about this now. "You have to kill the guardian and climb the ladder."

"What is this 'guardian' exactly?" Chris dared to asked, hearing nothing from inside the building.

It was making him more uncomfortable than he already was from the vibes of the city.

"Should currently be the Scarecrow," she said in return with a bit of thought. She leaned in a bit, and Chris leaned in to hear her. "In all honesty, I don't know why anyone hasn't done the obvious and tried to burn it yet. Makes the most sense to me."

She moved back, giving him a bit of space.

"So, I have to kill the guardian and climb the ladder out of Hell," Chris said as the doors opened. "Is that all?"

He was next in line. Heather gave him a smile before giving him a careless shove in through the doors.

"Good luck, Chris!" was the last thing he heard before the doors shut completely behind him and he was in darkness.

Chris sighed, wishing he could see something in the dark. He had no idea where he was meant to go and now that he knew a bit about what he had to do, he was more determined to find where this guardian and ladder were so he could just get back amongst the living. It would be nice to see some familiar faces again.

He began moving forwards, not having much choice in the matter. The sooner he got this done, the sooner he could get out of Hell and get home. It was all he wanted to do right now.

Hopefully, Heather was right and burning this scarecrow, or whatever she'd called the guardian, would do the trick and it would be over easily. Hopefully, it also wouldn't have any further consequences.

Chris continued to move forwards, seeing a small light up ahead in what looked to be another room. He headed for it, picking up his pace. There was a single entranceway that led into the room and Chris could see the ladder in the middle, the light coming from above where the ladder disappeared into the roof.

He cautiously entered the room, knowing that sooner or later he was going to run into the guardian. Maybe he could just make a run for it and get to the ladder. He didn't like his chances of that, though.

He was going to do this the correct way. He wasn't about to skip out by doing a half-hearted job and cheating his way out of Hell. He didn't know what the consequences would be if he didn't do everything right. If what Heather had said was true, anyway.

Once he'd stepped foot within the new room, the entranceway behind him suddenly disappeared, leaving nothing but the wall in its place. Chris glanced over his shoulder as another light suddenly appeared on his left, allowing him to see more of the room.

He was currently the only one in the room and it was making him uneasy.

He looked around, trying to figure out the best way to get something to light on fire. How he was going to do that was beyond him. Maybe that was why no one had tried that tactic yet. They hadn't been able to because there was nothing flammable and no fire with which to light anything.

Chris moved cautiously further into the room towards the ladder. He just wanted this to be over as soon as possible. A noise behind him made him stop where he was, a few paces away from the ladder. He dared to glance over his shoulder, seeing something large lurking in the darkness not far off to his right.

This wasn't good.

He turned slightly, seeing the figure shamble forwards. This was the guardian of the ladder.

The Scarecrow was at least seven-foot tall, towering over Chris more than he'd imagined it would. Chris moved backwards, his mind working over what he could do as the Scarecrow made its way over to him.

As the light touched it, Chris was able to see the features a bit more. Besides its height, the Scarecrow had very sharp, pointy teeth. That alone was enough to make Chris panic, and he worked hard to try to calm himself down so he could think. It looked rather ragged and, luckily for Chris, it moved at a slow pace. It looked like it had seen a few bad years.

Chris moved back slightly, still thinking as the Scarecrow kept advancing.

Surely there was something he could do. He needed to figure out a way to burn it and kill it so he could get up the ladder, but right now there was nothing to light it up with. If only someone like Zeke had been here in Hell with him, that would have made it a lot easier.

When that thought crossed his mind, Chris had an idea. Without any more hesitation, he put his hands out in front of him in his usual defensive position and the Scarecrow was rendered immobile.

Chris sighed with relief, glad his ability was still able to work down here. Hopefully that was going to buy him a bit more time and he'd be able to think through what he could do to finish this off.

He looked around, hands back by his sides, as he thought about his next move. Hopefully the Scarecrow would stay still long enough for him to figure out what he could set on fire and how he was going to do it. His gaze moved to the ladder, seeing that it was made entirely of wood.

Another thought crossed his mind. He moved over to the edge of the ladder, touching it as he looked at the opening below that led further down to the lower levels of Hell.

The moment Chris touched the ladder, he heard movement behind him, causing him to look back. The Scarecrow was mobile again, moving slightly faster than before.

Chris turned his attention back to the ladder. It was old, dry wood, and the rung he'd grabbed was already loose.

He pulled against the rung as hard as he could, feeling it give way moments later. He fell backwards, still gripping the broken ladder rung as the Scarecrow drew closer still. Now all he needed to do was somehow set it on fire.

He looked at the Scarecrow as it passed through the light. A frown crossed his face as something within the Scarecrow flickered. It looked like some sort of small flame.

Why would a scarecrow hold fire? It was a question that Chris would definitely have to think about later, as right now wasn't really the time and he didn't have any time left to think. He scrambled to his feet as the Scarecrow got closer. Chris moved and violently stabbed the broken rung straight into it, hearing it scream as the wood pierced its chest and hit something solid within.

Seconds later, Chris saw the spark within the Scarecrow flare and the broken ladder rung caught fire, forcing him to let it go and step back.

Moments later, the Scarecrow was entirely covered in flames. Chris winced as it screamed in agony.

The Scarecrow tried to move forwards but was unable to, collapsing to the ground moments later, completely engulfed in flames. The screams died down with the flames, eventually leaving Chris in the quiet.

The whole room suddenly lit up, making Chris shield his eyes. Once his eyes had adjusted, he looked at the ladder, glancing back at what was left of the Scarecrow before he made his decision.

He was going home.

CHAPTER THIRTY-SIX

Return to the Living

Gates frowned, seeing the look on Zeke's face as he sat opposite him at the table.

"You OK?" he asked hesitantly.

"Head just suddenly exploded in pain," Zeke said, putting his hand against his head as he winced and shut his eyes. "What the hell."

Gates watched him with concern, not sure what to say.

Eventually, Zeke opened his eyes, shaking his head a bit. "Something's not right," he said. He kept his hand against his head and shut his eyes again. "Goddamn it."

"Let's go see Jacob, try figure out what's going on," Gates suggested, already on his feet. He moved around the table and hauled Zeke to his feet, ignoring the wince of pain. "Come on."

He dragged Zeke out of the room and down the stairs that led to the front door of the lodgings. Zeke was obviously uncomfortable but, once outside, Gates made him keep walking through the outpost, getting a few odd glances as they passed by.

The sun was going down as they reached the church. Gates figured this was where they'd find Jacob. If he wasn't in the church, then they'd look somewhere else. Gates scanned himself in and Zeke followed him through the door, not caring if he left it open.

"What's Jacob gonna do?" Zeke asked, trying to ignore the pain in his head. He wasn't feeling too great.

"Don't know but if we can figure out what just happened, maybe we can figure out what to do," Gates said as he went in through the next door. He made Zeke descend the staircase at a quicker pace than Zeke was comfortable with. "You'll be fine."

Zeke didn't say anything as Gates went through the last door, making sure Zeke was through as well before it shut. Sure enough, Jacob was there with five others.

"We need your help," Gates called, the five of them looking over. Gates indicated to Zeke. "Something's wrong."

"What happened?" Jacob asked with a frown, indicating for the two of them to take a seat with them.

Gates dragged Zeke over to the desk and forced him to sit down as he stood behind the chair. Zeke leaned his head against his hand, wishing the pain would stop.

"We don't know," Gates said. "Sudden, terrible headache. Won't go away."

Jacob moved around from the other side of the table and looked at Zeke who didn't even bother returning the look.

"Any ideas what it could be?" Jacob asked.

Zeke shook his head, staying quiet as Matt rushed in through the door, Craig a step or so behind. Everyone except Zeke looked over.

"We think we know what's happened," Matt rushed, Craig off to his side. "Gonna sound real farfetched, but you've got to hear us out."

Jacob crossed his arms, looking between the two of them. "Alright, talk."

Remington enjoyed looking at the stars. It was one of the things he enjoyed most about only being able to come out at night. It was just a shame there were no stars in the sky tonight.

He frowned, sitting up quickly from where he'd been lying on his back in the middle of what had, unfortunately, become Banshee's End's local graveyard. He stayed silent, listening to make sure he wasn't mistaken.

No, he wasn't. That was definitely the sound of a beating heart. There was no question about it. He'd heard it so many times over the past six years that there was no mistaking the rhythmic sound of a living being's heart.

The frown stayed on his face as he looked himself over, temporarily wondering if he was imagining it. He was dead, there was no way it was his heart he could hear. That would have been remarkable, though. He would've been very impressed with himself if that was the case and he was alive again.

But sadly, it wasn't the case, and he was still dead. The living dead, as Matt never failed to remind him.

Remington sighed before going back to listening. Yes, he could still definitely hear someone else's heartbeat. But whose? He was the only one in this area right now and since it wasn't him, it had to be...

"Chris?" Remington looked down at the grave next to where he'd been lying on the dirt, raising an eyebrow in thought. "If it's not me, then it has to be you."

He moved, putting his ear to the top of the grave, just to make sure his vampire hearing wasn't deceiving him. Sure enough, whoever was below the ground was very much alive.

Remington scrambled to his feet, nearly tripping himself up as he did so. He knew they should have attached a bell to the grave in case this happened. It would've been a lot easier to tell if Chris somehow miraculously got revived.

"It's all good, I'll be right back. Don't suffocate for the love of God."

He rushed off to find someone who could help. He heard voices as he neared the church. Trust everyone to be down there when he needed to alert them to something drastic going on. He slowed his pace, still feeling the urgency as he neared the church's boundary.

He was going to have to guess at where it started, as Craig had refused to give him his boundary fence. If there had been a fence, he would've known where to stop.

Remington came to a stop as close to the church as he was game enough to get, listening to try and figure out who was down below in the operations room. That would be his deciding factor on who he tried to get outside to help.

"Abilities are a major part of someone's core," he heard Craig say, making him frown. Why were they talking about abilities? "Common ones are usually attached to some sort of ... anchor, I guess you'd call it."

"Something that ties it down?" That was most definitely Jacob.

Great, two of the people he needed were on holy ground and unaware that he was outside.

"I guess, if that's what you want to think." That was Craig again. "Common abilities, since they're not as unique to people and not specifically to that person, have to have a main core. That's why they're so common."

"OK? So, what's this got to do with anything?"

"We were trying to figure out how we could get Chris back," Matt said. Great, now there were at least three people below the church that Remington needed. "The Devil's Well was his best shot. You have to kill a guardian to get out of the well and we think this is what's happened."

"We think whichever guardian Chris has managed to kill, happened to be the fire ability anchor," Craig said, making Remington frown. That didn't sound good. "Anyone who had that specific ability won't have it anymore."

"Wait, let me get this straight," Jacob said, sounding rather confused. "You're saying that Chris was trying to get back to life through the Devil's Well and now he's possibly killed an ability anchor? Guys, seriously?"

Remington didn't have time for this so he stopped listening, trying to block it out as he tried to work out how he could get someone's attention. He looked around, still able to hear talking but trying hard not to listen. He moved back a bit, seeing a piece of stone on the ground that had fallen off one of the close buildings. He picked it up, moved back to his invisible boundary line and, without another thought, violently tossed it at the church.

The piece of stone went right through the closest window, and the noise was enough to make Remington wince as the glass shattered and fell to the ground.

"You guys hear that?" he heard Craig comment.

No one responded and he heard someone open one of the doors inside. It looked like that had been enough to get their attention. About a minute later, he heard Craig just inside the church, right near the door.

"You're kidding, what the hell?"

"Hey!" Remington called, urgency clear in his voice. "We've got a problem!"

The door opened and Craig came out, closely followed by Matt, Gates, and Jacob.

"The hell, Remington? You broke the damn window," Craig grumbled. "What are you doing?"

"That's the least of my concerns, right now," Remington said seriously. "If you didn't hold your operations under a church, I wouldn't have had to break the window!"

"What's going on? You said there's a problem?" Matt spoke up.

Remington looked at him and nodded, as Craig surveyed the damage done to the window, still not impressed.

"Chris is alive, and you need to dig him up before it's too late," he rushed. Everyone's attention was on him, now. "I was down at the graveyard, and I heard his heart beating. He needs to be dug up quickly or he'll suffocate and whatever he's done to resurrect himself will be for nothing."

"I'll grab a couple of shovels and meet you all there," Matt said, disappearing in the dark.

Not waiting for anyone to say anything else, Remington hurried back to the graveyard, the others following at a quick pace, hoping it wasn't already too late.

CHAPTER THIRTY-SEVEN

Deals are Made to be Broken

C hris had never been so happy to see a vampire in his life. The moment the lid of the coffin was removed and he saw Remington offering him his hand, Chris was accepting it and allowing himself to be hauled out of what had been his grave.

Ash rushed over, pulling him into a hug, making him wince as he felt a bit of pain, but he didn't mind. It meant he was alive.

She moved back, unable to believe this was happening, before pulling him back into a tight hug again.

"How in the world did you get back to life?" Jacob asked.

Chris shook his head, feeling drained and like he needed to lie down for a few hours.

"I don't know," he admitted, finally hugging Ash back. "Honestly, I can't remember a thing."

Ash refused to let him go as Matt looked him over. "You should go and get some rest," he suggested. "We'll try and figure everything out in a couple of days once you think you're OK and we know you'll be alright."

Chris nodded. He liked that idea.

Ash finally let him go and gave him a smile as she took his arm, making him head off with her so she could make sure he got to his room without any issues. Chris went without a word, leaving everyone else standing around in the empty graveyard.

When they reached the lodging house, Ash held the door open for Chris, before following him in. They headed up the stairs to the room Chris had been staying in, which was not far from the top of the staircase.

"I'll be down the hall if you need anything," Ash said, leaving him at the door. "Try get some sleep, OK? I'm only a few doors down."

Chris nodded and went into his room without a word. He shut the door behind himself and went over to the bed, lying down with a sigh and shutting his eyes. He couldn't remember anything. No matter how hard he tried, he just couldn't remember anything of what had happened between when he'd died and when he'd woken up in the grave. Was he even meant to know?

Chris shifted a bit, a frown crossing his face as he heard something crinkle in his back pocket. He opened his eyes and sat up, reaching into his pocket and pulling out a folded piece of paper. The frown remained on his face as he unfolded it to read what was written on it.

It wasn't *his* handwriting, he knew that for sure. When he realized whose handwriting it was, he read over what was written on the paper a couple of times before he folded it again and got off the bed.

He went a few doors down to Ash's room and knocked on the door urgently.

"Everything OK?" she asked.

Chris held up the folded piece of paper. "I think I know how to get Marion."

Craig looked out with a confused look on his face. He looked between Chris and Ash before settling his gaze solely on Ash, indicating to Chris.

"I'm a bit confused at why he's here," he said, making Chris frown. "Because you're here, but he's here, too. I'm pretty sure that's not my thing."

"I'm sorry?" Chris said, even more confused than Craig seemed to be.

Craig briefly looked him over before shaking his head and sighing. "Never mind."

Ash looked at Craig who reluctantly returned her gaze. "Chris thinks he knows how we can get Marion. Can we talk?"

Craig looked hesitant but moved aside, allowing them to enter his room. Ash gave him a smile, not getting one in return, and Craig shut the door once they were both inside.

"Alright, talk," he said, going over and sitting on the end of his bed, linking his fingers together as he regarded the two of them. He looked at Ash. "Also, you left something behind last time you were here."

He moved, grabbing something off the floor and tossing it to Ash. Ash awkwardly caught it, and Chris raised an eyebrow at her as he saw what it was. She gave him a guilty smile before looking at Craig with annoyance and throwing it back to him.

"Keep it until we're done talking," she said.

Craig rolled his eyes, tossed it back onto the floor, and looked back at Chris. "You think you can get Marion?"

Chris nodded, indicating the folded piece of paper he had in his hand.

"When I was dead, I think I ran into Heather," he began. The frown returned to Craig's face as he listened. "She wanted me to get her out of Hell but said she couldn't get out the same way as me. Something has to be done by someone on the surface because she doesn't have a body to return to."

"OK," Craig said slowly. "What's this got to do with Marion?"

"Heather wrote something down for me," Chris said, unfolding the piece of paper to show him what was on it. "Instructions on what to do to get her out. But she needs Carmen to do it, not me."

He handed the paper to Craig, watching as he read through it. Once done, Craig glanced up at Chris, before focusing back on the paper.

"So, she needs a witch to do whatever the hell kind of spell this is," he stated, Chris nodding as he talked. "Which should be able to reincarnate Heather as herself again." He looked at Chris properly, holding up the paper. "What's this got to do with Marion, again?"

"Carmen will want Heather back," Chris tried explaining. "Marion's *with* Carmen. We get into contact with Carmen and let her know I made a deal with Heather to help get her out of Hell. We arrange to meet up but you take Carmen out. Once she's out of the way, any barriers she has in place should disappear, which means we can then find Marion and get rid of her like we'd planned."

Craig sighed. This was all too complicated.

"Say this works, and say we can get Carmen to agree to meet up," he began, hesitantly. "She won't let anyone get close to her. She'll have protection barriers in place. I won't be able to get close enough to take her out. I'm sorry, Chris, but I don't think this is going to work."

"I might be able to help."

The three of them looked over to the doorway and saw Remington peeking in through the small gap in the door that he'd created, having silently opened it without anyone knowing.

"How?" Craig asked as Remington hesitantly pushed the door open a bit more, allowing himself access to the room.

"Ah, well, where do I begin?" he started, shutting the door behind himself. "For one, I'm immune to non-physical abilities, which counts for magic, too. Two, I'm a vampire which means I have top notch senses. Three, I wanna help somehow. I feel like I owe you guys."

Craig sighed, reluctantly staring at Remington as he thought.

"Alright, fine," he said eventually, Remington's face lighting up with a smile. "Track them down for us and let us know where they are, but don't get yourself caught." He looked at Chris and Ash. "This piece of paper stays with me. There's no way I'm letting Carmen get her hands on it because then she'll have Heather back. Once Remington knows where they're hiding out, we'll move out and grab Marion."

"How are we going to do this?" Jacob asked seriously. "If Carmen's there, we have to take care of that threat first."

"Remington's gone to set up the meeting, find out where they are, and offer Carmen Heather's escape-from-Hell instructions as long as she hands over Marion," Craig said, relaying the new plan. "It's the best we could do. Remington can find them, we can't. He's going to propose the trade to Carmen and, once we get Marion out of the way, Carmen will be as good as dead as long as I can get close enough."

Jacob seemed unsure, but he nodded anyway. "Where are we meeting them?"

"Coastline, the Dimension Portal," Craig said, making Jacob even more wary. "If worst comes to worst, I'll throw both Marion *and* Carmen in. I'm not taking any risks."

Jacob gave a hesitant nod. "Alright, get a group together and we'll head on out to the portal."

He looked around at everyone else in the operations room. The usual group waited for him to give his instructions.

"You heard him, let's get a move on and get to the portal on the coastline. We let Craig deal with Carmen and Marion. This threat won't be around much longer, and then we can focus solely on the Legion. Let's move out."

CHAPTER THIRTY-EIGHT

Setting Up the Rendezvous

"H i."

Carmen jumped at the sudden disturbance. She turned around quickly to see someone standing next to the closest sofa, hands in pockets as he looked around the room.

"I'm sorry, do I know you?" Carmen asked, crossing her arms as the man turned to look at her.

He gave her a grin, and Carmen saw the slight difference. The fangs were hard to see and that was the problem with vampires. It made it hard to tell them apart from normal people.

"Don't think we've met before, the name's Remington," he introduced himself. "Sorry for the intrusion, just wanted to talk."

Carmen shifted, looking Remington over as he admired one of the art pieces on the wall.

"I don't particularly like vampires," she commented.

"And I don't particularly like witches," he said in return. "You lot and your nasty hexes are not for me, but here we are."

He went back to looking at the painting on the wall, thought on his face as Carmen looked him over again, trying to figure out what a vampire was doing in her temporary hideout.

"What do you want to talk about?" she asked. He kept examining the painting, not bothering to look at her. "You said you wanted to talk, so talk. What do you want?"

Remington looked at her, a bit of a blank look on his face.

"Oh, yes, that's right," he said, shaking his head and giving her another grin. "Sorry, temporarily forgot the reason I was here." He indicated to the painting. "This is a nice piece, where'd you get it?"

"It was here when I arrived," Carmen said with annoyance. "Talk, vampire, don't make me force you."

Remington held his hands up. "Whoa there, missy, no need to threaten the lovely vampire. I just wanna have a harmless chat, that's all."

Carmen was not impressed and wished he'd just go away. Maybe letting him talk to her wasn't the best idea after all if he was like this.

"All you've done is avoid what you're here for. What do you want?" she snapped.

Remington moved, coming around the sofa and taking a seat on it, lazily lounging as he regarded Carmen.

"I've heard you're harboring a fugitive," he began. "Well, two fugitives, but I really only need the one."

"Marion?" Remington gave a nod as Carmen shifted her stance. "What could you possibly want with her?"

"Well, that's the mystery, ain't it?" Remington gave her a grin once again. "I have a proposal to make, something for you to think over, m'dear."

Now he had Carmen's interest.

"Is that so?" she said, getting another nod. "What's this proposal to do with?"

Remington pretended to think and looked around the room, before looking at her again.

"If I'm not mistaken, you lost a dear friend before the Emerald City fell," he said. Carmen's expression changed. "I know how to get her back."

Carmen scoffed. "Please, you think I haven't tried everything? You're a vampire, you don't know anything about coming back to life."

Remington pretended to be shocked upon hearing that, fake hurt on his face.

"Ow, that hurt," he said sarcastically. "Better than being in Hell."

Carmen scowled at him, not in the mood for fun and games. Remington shifted on the sofa, sitting up now and leaning forwards, linking his fingers together.

"I want you to hear me out," he continued. "If you have the time."

Carmen moved and sat on one of the chairs before waving a hand at him.

Remington took that as his cue to speak again.

"I know someone who's been to Hell and back recently, quite literally," he said. Carmen looked interested but partially bored. "He said he ran into Heather down there and she gave him instructions on how to get her back to life without her body being available. He has the instructions and is willing to hand them over ... for something in return."

"And that something happens to be Marion," Carmen said, Remington giving a single nod. Carmen shifted how she was sitting. "Which means that you most likely know the Banshee's End boys. They have their shit together down there, don't they? What does that make you? Their cute little errand boy?"

"I just happened to be in the right place at the right time," Remington said. "I don't work for them, they don't work for me. I do the occasional favor to keep myself alive and that's all I care about right now." He moved again, back to lounging on the sofa. "So? Marion worth having around? Surely, you'd rather have Heather back."

Carmen watched him for a few seconds before speaking.

"What happens if I hand Marion over to Banshee's End?" she asked, Remington glad that she was at least thinking over his offer. "I'd prefer Heather any day to Marion, but why should I give her up on this possibly false statement?"

"I have no reason to lie. If it wasn't true, you'd know. I can see you're thinking about it and that you *do* believe me, so that's a good sign."

Carmen wasn't impressed with this vampire. He was really getting under her skin, and she was sure that was his ultimate goal, but she did think he was telling the truth.

"Alright, where do we make the trade?"

"They're going to meet us at the portal," Craig said, putting his phone back in his pocket. He looked around at everyone. "We'll have a few days to prepare by the time we get there. It'll take a bit of time to make it to the coastline, so everyone keep alive and alert. Let's keep moving."

They'd ended up splitting into two groups, half going with Craig and the other half with Jacob. Each group had also taken a few recruits just in case something happened, so it wasn't just their usual gang.

Alex, Ash, and the four bandits were with Craig's group. Zeke had ended up staying behind, still not feeling quite right since the incident moments before Chris had come back from the dead. He was also quite depressed about having lost his fire ability.

As always, Alex kept close to Ash, not wanting to get lost or caught up in the small crowd. In a way, he was excited to see the coastline. Craig had explained to him what exactly the coastline was and, even though it involved mass amounts of water, which he hated, he was still excited to be travelling to somewhere so different.

"What do you think the coastline is going to be like?" Alex asked for the third time that day as Ash kept a few paces behind Craig, allowing a few of his recruits to separate the two of them.

Ash sighed. "I don't know, Alex. Lots of water? Just wait and see."

Alex nodded, still excited.

Danny and his other three gang members stayed near the back with the rest of the recruits. Ash was surprised they'd even agreed to come along, but maybe they were interested to see what was going to go down. Or maybe they were just bored.

"Think we'll get there before the others?" Alex asked, still chatting and trying to stop the silence from building too much.

"Maybe. Depends how long they stop for and where they stop on the way."

Alex nodded. "OK, that's true. You're right. Always right."

Ash rolled her eyes, not saying anything more. She watched Craig say something to one of the recruits who was walking just behind him. The recruit nodded and rushed on ahead, most likely scouting the upcoming area.

Ash increased her pace a bit, catching up to walk beside Craig, who glanced at her. Alex was not far behind and, when he caught up, he linked his arm with hers as he often did.

"Have you been to this coastline before?" Ash asked Craig, getting another glance.

"Yeah," Craig said in response. "It's nice, I think you'll like it."

Ash smiled a bit, getting a slight smile in return. She indicated to Alex.

"What about him?"

"Besides the water? Yeah, I think you'll be on board with it," Craig said, glancing at Alex. Alex grinned at him, and Craig couldn't help but smile back. "But before you get to enjoy it, you have to remember that we're there for a reason. Marion first, enjoyment later. Yes?"

Alex nodded furiously in understanding. "Yes sir!"

Craig had to smile again at his reaction, and he shook his head. "Once Marion's out of the way, you can take a couple days if you want and hang around for a bit. There's a small town not far from the coastline, where we're all going to be staying before we get out to the Dimension Portal. It's a nice place, worth visiting."

"You going to stay for a while after Marion's been taken care of?" Ash asked, getting another glance yet again.

Craig shook his head. "Can't. The Legion grows stronger every day, and we need to get back on top of it. I can't afford any time off."

"Surely you can take a couple of days," Ash tried. "Right?"

Craig sighed, wondering why she was trying so hard. "We'll see."

CHAPTER THIRTY-NINE

Waterwall Incline

The town's sign had come into view for Jacob's group a few minutes earlier. The bold lettering read 'WATERWALL INCLINE' in a dark colour, outlined by gold, making it stand out that bit more.

There had been no sign of Craig's group at all, and Chris wondered how long it would take them to get here, seeing as they'd taken a different route and had left a day later, just in case something happened back at Banshee's End.

Chris had never been this far out within the Oz county, and he was sure that none of the others in the group, apart from maybe a few recruits and Jacob, had either.

He knew Matt had never been this far, as he'd mentioned to Chris a while back that he hadn't even known about the coastline to begin with. If Matt hadn't known something, then it was rare that anyone they knew did.

Chris really hoped this plan was going to work. He was hoping Marion wouldn't see it coming and that there wouldn't be any complications or consequences to what they were planning. But, he knew, something always went wrong.

Just like it had at the Funeral Masquerade, something was bound to go wrong with this plan. Sure, they had Craig who could pretty well take out anyone he wanted with just a touch, but he'd been at the Funeral Masquerade and Chris had still died. Much like everyone else in the group, Craig was limited and could only do so much.

Chris was also hoping that Craig would take Carmen out for good. That way, nothing could happen in the way of tricks when this trade went down. The last thing they all needed was for her to have done something and for this whole operation to come crashing down around them.

The sooner they got rid of Marion for good, the better. She'd been an issue for far too long and, now that they knew she was stable and wouldn't keep killing off Wonderland, this was their chance to get rid of her once and for all, obviously without killing her out of fear that the counties would collapse if she died.

Throwing her into another dimension seemed like a pretty good option right now.

"Alright everyone, this is where we're staying for the next few days," Jacob said as they entered the town square. Civilians from the town either stood around watching the group or just went about their own business. "Try to keep a low profile. I'll take care of the accommodation. You're all more than welcome to have a look around but, as always, keep alert and if anything happens, come to either myself or Doug. Once Craig and his group gets here, you can also go to him or Cain. You're dismissed."

The recruits all headed off to do their own thing. Doug and Jacob headed off to an inn not far from where they were standing, while Chris, Abel, Matt, and Gates all stayed where they were and looked around.

"Well," Matt said, arms crossed. He looked at Gates. "You know what this reminds me of? England."

Gates gave a nod of agreement. The town square was neat and tidy, a few people around on the cobblestone streets and paved sidewalks. The sun wasn't out today; a lot of clouds had come over hours earlier and it looked like it was going to rain.

"Let's have a look around," Gates said, addressing Matt who nodded in agreement. Gates looked at Abel and Chris. "We're gonna wander off for a couple of hours. Guess we'll see the two of you back here later on."

"Probably when it gets dark! Don't wait up," Matt called as they headed off, keen to see what the rest of the town was like.

He gave them a bit of a wave, and Abel looked at Chris. "What do we wanna do?".

Chris shrugged. "Guess we just follow suit and go look around town."

"Didn't expect to see you out here."

Chris jumped and watched Remington sit down next to him on the rocks, before looking out at the ocean again.

Craig's group had arrived about an hour ago, but Chris hadn't seen any sign of Ash.

There was a bit of distance between them and the ocean, the sand and rocks separating them from the crashing waves a little way away. A cool breeze had started to pick up as the sun had gone down. The lights from the town only reached so far, but they gave them a backlight to see by.

Remington continued to stare at the water, mesmerized by the waves hitting the shore.

"I pretty well owe you my life, you know," Chris said, getting a glance before Remington went back to watching the ocean in the dark. "I know you were the one who realized I'd come back. I heard what you said before they dug me up. Thank you."

Remington gave a shrug, shifting to bring his knees up. He put his arms around his legs and rested his chin on his knees as he watched the ocean.

"I miss this kinda thing," he said, not commenting on what Chris had said. "Being a vampire stops you enjoying a lot of your existence. Can't really call it a life, since it's not. My life got ripped away from me when I died."

"The bite killed you, didn't it?" Chris asked.

Remington nodded, never once breaking his gaze.

"But it also saved me," he said quietly, the sadness in his voice. "As much as I hate to admit it, becoming a vampire was the better option for a scared, twenty-year old kid. Probably would have rethought it at the time if I'd been older."

"You ever regret it?"

"Sometimes. But I'd rather be the living dead rather than just dead. That's why I chose to go through with it in the first place. Your survival instinct comes into play, and you do things without thinking them through. Anything to save yourself from no longer existing. An eternity without pain, without any fear of dying. It's something you don't even consider the consequences of until it's too late."

Chris didn't say anything, not sure what the best thing to say was, or if it even needed a response.

"The vampire who turned me ... he was a very high ranking one, which is why I can turn people, now," Remington explained. "If you get turned by a high ranking vampire, when they die the next one in their bloodline inherits their ability to turn people. In my case, that's me. Their death triggers it within you somehow, and you also inherit their rank in the vampire hierarchy. If I turn someone and then die, that person will become the one who can then turn people. It goes down the line until everyone in that bloodline is wiped out. If I don't turn anyone, my vampire bloodline stops with me."

"*Have* you ever turned anyone?" Chris asked, looking at Remington, who was still resting his chin on his knees.

"Not yet. I don't want to; I never wanted to. I went through it, and I don't want to see other people go through it. I'm more than happy to let my bloodline die out. I don't want to be responsible for ruining someone's life like mine was."

"What if it was to save someone? I know you offered it to me before I died. What about that kind of situation?"

Remington finally tore his gaze away from the ocean and looked at him.

"Only for people I don't want to lose, good people," he said, and Chris understood what he meant. "As much as I don't want people to have to go through it, if they asked me, I'd do it because it's their choice. I won't do it without permission, though."

He fell silent again, back to watching the waves violently crash onto the shore.

"Where are you from?" Chris asked.

"Canada," Remington said with a bit of a laugh. The smile faded from his face as he looked out at the ocean. "I miss it, miss it a lot. I miss my home, my family. I can never go home, ever. I can't ever go back Upstairs."

"What if you got cured of your vampirism? You could go home, then."

Remington shrugged. "There's a very slim chance of that ever happening. I've never heard of any cure for vampirism. It doesn't exist, Chris. I appreciate the thought, but there's no saving me from this. I'm stuck like this and there's no going back."

"Surely there's got to be something out there that could potentially cure it," Chris said seriously. "You've just got to look."

Remington gave a slight unamused laugh, shaking his head.

"I'd know if there was anything like that out there," he said. "Believe me, Chris, if something like that existed, the Legion would have known about it a long time ago."

CHAPTER FORTY

Tricks of the Trade

"L et's move out, we're heading to the portal."

The sun was high in the sky and everyone who needed to go to the Dimension Portal got ready to head to the borderline of the town. All the recruits were staying behind on this particular mission. The less people at the portal, the better.

Chris wondered where Remington was, as there was no way he was going to be able to head to the portal with them while the sun was up.

The inn they'd stayed in overnight wasn't going to be able to block the sunlight, so he had to be somewhere else within the town.

Chris also wondered whether Remington would be at the meeting with Carmen and Marion. If it was during the daylight hours, he certainly wouldn't be.

Ash joined Chris as Craig spoke to Jacob about something, everyone else waiting impatiently to leave.

"Hey, didn't see you last night when you guys got in," Chris said.

Alex wasn't far behind Ash, and he hooked himself onto her as he always did. She didn't look at him, instead keeping her focus on Chris.

"We called it quits early, the travel was a bit too much," she admitted.

Chris noticed Alex glance over at Craig. "Fair enough."

Jacob finally joined them.

"We good to go?" Jacob asked Chris as Craig headed past them to the rest of the group.

Chris nodded and Ash gave Chris another smile.

"Let's go. I don't know about you, but I want to see this portal."

The Dimension Portal was a lot different to what Chris had expected. He'd expected it to be some odd hole in a wall or something, but he was completely wrong. The portal was impressive to say the least. It sat on a small hill and towered into the sky, like a huge mirror, with a stone border holding it in place. Whatever was in between each part of the border shimmered with different colours depending on the angle the sun hit it from.

Alex was speechless as he marveled at the structure. It had taken them the majority of the day to reach it; the small town of Waterwall Incline now nothing more than a small glow in the distance.

"How does it work?" Abel asked as they started heading up the hill.

"We don't know if there's a specific way to decide on the dimension or if it's just pure luck where you end up," Jacob explained as they walked. "For now, we're just taking our chances and doing what we have to."

"Which involves pretty well just pushing Marion in and getting rid of her," Matt noted. "You can figure the rest out later, right?"

"Right."

Abel shook his head as they reached the top of the hill. The ground immediately surrounding the portal was completely flat, in contrast to the hill they'd just climbed.

"About time you lot showed up." Remington gave them all a wave from the shadow of the portal. "I've been here for at least an hour. What took you so long?"

"How did you get here before us?" Ash asked in disbelief.

Remington looked at her with a grin on his face as he made some gesture with his fingers, accompanied by the words, "Vampire magic."

Ash rolled her eyes, crossing her arms as she stayed close by Chris. There wasn't a lot of room on the flat ground.

It was all rather too close to the portal for Alex's liking, and it was making him uncomfortable.

"I don't like this," he grumbled.

Remington perked up a bit as he heard something.

"Someone's coming," he said, looking past them all. "It's Carmen and Marion."

Jacob looked around at everyone, signaling for them all to move back. Remington made sure he stayed out of what was left of the sunlight.

It took a few minutes, but eventually Carmen and Marion appeared over the hill. Marion's face lit up in amusement as she saw what was going on.

"Well, who'd have expected this?" she said, the two of them coming to a halt not far from the others, as there wasn't a lot of room left between them all and the portal. She saw Chris. "Back from the dead, Chris?"

He didn't say anything in return, and Carmen glared around at all of them. "Which one of you has the instructions? I didn't come this far for nothing. I've held up my end of the deal, now you hold up yours."

Marion looked at her, a bit of a frown on her face. "What deal?"

Carmen looked at her as Craig moved away from the group slightly. He had the piece of paper with Heather's instructions on it. He stood in front of the Banshee's End group, between them and Carmen and Marion.

"It was either you or Heather," Carmen said to Marion with a small shrug. She switched her gaze to Craig. "You have it?"

Craig took the folded paper out of his pocket, holding it up to prove that he had it. Carmen gestured for him to hand it over.

"That was the deal," she said. "You hand me the paper, you get Marion. A deal's a deal."

"You hand her over and *then* you get the paper, that's the deal," Craig said seriously, bringing a scowl to Carmen's face.

"Fine." Carmen grabbed Marion, shoving her forward towards Craig who grabbed her, still holding onto the paper as Marion tried to break out of his grip. Carmen pointed at the paper. "Hand it over."

Craig stared her down, moving back and carelessly tossing the folded paper backwards without breaking the gaze. The paper went straight through the shimmering portal and was gone.

"You weren't ever getting that piece of paper," Craig said.

Anger was now clear on Carmen's face, and she growled in annoyance, shifting how she was standing.

"Craig, move," Jacob warned, seeing that Carmen was preparing herself for something.

Craig pushed Marion back to Jacob, quickly closing the distance between himself and Carmen.

Jacob took that as his cue to move as well, and he dragged a struggling Marion closer to the portal. He was having a bit of a hard time getting her close enough to avoid accidentally falling in with her.

By this point, Craig had a tight hold on Carmen and was out of her line of fire. She was struggling hard, though, and it was hard for him to keep his grip on her.

Chris, Matt, and Abel moved to help Jacob.

"A bit closer," Jacob said urgently, as Marion struggled more. "Now!"

Not needing to be told twice, Jacob released Marion and the other three helped push her backwards into the shimmering portal. Marion disappeared rather quickly.

Carmen kept struggling against Craig and managed to knock him off balance. They both fell backwards and tumbled down the hill, both disappearing from sight within seconds.

Jacob went to say something, but Chris spoke first.

"Guys," he said, everyone looking to him. "Something's wrong."

Chris felt himself being dragged him backwards towards the portal. Ash quickly grabbed him, trying to pull him in the opposite direction. Alex was next on board, but the invisible force kept pulling Chris backwards.

Remington moved from where he'd been standing, the sun having gone by now. The portal, though, gave off a lot of light, lighting up the surrounding area for miles.

"Let him go or you'll be dragged in with him!" Remington said urgently. Chris was now dangerously close to being dragged into the portal. "She's done a binding spell. He's tied to Marion!"

"Which means wherever she goes, he has no choice but to go too," Jacob said, realizing what Remington was saying. "Ash, Alex, let him go if you don't want to go with him."

Ash was reluctant, but she hesitantly let go of Chris, Alex doing the same.

Chris looked at Ash. "It's fine. I've gotten back once. I'll do it again."

Within moments of him saying that, he disappeared through the portal.

Everyone stood still, no one knowing what to do.

"Can we get him back?" Ash asked Jacob.

Jacob gave her a bit of a sad shrug, not sure how to answer.

They all looked over when they heard a laugh from the edge of the hill. Carmen had reappeared, albeit on her hands and knees. Craig was nowhere to be seen.

"Chris is not coming back," she said. "You thought we'd seriously come into this without something like that planned? The less people *you* have, the more chance *we've* got. This is only the start of things to come, just be warned."

She clicked her fingers and disappeared.

Jacob sighed in frustration, hands on hips. "Damn."

"Where's Craig?" Ash suddenly asked.

"I'm fine." Craig trudged up the hill and back to the top onto the flat ground, holding his head as he did so. "Still alive, don't panic."

"What happened?" Matt asked.

"No idea, flash knockout, I think, thanks to Carmen," he said, wincing. "She hit me pretty good with some kind of spell. Don't know what it was but, damn, it hurt."

"As long as you're alright," Jacob said.

Craig nodded. "Yeah, I'm fine. No need to worry."

Ash looked around at everyone. "What are we going to do about Chris? If he's spell-bound to Marion, we might not be able to get him back."

"You can if you kill Carmen," Remington said, everyone looking to him. "If she dies, the spell breaks and you can get him back without having to bring Marion back."

"That's the only problem, though," Craig said. "Fatal touch didn't work. She's protected. We can't kill her. Well, I can't, anyway."

"Well, we'll figure out how to," Remington said with determination. "Whether it kills us or not, we'll take her down and we'll get Chris back. That's a damn promise."